Copyright © 2025 by Torie Gaylord

Cover Design by Miblart

www.miblart.com

First edition March 2025

ISBN 9798992238914 (Paperback)

ISBN 9798992238907 (E-Book)

I0658743

To my husband – this wouldn't have happened without your encouragement.

THREE SECONDS AND GONE

TORIE GAYLORD

Chapter 1

A massive shake jolted me awake. Sitting on the edge of the bed, it took me a second to gain my bearings. I worked on blinking the sleep out of my eyes while trying to shrug off the remainders of sleep. Something was off. The TV was still on, looping through the same rom-com I had started before I fell asleep, but Daryl wasn't in the bed. I got up to check the bathroom to find that empty too. I didn't see his stuff anywhere around me either. *Okay, maybe everyone was upstairs getting breakfast going.* I threw on a sweater with some black leggings, finishing off the look with my signature messy bun before heading out of my room. I decided to check on the other rooms to see if anyone else was still down here. Mark and Lilly's room was empty, but at least it looked like they slept in it. Joe and Bev's room was in the same state. Jennie's and Chris' rooms were both tidy and neat. Another similarity between the rooms was that all their bags were gone. *They must have moved everything back upstairs.*

I emerged from the bunker into the basement to find the pool table as it was still waiting for Mark to finish his turn. I paused for a second to see if I could hear any chit chat floating down from the kitchen. There was nothing. Silence. My gut took this moment to remind me once again that something wasn't right.

I decided to head upstairs to look around the house. I opened every door, poked my head in every room, and there was no sign of anyone. I opened the curtains to look into the backyard just to find it empty. *No way everyone left ... I would have heard them. This has to be some sort of prank.* I went out the front door to see if there were any cars. To my surprise, nobody's car was missing. Something was different. Instead of the quiet, calm street with a view of the hills around my parents' house, there were a string of houses I had never seen before. Furrowing my brow, I went back into the house, locked the door, and proceeded to make my way to the backyard to see if that view had changed too. I grabbed the door knob taking a deep breath. *Three. Two. One.*

Once outside, I took a closer look at the city below me only to see it wasn't the same old city I had grown accustomed to seeing. Instead of the mix of old and modern, it looked completely modern with the sun reflecting off a lot of glass. The thing that stood out to me the most was there was no evidence of damage from the bombs that were dropping last night. *What the hell?* Everything was different and the city I called home was gone only to be replaced with something new and unfamiliar.

But, I'm getting ahead of myself ... to continue diving into the story of now, I need to explain how I got here ...

Friday Night

I decided it would be a good idea to get the friend group together for a weekend to forget about everything going on. Just us, games, lots of food and drinks, and the time to make some good, and some embarrassing, memories we would all laugh at later. The war and all the carnage it's leaving in its path was starting to take a toll on every one of us. I also needed a distraction from the mess I call my love life since I just ended my most recent "relationship" (if you can even call it that).

Jennie was the first one over to help me get things set up for the weekend and just oh so casually mentioned she would be bringing someone with her she wanted me to meet. She's probably one of the only people who knows the innerworkings of my mind, but that doesn't necessarily mean she can take a hint. I know she hasn't been the most excited about my choice in men, so she tries to intervene whenever she can. The current score on how that's working out you ask? Jennie – 0. She has good intentions and I often remind myself that, but when I heard she was bringing along a random guy, we'll just say I wasn't exactly brimming with excitement.

"He'll be great! Such a gentleman, and he can hold his own."

I couldn't keep my eyes from rolling as I crossed my arms, "Jennie, I've told you I'm not looking for anything right now. I just got done seeing someone and I need a break to reset. Plus, I want to focus on having fun this weekend. No strings attached."

"Quit it! I can hear your eyes rolling from here," she jokingly swatted the air in my general direction while she continued, "I would hardly call that seeing someone ... you slept with him a couple times then tossed him aside like yesterday's trash."

"Well, a couple times is more than I can say for most guys. There are far more important things to worry about right now."

I had to turn around to finish prepping the snacks so Jennie couldn't see the worry starting to cloud my face as I thought about my high-ranking military dad being caught up in the thick of the war. My mind kicked into overdrive trying to come up with ideas to change the topic, "Do you think we have enough drinks for the weekend?"

"Yeah, there's plenty," Jennie laughed, but I could sense she knew what I was doing. Thank goodness she didn't press the issue anymore. At least she got the hint this time.

I took a second to look around to ensure everything was in place ready to go – snacks set in the middle of the table, drinks and glasses lined up near the fridge to provide easy access to ice, and the house looking spotless. Dad would be proud. I was starting to get sentimental as the doorbell rang. Jennie sauntered over to the door, calling out over her shoulder, "I'll get it!"

"Thanks."

Turns out the first person to arrive isn't one of our friends, instead it's the mystery man. At least he's pretty punctual (about thirty minutes early) and I can appreciate that. I moved the sand bags that were my legs slowly towards the door to introduce myself. *Wait, is this nerves? Is that why it's so hard to move forward?* Thankfully, Jennie was here being her normal, bubbly self, giving me a chance to shake it off, "Chris! It's so nice to see you again! We're glad you could make it."

While Jennie and Chris were going back and forth catching up, I took a moment to take all of Chris in. He's tall, just under six feet with strong facial features and tan, so he's not a vampire unless he gets a spray tan. *Phew, don't have to worry about that.* I could tell he spends a good amount of time in the gym based on his muscle definition which means he could probably keep up with me. He has thick brown hair that he keeps a little messy and at a shorter length. However, there was something about him that seemed kind under his good looks, something I wanted to explore a little more – not what I was expecting. At all. Most of the guys Jennie associates with have massive egos, but I'm not getting those vibes from Chris. On the plus side, he seems like he can carry on a good conversation, but that could also be from Jennie talking his ear off.

Next thing I knew, they were both looking at me. Jennie with a big, expectant grin on her face and Chris with a shyer version of her smile.

"Sorry, I must've spaced for a second. What did I miss?" I asked as I pasted a smile on my face to mirror them.

Jennie chimed in now with a quizzical expression on her face that still had her grin fixed there, "I figured I shouldn't be rude and actually introduce you two. Chris, this is Valerie. Valerie, Chris."

I reached out to shake Chris' hand so as to not come off as rude, or more importantly, like a creep, "It's nice to meet you. Jennie's told me a lot about you."

"All good things I hope," he smiled returning the handshake. I couldn't help but notice he has a firm handshake. *Yikes, here we are both sounding cliché*. Jeez, I feel rusty with trying to actually make conversation without the help of beer. Feeling the heat rising to my face, I turned around to lead the three of us back into the kitchen, "Help yourself to any drinks and snacks."

I heard the sound of legs speeding up, and judging by the pace they were moving, it was Jennie who was probably here to quiz me about me zoning out, "Excuse us a moment, Chris. We'll be right back. I just realized we forgot to bring up some chips."

"No worries, J, I'll hold down the fort."

She grabbed me by the elbow leading me out of the kitchen down to the basement so there was no chance of Chris hearing us. In a hushed tone, the interrogation commenced, "What are you doing? Here's this guy who I've known for years, so I know he's perfect for you and you're over there zoning out like you're the captain of the space cadets."

"I can't take a second to look him over? And, hold on, you know this guy is *perfect* for me? Am I no longer in control of who I choose to date?" I took a step back crossing my arms over my chest.

"Not if it means your ears stop working, and let's be real Val, you've been striking out left, right, and center. It's hard seeing you in this never-ending cycle."

"Look, I'm sorry. I got caught up in his smile and looks. It seemed as though you guys have been close so I didn't want to get in the middle of anything," a smile crawled across my face while I relaxed my arms hoping that did the trick to get this round of twenty questions out of the way. "I'll be open-minded, but just know this is the last time you're setting me up. Especially since I feel like I'm the third wheel here."

She relaxed a little, "Sorry if we were making you feel excluded in any way. We've known each other since elementary school. He's practically a brother to me, nothing more. I want to see you happy and that starts with being with a guy for longer than a month."

I winked at her turning to head back upstairs, "Don't worry about me. I'll give him a shot, but I'll go easy on him since you two are so close. Don't forget about the chips!"

I wanted to sound convincing despite not being the happiest about how Jennie is trying to exert control over me. Again, I know she has good intentions, but sometimes it doesn't come across that way.

Smile still on my face, I made it back to the kitchen where Chris was sitting at the island taking it all in, "Jennie's coming with the chips. Took us a second to find them since my parents have everything so organized."

"No worries. So, this is your parents' house?"

"Yeah, they're out of town and asked me to look after it. Sure beats my tiny studio."

He leaned forward resting his arms on the island, "For sure. What does it take to have a house this nice?"

"My dad has a pretty solid job," I said quickly. Changing the topic because I didn't want to give too much information away, I continued, "Jennie mentioned you guys go way back."

"Oh yeah, I've known J forever. She's like a sister to me. Seems like she's worked her charm on you too."

I let out a nervous chuckle, "Yeah, she basically took me under her wing. Not like I needed it, but I can definitely appreciate her friendship. Drink?"

He nodded and I tossed over a beer just as Jennie was coming back with the chips. I could tell she was eavesdropping based on the smile on her face. Clearly, she thinks it's going well in the short amount of time we've been talking. I turned my attention back to Chris, "You sure got here early."

"Couldn't pass up on the chance for food and meeting this wonderful friend of J's. She's only gone on and on about you a million times recently, so you could say I didn't have much of a choice," Chris said with one of his eyebrows raised looking at Jennie.

I tried to hold back my laughter, "She's a bit persuasive."

"Better yet, she's unrelenting," Chris said.

Jennie took this moment to jump back in the conversation to change the topic, "Be warned, Chris, the group getting together this weekend can get pretty rowdy, I hope you can keep up," she continued as she jabbed an elbow in my side. "This one especially."

Now, both eyebrows were raised as he looked back at me, "Should be fun."

I made my way over to the drinks and grabbed a beer with the hopes it would make me more willing to be sociable. Meanwhile, Jennie was back to talking to Chris. I'm not always the best at making conversation around someone new, especially in a small group setting unless there's a competition, or alcohol, which reminded me of a couple things I still needed to take care of: music and cards. The plan is to start the night off with some poker, and let the rest of the friends weekend flow organically.

We've all been needing this little break with how intense this war has been lately. Everyone's on edge and it seems like every conflict contributing to the fighting is getting worse. Civilian routines typically consisted of going to work followed by heading home to lay low and check for any updates. The economy is tight and the fighting has been getting closer and closer to home which makes it hard for people to want to go out. I mean, it took a while just to get a small group of friends together, and even then, they only wanted to hang out at someone's house who has a bunker in case the bomb sirens go off. But I couldn't think of that right now ... I have to shake those thoughts out of my head and make sure I'm fun. Otherwise, I might scare everyone off. *I'm the host after all, right?*

"While we wait for the slow people to show up, shall we play a few rounds of Texas Hold'Em?" I asked as I sauntered back in the room, waving a deck of cards in one hand while I carried a case with poker chips in the other.

Chris seemed to perk up at the mention of playing cards, "I have to warn you, that's my game."

"This should be fun then. I don't think I've ever lost a game, and don't think those good looks of yours are going to end my streak. Jennie, can you grab my drink?"

I sat down at the table pulling everything out to get it setup. I nodded my head to get Jennie and Chris to head over my way.

A smile started to tug at the corners of his lips, "Good looks, huh? It goes both ways."

I gave a quick smile in return. All I need is a little competition to get my confidence back. The three of us snagged our spots at the poker table in a back corner of the house and Jennie volunteered to deal. It didn't take long to get in the rhythm of playing a few hands and tallying a win with each one. Poor Chris thought he had a chance of winning at least one hand, but what can I say? I'm something of a card shark.

Jennie started rambling so I took this opportunity to steal a glance at Chris, only to find he was doing the same thing, "Can I help you?"

He shook his head quickly shifting his gaze away from me, "I'm just surprised Jennie didn't introduce us any earlier, or that we didn't run into each other at the tables. Considering how I have no chance of winning, you must play *a lot.*"

Jennie giggled, apparently happy at the sight of me joking around and trying to flirt with Chris while she started dealing the next round. We went back to playing with Jennie occasionally checking her phone for any updates from our friends. Chris would throw some playful jabs at Jennie for not throwing him a bone with her dealing and I would jump in every now and then to try to get under his skin. Jennie finally placed an order for pizza when our stomachs decided to join in on the conversation making us take a break. She stepped away from the table for a moment to use the bathroom leaving Chris and I by ourselves, when he promptly scooted his chair closer to mine, "J wasn't kidding, you're a killer with the cards."

I guess he doesn't waste any time with trying to make a move.

"Eh, I guess it's a talent of mine or lady luck is on my side," I said taking my turn to shrug.

"I would have to say, lady luck's on my side tonight. I'm glad J talked me into coming."

This time I couldn't help but laugh, "You're starting to lay it on thick!"

Chris raised his shoulders up looking at me sheepishly, "I'm a little rusty. It's been a while since I've been on the dating scene."

"Why is that?"

"I've had other priorities. I've spent a lot of time focusing on my work and getting adjusted to a new city. J's really the only friend I have out here."

"I can see that, where'd you ...," before I got a chance to finish that sentence, Jennie came bouncing back in. "Pizza should be here in about thirty minutes and everyone should be here any moment. Did I interrupt something?"

Chris and I shook our heads with him scooting back to put more space between us. Done with cards, we moved our party to the couch to continue our conversation killing some time while we waited for pizza. It was mostly Jennie and Chris carrying the conversation, but that's okay considering there were plenty of other things occupying my mind.

The doorbell rang signaling the arrival of delicious pizza and I wasted no time jumping up to rush to the door. You would've thought I was starving with how quick I moved, but I wanted to step away from Jennie and Chris for a moment.

"Where are these other slackers?" Jennie asked checking her phone as I came back into the living room with pizza in hand.

Shrugging, I responded with my mouth full of pizza, "I'm not sure. They're late, but usually one of them would've said something by now."

Jennie's phone started ringing as if on cue, so she excused herself and walked out the back door, once again leaving Chris and I alone. This time wasn't feeling as awkward, but maybe that's because I had some pizza and beer in me getting me to return to my normal, confident self. Chris moved to sit next to me, just close enough for us to brush shoulders, and grabbed a slice. He started to eat, but didn't move away. I normally would've put a little more distance between myself and whoever was next to me, yet there was something there that was making it hard for me to want to move. The pizza and beer in me probably had something to do with that.

"You know, I almost didn't come over."

Raising my eyebrows, I replied, "That's not how Jennie makes it sound."

"We may be close, but she doesn't know everything. And she's definitely not in my head. No psychic bond or anything."

"Well, I don't know if having that kind of bond with Jennie would actually benefit you. I was dreading her trying to set me up, too."

He looked at me, face inches away, "Either way, I'm enjoying myself."

I started to smile while angling myself more towards him, "Me too."

Even up close, Chris was a good-looking guy and I could feel myself getting lost in his hazel eyes. Man, this is not how I expected this to go at all. He started to lean in, intensifying the magnetic pull I had been feeling.

Chapter 2

"I'm glad to see you guys are hitting it off this fast," Jennie remarked as she stood with her hands on her hips, a knowing grin creeping across her face. Yup, she knows she's about to have an "I told you so" moment.

Chris and I were moments away from sharing a kiss, and probably would have too, if Jennie didn't take that exact moment to come back in. Relief flooded me giving me the opportunity to sit back and not rush into something again. *Stop getting caught up in these moments, they get you into trouble.* I could feel the heat rising to my cheeks telling me I was blushing and stealing a quick glance towards Chris told me he was feeling the same way.

With that grin still on her face, Jennie mentioned, "Well, in case you both were wondering, Daryl's running later than usual and will probably be over in an hour. Something to do with work. He mentioned that Lilly needs a lift, so I'm headed out to grab her. Will you two kids be okay if I leave you alone?"

"Yeah, we'll be fine, mom," I mocked, rolling my eyes. "It'll give me a chance to show Chris around a little bit and maybe continue my win streak with something different, like pool."

"Alright, give me 20-30 minutes and I'll be back with Lil," Jennie winked while she grabbed her keys to make her way out the front door.

As soon as the door closed, Chris looked over at me as he sighed, "Alone at last."

Another laugh escaped me as I stood up from the couch gesturing for him to follow me, "Come on. Let me at least show you around so you know where the essentials are."

Chris followed as I started giving him the house tour. I started with showing him the room he'd most likely be sleeping in and where the bathrooms were. The guest rooms were all decent sized with queen-sized beds, a TV, and plenty of room in the closets. There were a couple of bathrooms scattered between the guest rooms, but only one with a shower and bathtub. We had made our way to the basement outfitted with a small movie theater opposite to the pool table and bar. When we were standing next to the pool table, Chris asked, "Where does that door go?"

I followed his finger to see where he was pointing, "Oh, that's to the bunker, or shelter, or whatever you want to call it."

We made our way over and I opened the heavy, airtight door revealing stairs that went down underground a little further. I flipped the light switch to reveal several doors lining the hallway, all open to show comfortable rooms with more bathrooms mixed in there: a queen size bed in the corner with a nightstand outfitted with a lamp, a small dresser on the wall opposite of the bed, a cabinet filled with non-perishable food, and another cabinet filled with over-the-counter medication for almost any ailment. Each bathroom had a small shower, toilet, and sink. Nothing special, but enough to cover the essentials. Everything has been kept in pristine condition almost looking like it came out of a staged house for a magazine.

"Wow, what does your dad do? Everything you would ever need is down here!"

I looked back into the room we were currently looking at, "Which is kind of the reason we decided to hold this friends weekend here with how tensions are in the conflict."

I ignored the first question to keep myself from sharing more information than I wanted to since I just met this guy today.

"Not a bad idea."

I turned off the lights and we climbed the stairs in silence making our way back to the main floor. We reached the sliding glass doors leading to the outdoor oasis my parents worked so hard to create. Chris gestured for me to go first and I felt the smile return to my face as I looked out at the backyard. What can I say? This is a great place to relax.

There is an infinity pool overlooking the city down below with a hot tub in one corner. Not too far from the pool, there is a fire pit with plenty of comfortable seating all in the glow of several outdoor string lights. In another corner, there's a gazebo with a huge flower garden on the outside almost taking it over, which now that I think of it, is quite a romantic hideout. We couldn't have asked for a better night. The stars were out in full force with the Milky Way trying to make an appearance. Crickets and birds were filling the night with their soothing songs, and there wasn't a lot of added noise from cars.

"Good thing I brought that swimsuit too. It's going to be seeing some use this weekend. This is incredible!"

I looked over to Chris to get the full effect of his reaction, "It's definitely the best part of the house. Want to grab the pizza and some drinks so we can move the party out here?"

He still had a look of awe in his face as he swept his eyes back and forth to take in everything.

"I think we should," he started working his way back towards the door, snapping out of the wonder he was in moments ago. "I'll go grab everything."

Smile still plastered to my face, I checked my phone to see how much time has elapsed since Jennie left. It had only been 10 minutes. I texted her to let her know how things were going (things were going great, by the way) adding in that we wouldn't complain if she took the long way back for good measure. The three dots popped up in the bottom of the screen only to be replaced with a couple of thumbs up and winking emojis. Okay, she had me there. Laughter escaped me and I responded letting her know where to find us where she returned with Lilly. She replied letting me know she'll pick up some more pizza.

The sound of the door closing caused me to stuff my phone back in my pocket, "Jennie will be a little while longer. She's getting more pizza."

Chris erupted in a smile while he set things down on the table clearly happy with more alone time, "Good, I was hoping that would be the case."

We headed over the to the fire pit to keep working on the pizza and I noticed he had changed into his swimsuit.

"Planning on a swim?"

"I was hoping that was in the plans."

"I think we can make that arrangement, but isn't there the rule of having to wait 30 minutes after you eat? Jennie will for sure be back by then."

I let the sarcasm ooze from me to see how he would respond.

He picked up on my joke adding in a wink for good measure, "I can break rules every now and then."

We let the evening sounds fill our space while we continued working our way through our pizza. Every now and then, I would sneak some glances towards Chris, sometimes meeting his eyes. Something felt different with him. Things felt easy making me want to explore this a little more.

"Since our current pizza supply has run out thanks to Jennie not ordering enough, I think I'm going to hop in the pool. Got to work my appetite back up."

I knew exactly what I was doing with slowly peeling my shirt off. *Guess my original plan is going out the window as per usual.* As I worked my pants down, Chris' eyebrows inched up, "You're prepared."

"What can I say? I like to be ready for every situation," I said sashaying over to pool fully aware of Chris watching me the entire way. Continuing to take advantage of showing off, I gracefully dived into the pool hardly making a sound. The moment I surfaced, I saw Chris walking over pulling off his shirt revealing his strong physique. The butterflies wasted no time taking flight in my stomach.

Chris got ready to dive into the pool with me, mumbling, "Fuck taking it slow."

I laughed hearing what Chris said. He must've had the same initial thought as I did with not wanting to rush into things. Funny how those plans can change.

It didn't take long for Chris to swim up next to me, and the moment he got by my side, his hand grazed my cheek finally resting at the nape of my neck. He gently pulled me in for a kiss. When our lips touched, muscle memory kicked in leading me to wrap my arms around his waist so I can close the distance between our bodies. Responding to my movement, Chris turned up the passion with his tongue gently grazing my bottom lip every now and then. Not being one to leave him hanging, I returned the favor.

I don't know how long we had been wrapped up in each other, but it was long enough for Jennie to return. Clearing her throat, she said, "Seems like I should've taken even more time than I thought."

Feeling like teenagers being caught in the act, we pushed away from each other blushing. Again.

"We were just enjoying the view."

"Hmph, some view you're getting behind closed eyes," she held up another pizza box. "Come get it while it's still hot."

Lilly, in the meantime, was trying to keep her laughter contained, "Why am I not surprised Val?"

"Hey," I said starting to feel a little defensive. "At least this is someone Jennie already approves of."

Chris jumped in at this moment, "I'm Chris, a friend of J's."

Lilly rolled her eyes towards Jennie, "Of course. I should've expected you to go and set up Val with a friend of yours. Tired of the scum she's always 'with'?"

Lilly, who's always full of sass, put air quotes around the last part of her question rubbing salt in the wound. I looked at Chris who was blushing and looking away then back towards Jennie and Lilly, "Lil, come on, no need to try to pick a fight. This weekend is about having fun and letting loose."

The tension in Lilly's shoulders started to melt away, "You're right, I'm sorry. Plus, that's no way to give a first impression."

Before I started to swim back over to the stairs, I turned to Chris further apologizing on Lilly's behalf, "I'm sorry she started off hostile. She's a little firecracker, and on top of everything else, she just went through a bad breakup herself. Unfortunately, that means she's taking it out on everyone. No excuse for her behavior, but I wanted to at least give you warning."

"Thanks. I'm just more upset about us getting interrupted."

I nudged his side with my elbow, thankfully under water so the other two couldn't see, "Me too. Just means we'll have to pick up where we left off sometime."

We made our way out of the pool and back over to the fire pit where Jennie and Lilly were sitting diving into the newest round of pizza. They were partaking in the latest round of gossip going around their office from the last week, which thankfully, seemed to have worked at diverting Lilly's attention from the events taking place when they first arrived. Jennie was good at easing tensions.

"So, Val," Lilly turned her attention to me. "It's been a hot minute since we saw each other. How's life?"

"Oh, same old, same old. Just house-sitting now."

"Obviously. When do your parents get back?"

I shrugged, not wanting to dive too much into the details around the lives of my parents. I turned my attention to Jennie, quickly changing the topic, "Jennie, have you heard from anyone else besides Daryl?"

As if on cue, Jennie looked back down at her phone, "Yeah, it sounds like Joe and Bev are going to be a little longer, but Mark is on his way."

"Is Mark still seeing that one lady?" Lilly asked while perking up at the mention of his name.

I couldn't resist asking, "Why? Are you hoping to sink your claws into him?"

Lilly was a good friend, but she was one I kept at a distance especially since she likes to take jabs at me when she can. I wouldn't put it past her to leave me hanging if I ever needed her help. I mostly remained civil for Jennie's benefit since she was the one who brought Lilly into this group. Plus, I've known about the crush she's had on Mark just by the way she perks up at the mention of his name. It doesn't help that Mark returns the attention making it obvious something's there. My guess is the timing has never lined up for them to act on their feelings, but you never know.

"You know me so well, Val," she shot back at me, lacing that response with some poison.

I put my hands up in surrender, "Hey, I was just getting back at you for the comments earlier. Call us even now."

"You're right. I did deserve that one. You do know how I would love my chance at Mark, though."

"Mmhmm. Jennie, can you let them all know to come around back?"

Jennie nodded her head, "Already did. Lil, come with me to bring more stuff out here. It's such a beautiful night, we can't let it go to waste plus I want s'mores."

Jennie and Lilly started to walk away when Jennie turned her head to wink at me. She wanted to give us more alone time before the rest of the chaos arrived, and for that, I was appreciative. As I turned to Chris, he asked, "Is the dynamic between you and Lilly always so tense?"

"Eh, kind of. She can be intense and will walk all over you if you aren't careful. Another thing to watch out for with her is that if she finds you attractive, she won't hold back, so don't let your guard down around her."

"No need to worry about that."

I ignored that last comment to jump into telling Chris a little more about the group joining us tonight, "As for our other friends, I figured I should give you a head's up about them too. Daryl is a higher up for a financial company and can be protective of his friends which means he can also be a little intense. Don't start talking financial numbers unless you want him to talk your ear off. He's a lot nicer than Lilly, though, and doesn't come out swinging. Joe and Beverly, or Bev, are the token married couple and some of the nicest people you'll ever know. Then there's Mark, who's the playboy of the group and the current focus of Lilly, as you can tell. He's a little bit of a clown and likes to joke around a lot. I think you'll fit in with them."

He smiled back at me, "Sounds like a good mix of people. How do you all know each other?"

"We kind of all just stumbled across each other. Jennie and Lilly work together. Jennie and I met when we were in college. She was actually dating a brother of one of my ex's at the time and we just ended up bonding over how terrible they were. Daryl met Jennie and me in college too and we kind of became the three musketeers. I honestly wouldn't be surprised if those two started something. Joe and Bev came into the picture through Daryl – Joe works at the same company as Daryl and they became really good friends, so naturally, Bev ended up becoming part of the group too. Then, there's Mark ... he came into the picture because of Lilly and we've somehow enjoyed the chaos he brings."

Chris nodded for a moment, "Well, hopefully I can mesh with the group too. I've at least enjoyed getting to know you a bit more."

I returned the smile, "I hope so. I'm sure everyone will like you."

I stood up to grab my clothes as I heard the sliding glass door open. Looking up thinking it was Jennie and Lilly coming back outside, I was pleasantly surprised to see Daryl making his way towards me with his usual lazy grin on his face, "Val, long time no see!"

Forgetting my clothes, I ran over to him with arms wide open for a hug and a huge smile on my face, "Daryl! It's been way too long. Where've you been hiding?"

We embraced in a tight hug swaying on our feet for a while before conversation resumed. It had been at least a year since I had seen him last which has been the longest since we met freshman year of college.

The story of the three musketeers begins at orientation where Daryl and I were in the same group for one of those introduction games they make you play. We kept joking around with one another until we decided to grab some dinner off campus. During those conversations, we found out we had a lot in common including being in the same dorm. We spent countless hours with each other, so I guess you could say we kind of had a thing, but nothing ever evolved. There was one night Daryl and I kissed. I think that was the moment I decided we should remain friends. After that, I started dating around finally landing a guy I could picture forever with. In the midst of that, I met Jennie and the three of us ended up hanging out during late night study sessions fueled by pizza. From there, the friendship blossomed and we've been tight ever since.

"Just didn't want to scare away any of your dates," he mentioned while we separated from each other. "Although, my streak may be over. Who's the new guy and didn't you just get out of a relationship?"

"Come on over and meet Chris. Jennie brought him over because she felt the need to set me up with someone better."

As I turned to head back over to Chris, I ruffled Daryl's messy, thick brown hair a bit just to annoy him a little in return for the question about my dating life. I couldn't help but notice something behind that easy grin of his, there seemed to be some sadness in his eyes. *Did I say something wrong?*

We headed back over towards the fire pit where Chris was watching us closely. When we were back in the circle, I tossed Chris' shirt to him and introduced the two guys. Daryl, being the easy-going person he was, casually stuck out his hand and shook Chris', "Hey man, I'm Daryl. It's nice to meet you. I hear Jennie dragged you here for a weekend of torture?"

A smile cautiously made its way across Chris' face, yet I could tell there was some tension underneath the surface, "Nice to meet you! I'm Chris. Valerie was just telling me about all you guys in this group. It seems like it'll be a fun weekend at least."

I'm starting to wonder if Chris saw something there too and it's bugging him. I'm not sure why it should, though, considering we just met. I headed towards the house to remove myself, "I'll be back. I'm going to grab some towels for everyone and see what Jennie and Lil are up to."

I got back inside the house to find Jennie and Lilly hanging out at the island chatting each other up. I gave a little finger wave then made my way upstairs to the linen closet to grab towels. I heard some voices coming from one of the guest rooms that sounded like Joe and Bev getting settled in with dropping their bags off, so that meant Mark was the only one who still needed to make his way here. With my arms loaded up with towels, I popped my head in the open doorway to say hi to the two of them. It had been a while since I had seen them too since they usually only came around when Daryl did.

I made my way back to the door to see that Mark had joined the crew. All three guys were standing up chatting around the fire with beers in hand. Mark and Chris seemed to be getting along just fine since they were both laughing at something I'm sure Mark said. What really caught my attention, though, was Daryl who was standing in a way that he could have full view of the sliding doors while still being a part of the conversation. And he was staring right at me in a way I hadn't seen in years. I paused with my hand on the door waiting to open it.

I took a deep breath to remind myself that Daryl and I tried the relationship thing back in college only for it to not work. *What was going to make it any different now?* Besides, I was hitting it off with Chris who was charming and easy on the eyes. Plus, Jennie's been wanting a shot at Daryl and I didn't want to come in between that despite his stare telling me otherwise.

I snuck out of the house as best I could and placed the towels by the pool, taking my time before making my way back over to the guys. Time to be the good host and at least say hi to Mark.

Mark's infamous million-dollar smile grew even bigger when I joined their circle, "There she is!"

"Hey Mark, you know Lilly is stewing over you right now, right?"

He winked, "Yeah, that's the plan. She's more fun when she's feisty."

"Don't let her stew too long, I don't want to deal with an angry Lilly more than I already have," I clapped back rolling my eyes. "I think everyone's here now, so let the games begin!"

It was like that was everyone's cue. Jennie, Lilly, Joe and Bev made their way outside with more food and drinks, but most importantly, the s'mores supply. I turned up the music to let the party vibes take over. This was the first time in a long time since all of us had been at the same place for more than five minutes and I was starting to realize how much I missed everyone. I pulled out my phone to capture a selfie to remember this exact moment. Thankfully, I put my phone on my seat right as Daryl scooped me up, ran over to the pool, and threw me in, "Hey!"

Before he could respond, he was jumping in too. A mix of happy squeals and laughter took over everyone else as they started making their way over to the pool to join us. Treading water, I felt a familiar arm grab me by the waist and lead me over to the far end where I was at not too long ago, "I couldn't let a tradition die. And I wanted a quick second with you before everyone else is in range. I've missed you. I've missed you a lot Val. I couldn't be around you for a while because ..."

Before Daryl was finished, everyone else caught up with us. Good timing too, I don't think I was ready for where that conversation was going. There was something different about the way Daryl was acting tonight. There was an intensity behind his actions and a fire in his stare. I wiggled myself away from him and went over to Jennie who was on the opposite side of the now forming friend circle with Chris. She could tell something was up despite my best efforts to keep my poker face on.

I think Jennie may be the only one who could read me all the time. I shook my head no to signal there was nothing to discuss and nodded towards the hot tub, "Chris, want to join Jennie and me while these goons keep a tradition alive?"

"Sure! What tradition?"

Jennie laughed, "You'll see. Best to have a vantage point though. You don't want to be drug in right away."

We hauled ourselves into the hot tub and I took this moment to discard my soaking wet clothes since I didn't get the opportunity to keep them dry.

"Let the games begin," I yelled again as I got comfortable between Chris and Jennie.

Chapter 3

It was like a referee blew the whistle. Lilly and Bev wasted no time getting on the shoulders of Mark and Joe while Daryl started reviewing the rules, "Alright, it's been a while since we were able to partake in the tradition to kick off a friends weekend. Let's review the opening ceremony rules. Ladies, this is a standard chicken fight. Whichever team gets knocked over first is the loser and is out of the next round. Whoever wins takes on the newest couple in the arena," he gestured over towards the direction of Chris and I as he continued, "our wonderful hostess and the newcomer."

I jumped in here, "Hold on, this wasn't part of the agreement ..."

"You don't think we can take on the winners and be crowned champions?" Chris asked with a competitive look on his face making me feel confident we could win anything.

I put up my hands in surrender and gestured for Daryl to continue.

"That settles it. The first losing team is in charge of keeping our food and drink supply stocked. You may begin."

Daryl stepped back as the two teams started towards each other. Mark and Lilly looked determined while on the other side, Joe and Bev looked like they were completely enjoying themselves. Based on that, I already knew how this first round was going to go. I leaned over to Chris to start prepping him,

"I'll tell you right now that Mark and Lilly are going to be the winners of this round. They're too competitive and Joe and Bev are too nice."

"So, you guys all know this and just make Joe and Bev be your glorified waiters?"

Jennie chimed in, "Eh, they do it regardless because they're saints. Might as well make it fun."

He laughed and we settled in to watch the battle take place. We didn't have to wait long, however. Lilly saw her opportunity and took it. She lowered her shoulder as Mark charged over to Joe and Bev ending that match. A loud splash was accompanied with Lilly and Mark pumping their fists in the air celebrating. Laughter and cheering erupted as Daryl coined Mark and Lilly as the champions of the first round. I stood up to make my way out of the hot tub, looking back at Chris, "You ready for this? I haven't lost a match yet and I don't plan on it today."

"Oof, no pressure or anything," I felt him nudge me in the ribs, surprised at how quickly and quietly he moved. *I think my record is safe today.*

We entered the pool taking a moment to adjust to the different temperature then swam over to where Mark and Lilly were trying their best to look intimidating. Chris didn't hesitate with getting me on his shoulders, and the next thing I knew, I was at Lilly's level. Daryl chimed in, "Alright, this is the final match for bragging rights. Will Mark and Lilly be crowned the new champions of the weekend? Or will Val and newcomer Chris continue Val's stellar record? There's only one way to find out and that begins now!"

Mark and Lilly took some time to try and size us up foregoing their original plan of attack they used against Joe and

Bev. Their hesitation was exactly what I was hoping for. I subtly tapped Chris on the back to indicate it was time to move forward. Thankfully he picked up on the message without revealing anything. I knew he'd be good at keeping a poker face the way he played me earlier at the table. Thanks to Chris' stealth moves he casually demonstrated earlier, I was able to grasp Lilly's shoulders quickly to catch her off-guard. Next thing I know, her eyes got big and then there was a splash, "Dang it!"

I punched the air, "Woo! The record is safe!"

I climbed off of Chris' shoulders to turn around and give him a high-five. Chris was smiling returning the high-five but not letting go of my hand, "You're welcome. I hope I did my part to keep your record safe."

I blushed, "Why, thank you mighty sir." I turned to Daryl, waiting for his announcement of the reigning champion to find a shadow clouding his face that I knew I was only meant for me to catch. Daryl turned back to everyone, the shadow disappearing as he announced, "Looks like the record is kept safe and Val has bragging rights through the whole weekend."

Joe and Bev didn't wait long to return with a couple of drinks, "For our champions." They jokingly bowed, "We are indebted to you."

Chris and I graciously accepted our drinks with a small curtsey, "Why thank you."

Normal conversations returned and everyone broke off into their little groups. Jennie, still in the hot tub, was now joined by Lilly and Mark. Daryl, Joe, and Bev were hanging out right next to the hot tub engrossed in their own conversation, but would chime in with the ones in the hot tub every now and then. Chris and I were a little further away at the edge of the infinity pool once again looking at my favorite view: the twinkling city lights of downtown below with the stars shining brightly above. As I took a drink of my beer, Chris wasted no time jumping into conversation, "So, I may be overstepping my bounds, but what's the deal between you and Daryl?"

For some reason, I felt a little nervous. There should be nothing making me feel this way, and normally there wouldn't be, but Daryl came into the house acting a little different than usual.

I shrugged off the question avoiding any eye contact with Chris, "There's nothing. We've been good friends for a long time. When we first met, we tried to see if we could be something more, but that just felt awkward, so we agreed to keep things platonic."

Chris panned his gaze back out towards the city, "Doesn't seem like he got the message though."

I decided to try to make this more light-hearted and poked his shoulder, "A little jealous? Need I remind you we've already kissed and I've only met you a couple hours ago."

He chuckled, "There's something about you I can't quite put my finger on, but I can't get enough."

"Ah, you're experiencing the Val effect."

We both jumped at the sound of Mark's voice, breaking the little bubble we thought we were in.

"Sorry to interrupt this, ah, session, but your audience is getting ready for s'mores and figured you two didn't want to be left out. I have a hunch there's not going to be a lot left if you wait."

Chris grabbed our drinks following Mark when he asked, "What's the Val effect?"

"Ah young student, wise question," Mark said as he threw an arm over Chris' shoulder leading him away from me. "Val has this allure that can draw anyone in if you're not careful. She consumes your thoughts and when you're around her, you just want to be caught up in every inch of her. She's a modern-day siren, or kryptonite, whether you consider yourself a sailor lost in the sea of love or Superman. Judging by the way you carry yourself, I'd say your Superman who has found Luthor's stash."

Their voices trailed as they walked further ahead. My feet were cemented at the bottom of the pool and I'm sure I heard an echo from the sound of my jaw dropping. *What was Mark rambling on about?? A siren? Kryptonite?* Despite the nonsense Mark was rambling on about, I was happy he interrupted.

I took a few more seconds to gather myself before making my exit out of the pool. I grabbed the remaining towel and checked on the marshmallow supply before finding my seat, "Do we need any more mallows or anything else for the s'mores? I see you all wasted no time diving into them."

Jennie looked at me with a smile like a little kid who just tried their first s'more ever, "There's more?! Bring it all out here!"

"Sure thing," I laughed as I turned to head inside.

Back in the comfort the four walls of the house provided me, I took a deep breath to try to center myself. I started digging through the pantry pulling out the requested supplies when I heard footsteps joining me in the kitchen. I looked up expecting to see either Daryl, Chris, or Jennie, but was surprised to find Bev and Joe, "What's up guys?"

Bev started grabbing what I had pulled out while Joe responded, "Nothing much. It's been a while Val. It looks like you're doing good though."

Joe leaned against the island, "I just wanted to give you a head's up about something."

Feeling the conversation shift to a more serious tone, I paused what I was doing and looked over to Bev before looking back at Joe, "Is everything okay?"

Joe smiled, "Oh, it's nothing to be worried about. We're good! I just wanted to give you some more insight as to why Daryl has been a little M.I.A. lately."

"Yeah, what's up with that? He's been turning down invites from Jennie and I. That's not like him."

"Well, there's been some developments in the feelings department for Mr. Chill-As-A-Cucumber."

I raised my eyebrows, "Oh really? Did he finally find his one-and-only?"

"It might be something like that. Look, in all seriousness, Daryl started to realize he had feelings for –"

Cutting him off, I got excited jumping right in to attempt to finish his sentence, "For Jennie?! Oh, I knew it! And he's been acting weird because he thinks it'll bug me."

Joe glanced at Bev who just shrugged, "Um, not exactly. I'm just going to get straight to it. Val, he realized he has feelings for you, and not just any type of feelings, strong feelings. A big reason why he decided to come tonight was because he wanted to shoot his shot, but I can see Jennie is cock-blocking with the friend she brought who can't seem to keep his eyes, or hands, off you."

I felt like someone reached inside my lungs taking all of the air out of me. And I mean all of it.

"Hold on, what?"

Bev took this time to chime in, "Val, it's hard to understand especially when you thought his feelings would be directed towards Jennie. You two would make the best match though, and the way he describes it, it's always been you."

"This feels like the most cliché rom-com story line. There's no way, he's always made it clear he's good with just being friends. What changed?"

Joe chuckled, "Nothing ever changed, you just didn't want to see it. Either way, take some time to think on it. Seems like you have some options, but just so you know, I'm rooting for team Daryl. Chris is nice and all and could be a great addition to our group, but there's just something about you and Daryl."

I nodded indicating I would be thinking on this. I guess I just didn't want to admit there could be something between the two of us.

"Thanks for telling me, guys. You two always know how to look out for others."

Bev came over and gave me a hug, "We just didn't want you to be blindsided, that's all. We care a lot about you two."

We finished our conversation then took everything outside. In light of the recent conversation, I decided to settle in next to Jennie rather than succumbing to every urge telling me to go sit with Chris. I didn't want to muddy it up any more than what it already was.

The night was filled with laughter, games, a lot of jokes, and a lot of confused looks from Jennie and Chris. It was getting to be around midnight when we were all settled in to the family room watching a movie. We buried ourselves under blankets with several bowls overflowing with popcorn. I took a moment to look around once again appreciating my friends when a yawn took over. I didn't realize how tired I was getting. Before I fell asleep here, I got up and gathered my blanket. Jennie paused the movie, "Don't tell me our champion is getting sleepy?"

"I'm afraid so, but don't let that stop you guys from finishing the movie. I think I'm going to get my beauty sleep."

Mark chimed in with one of his usual jokes, "We can't let our Siren miss out on her precious hours of beauty sleep, can we?"

I jokingly threw my pillow at him, laughing, "Shut up, Mark."

Jennie chimed back in, "Well, good night, Val. We'll see you in the morning."

"Good night, guys," I said turning around to make my way to my room eagerly looking forward to being able to hide out in my sanctuary.

I got up to my room, finally able to have more than a few moments alone. I've always loved my space at my parent's house. It was a pretty decent sized room, which I've always been thankful for knowing I was lucky enough to have, with its own full bathroom (again, my dad has a really well-paying job) and a balcony overlooking the backyard. There were vaulted ceilings making the room even more spacious like my own castle. I knew I had a great life growing up, and I'm definitely appreciative of my parents for everything they provided, but I'm also glad I made it clear I'm doing things on my own now. Boundaries and what-not. Standing here, I realized this room is bigger than my apartment, but my apartment is my true palace.

I was trying to avoid thinking through everything that has happened today. Meeting Chris, kissing Chris, seeing Daryl, learning about his feelings about me even though those admissions didn't technically come from his mouth. I think I'll wait to hear it from Daryl before putting too much stock into what Joe and Bev explained. Thankfully, Chris doesn't know where I'm sleeping and it's at the complete opposite end of the hall or I don't think I'd be getting much sleep tonight. But Daryl knew where I'd be. He also knows he could get me alone to talk which didn't necessarily bother me.

On my way to the bathroom, I opened the balcony door to let some fresh air in bringing the refreshing outdoor sounds with it. I paused before starting my nighttime routine wondering if I should go back down to ask if they could all lock up the place and close everything down, but they've been here enough to know the routine.

As I was wrapping up my oral hygiene, a light knock came from my door, "Come in."

I knew exactly who would be closing the door as I made my way out into the main room area. I had the TV playing the same movie they were all watching downstairs so I could fully be involved in the conversation about it tomorrow. Daryl smiled as he drew his eyes away from the TV and over to me, "Can we talk?"

"Sure. Want to take it outside?"

He answered by moving towards the door, grabbing the blanket I was using earlier, and gesturing for me to sit in the chair next to him.

"What's up?"

By the look on his face, I knew I was about the get the conversation I hadn't yet had with him.

"Um, I'm not sure where to start, so I'm just going to jump right in," Daryl nervously ran his hand through his hair again, making it even messier. "Val, I've missed you like hell, but I couldn't be around you until I sorted through everything that was running through my head and heart. In college, when we kissed, it was like everything stopped. Every part of me wanted to be with you. You were so quick to say that we should remain friends that I didn't want to blow the opportunity to be in your life, so I agreed. It wasn't until I saw you last year when you, Jennie, your guy of the month, and I were hanging in the bar that I couldn't stand seeing you with someone who wasn't me."

Realization sunk in as I was absorbing his words. That was the last night I had seen him until now. This entire time, I thought he was just beyond busy with work. At least, that's how he made it sound every time Jennie or I tried to reach out. He continued, "And then I come here tonight, hoping to get a second chance to see if we could be something, but Jennie had to bring over her friend who is clearly into you. It was like she had this planned."

That got my attention. It wouldn't be the first time she's tried something like this, but I thought we had moved on from that time in our lives. I held up one of my hands signaling him to stop, "Wait, what do you mean?"

"I told Jennie months ago what was going on when I turned down her invitation to grab a bite only because she got all up in arms about it. She hounded me with questions about why I wasn't spending time with you guys anymore. I couldn't deal with it, so I told her everything about the feelings I've had for you which must have pissed her off."

I remembered Joe's words about Jennie cock-blocking Daryl, but they didn't register until now, "Daryl, you do realize Jennie has been trying to get with you for a while now, right?"

He just shook his head sighing, "I know, and so by me confessing what I did, she got mad and was doing her best to make sure I had no chance."

Realization dawned on me, "So that's why she's been pushing me towards Chris. I thought that was weird. It's not that she wants me to be with a better guy, it's so she can keep me away from you."

Daryl looked me dead in the eyes, "You think Chris is better than the guys you've seen in the past?"

"I thought he was."

"Val, you always try to see the best in everyone, so much so that you don't see the faults. He's exactly like every other guy you've been with. Plays the prince charming card just so he can get in your pants."

I forced myself not to get angry with him for saying that and instead let his words sink in. Chris was so quick to try to get me alone and wasn't afraid to let his jealousy show even though we had just met almost as if he was being possessive. The same routine I've been going through the past couple of years.

Daryl continued, "I don't care anymore, though. Val, I want to explore a relationship with you and I can't stand the thought of not being with you. You've made things so much better in my life. You do have that effect Mark said, and I have to admit that out of all the crazy shit he says, he hit the bullseye on that one."

We both chuckled at that. I reached over to place my hand on top of Daryl's, noticing an electric current I hadn't before. I don't know if that was from his confession or if that had always been there. With everything that had been said tonight, I was second guessing a lot of what had happened in my past. I brought my eyes to his to see he was waiting if I had anything to say.

"Daryl, this is something that would be entirely new to me. Tonight has been a lot with so much to process, but I'm really happy you talked to me. It's good to hear it come from you." Daryl cocked his head to the side furrowing his brow a little bit. I wasn't planning on saying anything, but I decided to give him some insight, "To be honest, Joe and Bev gave me some warning."

"Damn those two," Daryl nervously laughed, "I tell them one piece of juicy news and they couldn't wait to spill the beans."

"Well, I'm glad they did because I told myself if you came to talk to me about your feelings and those feelings matched what they were telling me, I'd explore this more."

"Really?"

"Mmhmm," I confirmed as I scooted myself closer to him. Instead of waiting for him to make a move like I always do, I leaned in lightly kissing him, testing to see what he would do. You might have noticed by now that physical touch is my love language, but I know it can be off-putting. Daryl is analytical, so I wouldn't have expected him to kiss me back right away. I told myself to be okay with that. What I didn't expect was for him to circle one of his arms around my waist to pull me to him while cupping my cheek with the other. "Come here," he whispered against my lips.

He said that in such a gentle way, a way that no man has ever spoken to me before. What can I say? I'm a romantic. The next thing I know, we're entwined on his seat on the balcony, kissing passionately.

Daryl locked his arms under my legs and stood up, carrying me back into the room. He laid me on the bed, locked the door leading out to the hall, then made his way back over to me. We wasted no time picking up where we left off, and before I knew it, we were completely lost in each other. We went a couple of rounds keeping our steady rhythm thankful for Lilly and Mark being in the room next to us so that no one would hear us over their symphony. I knew I'd be sore in the morning, but I couldn't wait to feel the ache of what being loved by Daryl felt like.

Chapter 4

I guess you could say Daryl and I woke up early, although it's hard to wake up when you didn't really sleep. The house was quiet and bringing a different kind of peace. Maybe it was because I was lying next to someone who really wanted all of me and not just for sex. I smiled at that thought. He kissed my forehead causing me to murmur a good morning to him.

He kissed my forehead again and tucked a strand of hair behind my ear, "Good morning, beautiful."

The sun was starting to rise with streams of light filtering in through the curtains creating a warm glow in the room. I wanted to be stuck in this moment not wanting to move, but my stomach ruined it by growling. Daryl propped himself up on his elbow to ask, "Do you want breakfast?"

"Hmmm, that sounds nice," I said stretching. "Let's go downstairs and make some."

"Even better, let's eat outside by the fire pit."

I gave him a quick kiss of approval before rolling out of bed. As I predicted, I was sore and every single one of my muscles were tired, "Wow, I haven't been this sore in a while."

He made a little noise when he stood on his feet, "You're not the only one feeling it, but I'll take this kind of soreness any day."

I grabbed some clean clothes out of my duffle bag to get dressed while he put on yesterday's clothes, "Guess I need to grab my bag from my room."

We giggled like a couple of teenagers. He poked his head out the door, "All clear."

We tiptoed to his room then back to mine, softly closing the door. He wrapped me up in his arms and kissed me passionately for a while before letting go to get dressed. Once clothed, we quietly made our way back downstairs so we didn't wake anyone else and looked at the mess that was left behind. I sighed, "I guess I'll start cleaning things up if you don't mind opening up the place?"

"Sure thing."

We got to work eventually making breakfast. I started on the pancakes while he took care of the sides ending up with plenty of food for everyone else when they decided to get moving. We took everything outside not wanting to wait for the others.

Joe and Bev were the first to join us smiles plastered on their faces as they asked in unison, "So? Any new developments?"

Daryl was the first to answer, "I think you two may know the answer to that since you decided to steal my thunder."

Joe winced a little bit, "Whoops, sorry bud. I just didn't want Val to be blindsided or put too much attention on the wrong person."

"It helped," I chimed in.

We continued our conversation for a little while longer until we were joined by Mark and Lilly. They had their plates piled high with food causing Daryl and I to give each other a knowing side glance. Mark and Lilly were so caught up in each other they didn't even notice Daryl and I. Bev spoke up, "You two seemed to have a good night."

Mark didn't hesitate, "It was something alright."

We all started diving into conversation catching up on events since it had been a while. It was nice to finally feel some normalcy even with all the new developments within our group. The only two remaining to join us were Jennie and Chris who came in that order about 30 minutes after Mark and Lilly. While the three of us couples were chipper, Jennie and Chris looked like they hadn't slept a wink. I knew what it meant when Jennie didn't have a lot of sleep in her, and it wasn't a good thing.

"Did Mark and Lilly keep everyone else up too?" she grumbled as she started aggressively stabbing a strawberry onto her fork.

Mark puffed his chest out a little more while Lilly blushed. Daryl and I coyishly grinned to one another knowing our secret was safe for now. It was Joe and Bev who finally responded, "Yeah, but what can you do about young love?"

"Young love my ass."

"Woah J, don't take it out on them," Chris piped in.

She sipped on some coffee before sighing, "You're right C, I should be happy for them."

As she said that, I knew instantly she was annoyed because she didn't have any company last night. *Tally one for me.* Daryl and I were able to work past the blockade she tried to put up in a selfish way to keep us from being together. I was also still a little mad she was putting herself before me when that was all I did for her. Even when she tried to pull this stunt before, I always wanted her to be the happiest and did whatever I could to make sure obstacles were removed from her path until now.

Thankfully, she hadn't realized what was going on between Daryl and I. I didn't want the bliss from last night to be over just yet. I also wasn't ready to confront her when we were trying to have a weekend focused on happiness.

Chris looked over at me longingly and I had a hunch he knew something was up. I also somehow had a feeling he wasn't going to say anything to Jennie. That could mean one of two things: he knew of her plan and was just a pawn, or he was genuinely happy for me. I nodded to him hoping he would pick up on the signal to keep his mouth quiet. Jennie kept going on and on about things that frustrated her and the last thing we all wanted to do was to add to that. Except Jennie completely changed the topic and directed the conversation to Daryl. She pointed her fork directly at him, squinting her eyes in the process, "Where did you sleep last night? Your room was completely empty this morning."

"Why were you looking for me?" he asked, calm as ever.

"I – I wasn't," she stammered, blushing and looking away. Realization slowly started to dawn on her. I watched her face go from thinking to confusion to hurt to rage in about five seconds, "Wait a minute, did you two?" she asked alternating who she was pointing to.

Mark spoke up first fist-bumping Daryl as he said, "Oh shit! That's what I'm talking about."

I jumped in directing the conversation back at Jennie before anyone else could, "Why would you try to interfere with someone's feelings?"

"Honestly, Valerie, I've been crushing on Daryl since I first met him. All I could see was how he looked at you and how you were oblivious to it, chasing these assholes and hurting him every time. I just wanted to take that pain away."

I knew how irritated she was feeling since she called me by my full first name. I narrowed my eyes, "I think your judgement got a little clouded in what you were trying to do. You were just going to cause him more pain by setting me up with Chris. That's low."

Instead of putting up a fight I thought she would, she hung her head, "You're right. I didn't think of that, I'm sorry Daryl."

Daryl shrugged it off. We all sat there in an awkward silence for several minutes. I think I came to the realization I was losing my best friend and it sucked, but it was all due to her actions trying to toy with everyone here. Jennie excused herself, followed by Chris and the rest of us were quiet for a little longer before Mark chimed in, "Well, that was awkward. And low, but on to better news. Lilly and I are going to try and make this work."

He put his arm around Lilly and I think that was the happiest I had seen her. *It's about time.* I raised my mug to them to convey my congratulations. Daryl, Joe, and Bev all did the same. We were able to go back into relaxed conversation enjoying each other's company. Bev went inside to grab the bowl of fruit, but we all knew she was checking on Jennie and Chris. There was no better person than her for the job. I was happy to see things working out for the majority of our group and was starting to wonder what this would do to our dynamic when a couple of fighter jets flew over. My attention shifted to the war. This was the first time in weeks we had seen any military action in the city, instantly reminding us all there was still a war going on.

We all took this moment to move the party inside to start brainstorming what we were doing for the day. It didn't take long for us to fill our day with games, time out on the pool deck, and delicious food. Jennie had simmered down and was joining back in on the fun with Chris in tow.

Time quickly passed. We were eating dinner in the living room watching TV when a breaking news broadcast came over. Most of the time, I didn't like to watch cable because of the nightly war updates, but we didn't want to get too engrossed in a show or movie when we were just going to get back in the pool. This time though, the newscaster gave a warning there was a good chance the sirens would be going off tonight due to some extra air activity during the day. We paused what we were doing to move our weekend bags down to the bunker, claiming our rooms. *There go our plans of hanging out in the pool tonight.* We also added in some of our favorite snacks and anything else we deemed as necessary before moving to close down all the blinds and shut off all the outdoor lights that way everything was ready to go in case the sirens sounded.

We sat back down to finish our dinner and I couldn't keep quiet, "I'm sorry guys. I was hoping we would've been able to shut out the nonsense of the world for one weekend."

Bev gave me a reassuring smile, "Nothing you can control, so you don't need to apologize. Isn't a big reason why we descended on your parent's house because of all the safety features your dad has built in?"

"I guess you're right."

"Let's get back to having fun."

And we did. That's one thing Joe and Bev always brought to the table, the ability to brighten the mood by always bringing the light. Plus, I didn't want to detract from all the good that has come out of this weekend so far. I looked around at everyone and smiled: Mark and Lilly were non-stop flirting with one another,

Jennie and Chris were reliving the glory days of their friendship while Joe and Bev gave them their undivided attention, and Daryl laughing at Mark while keeping a hand on my knee.

"Y'all ready to lose in some pool?"

"No way, Val. You may run the poker tables, but I'm the king of pool," Mark said as he mimicked the motion of hitting the balls.

"You're on!"

We cleaned up wasting no time getting downstairs to start the rounds of pool. While Mark was setting up for his first match against Daryl, I went back upstairs to make sure no lights were on and visible from the outside. Safety precautions, you know. Plus, I had to take this opportunity to grab Daryl's favorite drink as a motivator when Chris came upstairs looking for drinks as well. He paused when he saw me alone debating about whether to avoid any conversations or to take a moment to talk to me. He decided he wanted to continue on his mission and chose the latter option, "Valerie, I'm sorry about earlier and yesterday. Jennie mentioned something about what she was trying to do and being the friend I am, I didn't want to let her down."

"She has that kind of hold on you too, huh?" I asked casually leaning my hip against the counter.

"I guess so," he chuckled. "But, I can't deny the fact that you're a pretty damn good kisser. And what Mark was saying last night about the 'Val effect'? Totally real. There's something super alluring about you. Daryl's a lucky guy."

I nervously laughed, "Well, thanks, I guess? Either way, I'm sorry you got caught up in all this drama. I hope you can still enjoy your weekend."

"I intend to."

We grabbed all the drinks we needed and headed back downstairs. The game was well under way at this point. Mark went from his light-hearted self to focused and competitive. Daryl, on the other hand, was his usual laid-back self who smiled the moment I walked back into the room.

I waved his favorite beer and asked, "Want some?"

"Ha! That's a loaded question, but yes, I'll take the beer."

I opened it for him and handed it over before I settled into one of the many cozy seats around the table. These two were pool sharks, so it was going to be a while. It wasn't a common sight to see the goofy Mark turn into someone who was calculating, but he was really into this game. Funny how a guy wants to show off for his new girl even though they've known each other for years. Romance can do that to people.

Mark was getting ready to take his shot to sink another solid when the sirens went off.

"Damn it!"

We all felt the same way as Mark in this moment, except everyone else looked around in a panic. I'm sure we were all pale as ghosts. I found Daryl's eyes and knew our friends were looking to me to be the leader, to tell them what to do next, "Alright, Mark it was your turn. Let's remember that for when we get the all clear. For now, let's settle down into the bunker."

I headed over and unlocked the door, letting everyone file in before me to make it to the rooms we selected earlier. I popped back out into the hallway to make sure everyone was settling in okay, but they were all poking their heads out their doors saving me from having to walk around.

"We can either head to the biggest room at the end of the hall and start working through the games we brought down here, or we can just hang out in our rooms for a while. Thoughts?"

I felt as if I was leading a meeting at work with how quick I got down to business, but that's what happens when everyone is looking to you to call the shots. Jennie was the first to speak up, and I couldn't help but notice Chris was with her in her room, "I vote we just hang out for a little bit to process."

Lilly was the next to speak up, "I second that."

I looked around and saw everyone else nodding their heads, "Alright, that settles it. If anyone changes their mind, just give a knock on my door. This'll be over soon."

Doors started to close. As I turned around, I was hoping I was right.

The last time the sirens went off was a couple of months ago and everything ended up being fine. There were some planes that flew over, but nothing dropped. Maybe it'll be the same this time. Either way, it felt good to turn into the bunker room to find Daryl there with me so I wasn't alone. He patted the space next to me on the bed and turned the TV on. I joined him grabbing the iPad that controlled everything down in the bunker to make sure all the levels were as they should be. The generator was ready to kick in just in case we lost power and there was plenty of air flow to make things comfortable.

"What do you want to watch?" Daryl asked.

"Hmm?" I responded still distracted by the iPad in my hand.

"Movie, show?"

"Let's go with a movie. You choose. I just want to enjoy being here with you."

"Sounds good."

Daryl chose a random rom-com, my favorite genre when I'm not in the best of moods, and propped up some pillows so we could get comfortable. I turned off the lights and returned to the bed to nestle into the crook of his arm when the first bomb hit shaking the ground. I flinched causing Daryl to bring me in closer, "It's okay, that one was far off."

I nodded, but still couldn't bring myself to say anything. I closed my eyes counting to five as a way to bring my heart rate back down. Before I opened them, I took a deep breath, inhaling the way Daryl somehow smelt like the ocean and his own unique smell. I took special care to remember the feeling of security his arm provided me which finally helped me break the panic starting to rise in my throat. I opened my eyes and looked back up at him to see he was glancing down at me to make sure I was okay. Once he realized I came back to planet Earth, he placed a gentle kiss on my forehead for reassurance. About 20 minutes elapsed before the next bomb hit, feeling closer based on how much the house above us was shaking. Another one fell immediately after that. I flinched and huddled even more into Daryl, letting out a little whimper as I did. *Way to keep your composure.*

He angled himself so he could wrap both arms around me and started rubbing my arms, "Shhh, it's okay. I appreciate you being strong for everyone else out there, but you don't need to put on that armor in here."

That was all I needed to hear for the tears to start falling. All the worry I'd pushed down between today and yesterday came boiling over. This war was real, we weren't untouchable, and my father, who I was really close to, was out in the epicenter of it without me knowing if he was okay. On top of that, I finally felt like I was going to enter a good relationship for the first time in a while and now even that was threatened. It was too much for me to process all at once. Thank goodness this isn't the first time Daryl has seen me cry, so I didn't need to worry about breaking that barrier. He was sitting there comforting me as he knows how to do when there was a knock on the door. Leaning down to give me another forehead kiss, he whispered, "Hold on, I'll be right back."

He got up to answer the door to see Mark there, "Dude, it must be bad if it's you answering the door."

Ignoring what Mark said, Daryl asked, "What's up?"

"Do you think we'll get the all-clear tonight?"

There was a pause as another bomb hit before Daryl responded, "I'm honestly not sure. This is the first time they've hit us. It doesn't seem like they're too close."

"True, I guess I'll let Lil know that we're probably sleeping down here tonight. Do we have enough reserves in case the power goes out?"

I knew Daryl wouldn't be able to answer that one, so I took a steadying breath and wiped my face, "Yeah, there's plenty for us to be stuck down here for a week."

Mark nodded turning to walk away, "Okay, I'll pass that along."

"Thanks, Mark," Daryl said.

Mark left and Daryl closed the door. He made his way back over to me to settle back in, "We'll make it through."

It sounded like he was trying to reassure himself as much as he was trying to make me feel better. Let's admit it, this is a first for all of us tonight and it made us question everything. Instead of dwelling, I burrowed myself deeper under the covers turning my focus to the movie playing on the TV. It had been at least 30 minutes since the last bomb had hit. I was starting to wonder if the all-clear would be given, so I propped up on my elbows to see if I could hear to anything only to have my questions answered by feeling the rumble of some big planes passing over head. I cuddled back into Daryl's arms hoping there wouldn't be anything else and kept my curiosity in check until the movie was over. When the credits started rolling, I flipped over to the news only to see the black screen telling me we weren't out of the woods quite yet. I put on another rom-com and looked back at Daryl. He gave me a smile followed by a kiss before mumbling, "I'm starting to fade, but I'll be right here if anything happens. I won't let anything happen to you."

"Okay," I whispered returning a soft kiss.

His arms wrapped around me tighter and I turned my focus back to the TV. With everything that has happened over the past 24 hours, my mind was spinning. I guess this time in the bunker is good for at least letting me process and figure out what my next steps are. I have Daryl who's made it very clear he wants to be with me with no intentions of going anywhere. The thought of having that kind of commitment is reassuring, but nerve-wracking. On top of that, there was Jennie who, yes, is or was my best friend depending on how you look at it, but her actions this weekend are making me question all our years of friendship. She admitted she's had feelings for Daryl since day one and how she didn't appreciate seeing her chances with him go down from little to none since he focused his attention on me. Did she actually want to be my friend or was she taking advantage of the way I did "relationships" to wear Daryl down to get him to turn to her? No matter how I tried to explain her actions, it didn't change the fact she hurt me. There's no way of recovering from that. Jennie also showed her true colors with how she's not afraid to use people to her advantage as pawns in her overall scheme.

The rhythmic, soft snoring sounds behind me were making my eyelids feel heavy distracting me from sorting out everything running through my mind. After a couple minutes of trying to keep sleep at bay, I finally succumbed to dreamland consisting of flashes of the previous night with Daryl and hopes of what the future may hold for us.

Now we're back to where we started this journey ... waking up to something completely different and none of my friends with me. I'm staring at the landscape in front of me only to see a city I didn't recognize. I have no idea how I got here or what even transported me here. I have no way of knowing if any of my friends made it with me or if I have any way of figuring that out.

Chapter 5

Where the hell am I? The house and outdoor property looked the same, but everything else around me was new. None of the group was here anymore either. *What happened? Were they out exploring the new city?* I locked myself back in the house and closed all of the blinds before pacing through the living room. A million questions were running through my head but pacing wasn't going to solve anything. I had to go out there to figure out what was going on. I opened the garage to see if I could pull my car out, but thanks to Mark, I was trapped. *Great, so now what are my options?* I scanned over everything in the garage hoping my parents didn't get rid of my motorcycle. I was starting to think they did when I spotted the beige cover tucked away in the farthest corner right in front of the third garage door. Smiling to myself, I let my hair down and headed over to my familiar friend. It had been years since I last rode my bike. Everyone hated it. My parents, Daryl, Jennie, everyone. But I felt unstoppable on there.

I threw the cover on the ground relishing in the condition she was still in. The bright blue paint still sparkled like the first day I got her. My Yamaha YZF-R7 was perfect. Running my hands over her, I whispered, "It's been a long time. Ready to get back out there?"

I opened the garage, grabbed my helmet and got her started. My smile came back just listening to the purr of the engine. This was going to be good. I eased her out of the garage and headed towards the city feeling like nothing could stop me. Instead of getting lost in the thrill of being back on my bike, I reminded myself to take in the surroundings.

Everything was different: the buildings were more modern, the sidewalks clean, cars more updated. There was a lot of white and a lot of glass, but everything was pristine. Skyscrapers towered above me making it clear I was now heading into the heart of the city. I slowed my speed a little to admire how well the landscaping was cared for – there wasn't a leaf out of place on the trees or bushes. It was almost like someone had copy and pasted all of the shrubbery to be in perfectly manicured rows. There wasn't a piece of trash on the streets, no homeless. At least the people walking around looked normal, either on their way to the next shop, tourist destination, or to lunch during their workday. *Hmm, lunch.* The thought of food made my stomach growl reminding me I hadn't eaten anything for quite some time. I stopped at a light, my attention being drawn to the massive skyscraper a block ahead of me. Everyone walking in and out of there was expensively dressed, looking serious. Must be a big-time business.

I looked across the street from the building spotting a nice-looking pizza shop that didn't seem too modern and didn't seem too much like a hole-in-the-wall. A happy medium so to speak. As soon as the light turned green, I jumped to the next block flipping a U-turn to park in the open spot right in front of the pizza place's door. Taking my helmet off, I looked at the sign to see if I was familiar with this shop. I don't know why I would be, but I guess I was hoping for something a little normal. The faded blue sign had Lou's painted in white lettering. *Never heard of it, but no time like the present to try something new.* The windows were all pretty tinted so it was hard to see in to see if there was any life. The door on the sign said it was open, so I made my way into the restaurant. Maybe I could even figure out where I was.

Well, maybe there wasn't a lot of life in here. And it was dark. The lights were dim, classic rock was playing softly over the stereos, the tables had the classic red and white checked table cloth with parmesan cheese and pepper flakes flanking a tealight candle. There was a sense of warmth and familiarity with this place not being the harsh clean white with modern touches everywhere. It looked like you could sit anywhere, but I headed in the direction of the bar so I didn't take up a table. Not like it seemed that business would pick up in 30 minutes – there were only two other tables that had four people total, five if you included me in here. I was more focused on getting answers than trying to determine if I should turn around and leave.

As soon as I sat at the bar, a man walked out from the back wiping off a beer glass. He glanced at me, "Be right with you."

"Yeah, no rush."

I took a long look at him to see if there was anything I could recognize about him and nothing came to mind. A little bit of panic started to bubble in my stomach. Here I was in a completely new place with no one I know around me. I have no idea where my friends went. Somehow my parent's house got transported to another area completely. Who knew how that happened. I didn't even know if I could get answers to any of the million questions going through my mind.

The waiter tapped on the bar top a little impatiently, "You okay? Anything I can get ya?"

Jumping, I stammered, "S - sorry, it's been a weird day so far. Could I get started with a couple slices of cheese pizza and a light beer? Whatever you have on tap should be fine."

He looked at me somewhat puzzled as he turned to grab a clean glass, "Sure."

I couldn't help but notice he was tall. At least over six feet. He was rugged, too, with a sort of lumberjack look about him. His dark blond hair was short and messy. He had some scruff on his face that came with not shaving for about a week, but he didn't have a long beard so he must have trimmed it. He was strong with his plaid shirt hugging his muscles tightly. And I couldn't help but notice how well his jeans fit him too.

He leaned over the bar growling as he handed the beer to me, "It's not polite to stare down people you've never met."

I broke eye contact and looked down into the beer in front of me feeling very unsettled, "I - I didn't mean to. Just trying to take in my surroundings, that's all."

I've never felt this intimidated by someone before. I can hold my own and haven't been afraid to step up to the plate, but I couldn't help but get the sense I was crossing a major line. Was I going to be able to even ask some basic questions?

His footsteps trailed away from me, but I didn't dare look up. Maybe this wasn't a warm place after all. I should eat my food and head out. Just as I was wondering where my food was, soft footsteps approached and placed a plate in front of me, "Thanks," I mumbled still looking down at my beer. I was starting to feel like I wasn't welcomed, and honestly, that made it easier for all of my negative emotions to come crashing down on me. My shoulders slumped keeping me from trying the food.

"You gonna eat or just count the bubbles in your beer?"

I didn't realize he was still there, "Jeez, yeah. Talk about customer service."

I heard the sound of a barstool being drug closer to where I was sitting. Without looking over, I could tell Mr. Ray of Sunshine was taking a seat all while staring me down. My sass was going to get me in trouble which was the last thing I needed right now. I told myself to keep that in check, but it didn't take too long for my mouth to open, "Is it customary to watch your customers eat?"

"Makes sure I get my five-star ratings."

"Yeah, by pure intimidation."

"Problem?"

I took a chance and met his eyes. Took some guts considering how close he was to my face. I set my shoulders raising my chin a little bit, "Yes. You would think you could give some space."

He shrugged and grinned a little bit, "I don't think I can. I feel like you're challenging me. As the owner of this establishment, I at least get to know if my pizza is any good. Otherwise, how am I going to keep all my happy customers satisfied?"

He swept his arm over the nearly empty restaurant. I couldn't tell if he was joking or not, so I raised my eyebrows, "Seriously?"

He sat there for a moment before dropping his arm to the bar top leaning even closer to me, allowing me to see the different shades of grey in his eyes. His pupils dilated just a little bit before returning to normal, "You don't look familiar and this is a place for regulars. What made you stop here for food instead of one of the trendy places down the street?"

I broke eye contact again since he finally seemed to be calming down. Gosh forbid I keep stepping on his toes. As much as I didn't want to admit it, I needed help and I might as well start here. I took a bite of one of the slices. It was pretty damn good pizza. It brought me some comfort which helped make me lose my defensive edge, "Pizza's good, so you can rest easy knowing that. Clearly you can tell I'm not from here. I have no idea what's going on. One minute there were bombs dropping around my house and the next, I woke up alone in a completely new city."

Before I could continue, he dropped his head and shook it, "Shit."

This made me pause. Did he know something? Maybe I stumbled in here for a reason, "What makes you say that?"

"I don't think you answered my question," he responded as he raised his head.

"Fine. I'm not some woman who survives on salad. I need cheap food, preferably in the form of pizza and beer. I was hoping I could find a friendly pizza shop owner who could at least answer some of my basic questions. So, I'll repeat myself. What makes you say 'shit'?"

"Before we dive into this, we're going to want to move into that back corner booth over there. It'll give us more space because I'm bringing out more food for this conversation. Second of all, we've talked too long without introducing ourselves. I like to know the names of the people I'm feeding."

"I take it you're Lou?"

"Normally people would call me Louis the first time we meet, but I'll let this one slide. Your name is?"

I stood up getting ready to move, "I'm Valerie, but since the whole nick-name barrier has been broken, you can call me Val."

"Nice to meet you, Val. Go ahead and move over there. I'll be back in a couple of minutes."

I grabbed my plate and beer then made my way to the side of the booth facing the door. My dad taught me well enough to know not to have my back to the door in an unfamiliar environment. I took a few more bites of my pizza waiting for Lou to return and couldn't help but think about how rough he was. For owning a restaurant, he clearly didn't have the best social skills. No wonder this place wasn't brimming with people. It was also apparently during a time of the week where a lot of people were working despite it being a Sunday. *Maybe this place doesn't follow the same calendar.* Either that, or the building across the street just never sleeps.

Lou came back with a large pan of freshly baked pepperoni pizza, a pitcher of beer, and another glass for himself. He settled in and took a bite following that with a big gulp of beer.

"I must be getting special treatment if the owner is sitting and having a beer with me."

"Don't let it go to your head newbie. You're in it for the long haul for this conversation."

"Newbie?"

"Eh, I don't know if that'll be the one that sticks, but we'll go with it for now," he took another bite making me wait even longer to start the conversation I've been wanting to dive into for a while now. "So, can you start from the beginning? You mentioned bombs dropping?"

I looked around to see if the other people were still here only to find they left at some point when Lou was berating me. Good, we were alone. I didn't have to feel like I was going to be airing out my dirty laundry. I panned my gaze back over to Lou feeling like I could look him in the eyes now, "Yeah, there's a war going on, or at least there was where I was at. I decided to throw a friends weekend so we could take our minds off the stress of what was going on. We were all having a good time despite the drama that came up. I finally felt like I could start a relationship with someone that had more substance than just sex," I trailed off for a second thinking about Daryl causing my heart to ache a little bit. I wasn't in love with him yet, but it still hurt to feel like I was missing someone who quickly became very special to me. I love hard and fast, I guess.

"As much as I'm sitting on the edge of my seat wanting to hear about your sex life, what happened next?"

Shaking off the ache, I continued, "The bomb sirens went off and we decided to hunker down in the bunkers underneath the house to ride out the raid."

Lou nodded as if in agreement, "Good choice, that would've been my plan."

Ignoring that, I finished the last little bit of my story, "We started to feel some bombs hitting the ground around us, but none of them felt like they hit the house. I ended up falling asleep since it didn't seem like the all-clear was going to be given any time soon. When I woke up, everyone was gone and I was here, house and everything. Do you have any idea how I could've been transported to a place where there seems to be no war and everything is pristine?"

Lou leaned back and chuckled a little bit, "Honey, there's always a war going on whether or not you can see it. You just don't know enough about here yet," he leaned back in to continue. "In all seriousness, though, you're not the first one that's told me something similar, although it's usually without the relationship crap. There's been a recent rise of newcomers to our city and the majority of them have a similar story if they can remember anything at all. You're lucky your house came with you."

I couldn't be patient anymore, "So you know what's going on?"

He held his hands up, "Slow your roll. I'll tell you what I know."

I impatiently gestured for him to continue while I took a large swig of my beer.

"The first time I ran across a new face was about a year ago. They mentioned something about bombs falling and waking up here, similar to what you've said. However, they didn't have anywhere to live. Their house didn't come with them and they were having to completely start over. After that, there would be groups anywhere from five to twenty to fifty people. It was random who had their house and who didn't, but I think it has something to do with whether or not their house got leveled by a bomb. So, it's safe to say your house probably didn't get hit in whatever world you came from. The other thing is that even if people were together, they got split up and some people couldn't find the rest of their group at all. I'm sure that's not what you want to hear given your new lover and all."

He took the words right from my mouth. I could feel that ache coming back, and if I wasn't careful, I was going to start crying. Lou seemed like the type of guy who didn't tolerate tears splashing on his food.

"Anyways, that's about all I've gathered with what's going on. I don't know what's causing people to jump ship from their world and end up here, but it's been happening since those bombs started falling. I figured the best I could do is try to help new people out if they stumbled in here like yourself. There's a lot of complexities here that I know you haven't had to face yet or have even thought were real. I'm here to help you out if you want, but at the end of the day, that's your choice."

Whatever was going on, it's weird. I thought carefully about what my next words would be before diving in. I could use help, but I was also more curious about the complexities he mentioned. I stuck my hand out across the table, "I'll take you up on your offer for help."

Lou looked at my hand with the corners of his lips twitching. He shook my hand signifying a deal and I took my hand back, "What did you mean when you said complexities?"

"Hmph, I don't know if you're quite ready for that side of it yet. You did just get here after all. At least finish your first glass of beer," he said as he tilted his head back to eat.

I did as I was told, grumbling as I did so, "Treating me like a kid. The best way for me to know how to adapt is to know what the hell I need to look out for."

He turned to me nostrils flaring, jaw muscles twitching, "I'll tell you, but you need to understand that you're doing this my way. I've been chewed up and spit out in a way you wouldn't understand and I don't want to see that happen to anyone else. Don't mistake this as me treating you like a child. There are some monsters out here that wouldn't hesitate to torture you until you wished you were dead."

For some reason, this snapped me out of any foul mood I was in. I may not have known Lou for long, but I could tell he was wanting to look out for me and was putting me under his protective wing. I wouldn't complain because he doesn't look like someone to be messed with. I held up my hands in surrender, "Look, I'm sorry if I've crossed a line. You're right; I'm dealing with a lot right now and despite wanting to know everything that's going on, I'll respect the pace you want to move at."

"Good."

We sat in silence for a moment drinking and eating until I started wiggling. He raised an eyebrow, "I guess we can get into it. Does your world mention anything about werewolves?"

I giggled, "Werewolves? Only in movies and books. There's no such thing."

He sighed leaning back and placing his hands on his hips, "You're not in Kansas anymore, Dorothy."

"Wait, are you implying that werewolves are walking among us here?" I asked feeling my eyes widening. This can't be real. A part of me wanted to lean into him just messing with me because there's no way the man-wolf beast I've heard so much about is real.

He narrowed his eyes a little bit, I suspect catching the sarcasm that was creeping into my tone, "Would you believe me if I said yes?"

"I mean, I guess so?" shrugging my shoulders.

Lou leaned forward taking up the majority of the table and lowered his voice, "Look, I'm just going to dive right into this and rip off the band-aid. You can do what you want with the information. There are werewolves here. There are some who will leave you alone, even when they turn, and there are some dangerous ones that will torture you if they get the chance."

Of course there's werewolves. Everything else about my life is completely different, why not add one more thing? *Might as well keep rolling with the punches here.* I held up my hand signaling him to pause and he leaned back in his seat, "Lou, I know I wasn't convincing half a second ago, but I'll believe you. You already seem to have a pretty good idea of what's going on here and I'm completely alone. I need to have some idea of what's happening here so I can find my way home. What do I need to know?"

He gave a quick nod of his head to show he was convinced then proceeded, "There are two main packs here. One's giant, the other one not so much. The giant pack is the one you need to watch out for. Their leader is dangerous, cold, and nothing will get in his way when he wants something. The other pack, mine, is more focused on helping people around here."

"So, if I'm hearing you correctly, you're the alpha?"

"Glad I don't have to explain pack dynamics to you. And, yes. My pack consists of around 20 main people and we also help take care of the stragglers who may not feel like pack life is cut out for them."

"Very thoughtful of you."

Lou shrugged, "Eh, what can I say? I'm a community man."

Based on the cold welcome I received not too long ago, I wasn't entirely sure if I could buy into that.

He finished off his beer and started to refill his glass giving a nice pause in the conversation to let everything settle in a bit. It made sense now why I couldn't look him in the eyes for very long. It also explained the quick temper of his.

"Ready to continue?" he asked.

"Yeah. What can you tell me about this other pack?"

Lou pointed his thumb over his shoulder towards the door, "That big, fancy office building over there? That's where the other pack leader hides out. He runs the biggest tech firm in town and is probably the richest bastard here. His pack? At least over 100 that I've been able to figure out, but there's probably more wolves than that. The main difference is he only wants power and the way he thinks he's going to get that is by controlling the most wolves."

"Sounds like a peach. How has he not taken you over?"

Lou looked down the edge in his voice back, "We have a sort of agreement. I don't cross him and he doesn't cross me."

I sensed there was something else beneath the surface of that response. I asked, "Seems like you two may have some history."

"It's more than that. The other thing about him that makes him really dangerous is he's not afraid to turn someone and leave them to fend for themselves during their first change. So don't get caught in a situation where he can do that to you."

"How do you turn? Is it a scratch or something?"

Lou was staring me down at this point while saying, "Usually a bite, but I've noticed it doesn't have to be an intense one. All it has to be is something to draw even the slightest amount of blood so the werewolf's saliva can get into the blood stream and start causing the changes."

"Hm, like vampires," I said thoughtfully. "So how did you change?"

Lou sighed, his face clouding over, "I had a feeling you were going to ask that."

I reached across the table, not knowing if this was the right thing to do or not, and placed my hand on his arm, "You don't have to tell me if you don't want to."

He didn't pull away which I took as a step in the right direction. He started, "It's important, just doesn't change the fact I don't like to relive it," he rolled his shoulders back, but didn't move his arm out from under my hand. "I know first-hand how dangerous the other pack leader, Warrick, can be. I got a huge break in my career and landed an interview for a high-ranking position at his company. My only interview was with him. At the time, I didn't know he was sizing me up for his pack. I knew about the werewolves, but had no idea who was who. Anyways, I started working there and got stuck in the office late one night with Warrick facing a tight deadline. He wasn't in the best mood and wasn't happy with the fact I wasn't working faster. In the end, he decided to pick a fight. Mind you, it was also the night before the full moon, so tempers were higher than normal."

"Were you guys yelling at each other?" I asked wanting to hear more.

"There was a lot of yelling. I was holding my ground with an opposing viewpoint. As you can imagine, alphas don't like that and, so, instant trigger. Next thing I know, I was on the ground with him pinning me down and he bit me. Something totally unexpected. That stopped me in my tracks more because I had just been bitten by someone in a fight rather than being hit."

"I would've been caught off-guard by that too. Not something that usually happens in a fight."

"Especially when you don't know much about werewolves. Either way, with the full moon being the next day, I was screwed. After he bit me, he laughed and let me go, explaining what just happened. He admitted to keeping tabs on me for a couple of reasons: I was big, could hold my own, and take control if needed. Naturally, he wanted me to be his beta. In order to get to that point, though, I was put through a lot of trials that nearly broke me."

Lou paused and pulled down his shirt just a little bit to reveal the top of a nasty scar. He pointed so several other scars on his arms and ended with the one going from about a half an inch above his eyebrow, down his eye at an angle, and finishing at the top of his cheekbone. He continued while pulling his shirt back up, "Warrick took pleasure in bringing me near death. Every time he did, he reminded me how much he was preparing me for the pack and building up my thick skin. Didn't realize thick skin meant scar tissue. I've lost count the number of times I was left lying in my office bleeding out just waiting for the healing to kick in or for death to finally make its presence known."

My eyes were wide again, "I'm so sorry. No one should have to go through that. How were you able to get away?"

"It took a lot of fighting. There was actually one time I almost overtook him."

"Which means you could've become alpha of his pack."

He nodded while repeating, "Which means I could've become alpha of his pack. For someone who's power hungry, they aren't going to let that happen. With the way pack bonds are, the pack felt the ripple of power."

"I still don't understand how he didn't just end you," I said shaking my head in disbelief.

"I don't know to this day why he didn't. Maybe the sick part of him wanted someone to give him a run for his money so he could have some competition with another pack."

"That's weird, but okay."

Lou shrugged, "Not what I would've done, but he doesn't like to be predictable either. So, he let me go. From then on, I vowed I would never employ his practices and I would give a safe place for people going through the change. Plus, there's a lot of us who didn't cut it in his pack due to his cutthroat nature."

"So, I take it Warrick's pack is primarily his employees?"

"Don't work there unless you want to get turned. Should be their slogan. Theres more employees than there are werewolves, but it's part of keeping the façade for who's in the packs. All I know is high-ranking positions are for sure his wolves. The higher they are, the more powerful of a wolf they are."

"Got it, so don't mess with him."

"You got it."

Our eyes lingered on each other's for a moment and I could tell the gears were turning in Lou's mind. I noticed he still hadn't pulled his arm away from my touch, and I wasn't necessarily complaining either.

It didn't take long for his brow to furrow and for his face to harden. Confused, I asked, "What's wrong?"

Taking no time to get on his feet, he growled. "Quiet," he said turning to the door. He positioned himself so I couldn't have the best view, but I recognized the protective posture. The door swung open and voices carried in, but one voice carried above the rest, "Well, if it isn't the saint of Broadway."

The rest of the group chuckled and the hairs on the back of my neck raised. I was wondering if this was the group Lou warned me about. I definitely didn't want to be here.

"Warrick, to what do I owe the pleasure?" Lou asked calm and composed.

"It's lunch, I'm here for my usual order. I got to show the new guy where to find the best pizza."

Curiosity got the best of me. Between the British accent and the mention of someone new, I poked my head around Lou to see if I could get a good look of who was here. My eyes were met with a small group of four people. I could only assume the man in the front was Warrick, who was leaning on the bar with a cocky smile. He was tall and built too, but unlike Lou, he was clean shaven with black hair that was slicked back. The rest of the crew looked the same, just a little shorter and not overly muscular. There was one who stuck out like a sore thumb with messy brown hair and no suit. Something about this one was familiar. I started to get out of the booth to try to get a closer look, but I wasn't sneaky enough.

Warrick stood up to his full height leveling his icy blue eyes on me, sending a chill down my spine, "Who's this? Very rude of you not to introduce us Lou, you should know better than that." He gave a wave of his hand telling me to move towards him, "Come on out, love."

Lou dropped his head and side-stepped out of my way, "She's our new waitress."

News to me, but I decided this wasn't the best time to ask questions. Instead, I walked over to Warrick and stuck out my hand, "Nice to meet you."

The cocky smile that was there a moment ago was replaced with something a little more sly. Every muscle was telling me to run. He grabbed my hand in a firm, but gentle handshake using it to pull himself closer to me, "Nice to meet you, too. With someone like you working here, I may have to stop in more often."

I could tell what Lou was meaning when he said Warrick was dangerous. My gut was screaming to get away, but his presence was alluring. This was someone who had power knowing he could use it to do whatever he wanted.

I ended the handshake and walked away before giving him too much satisfaction. I wanted to do my best at making sure he didn't think he had complete power over me.

Lou stepped back in, thankfully, "Your pizza will be out in about five minutes."

I took that as my queue and headed to the back area. I had no idea what I was doing, but didn't want to make a mistake here. I stepped into the kitchen, tying my hair back to be met with a brightly lit, immaculately kept space. I don't know what I was expecting, but this wasn't it.

Alright, making a usual order in five minutes. Looking around, I finally laid eyes on a couple of pizzas sitting next to the oven, silently thanking Lou for making this easy. All I had to do was pop these in and get them cooked. I slid them into the already hot oven, got a couple of boxes ready, and leaned by the doorframe to see if I could pick up on any conversation. Warrick was the one speaking, "About time you got some help around here. I was tired of always having to wait."

"Business is growing. I can't do it all on my own."

Warrick let out a quick laugh, "I can tell."

"Who's the new guy?"

I wanted to get another chance to see who this new person was, so I checked the pizza's hoping they were done. I cracked open the oven relieved to see a perfectly golden pizza. One hell of an oven he has back here. I quickly packaged the pizza's up and came back out into the main dining area, "Here you go."

Warrick's gaze drifted over me again, "She's quick on her feet, too."

It rubbed me the wrong way. Before I could stop my stupid mouth from opening up, I shot back, "She's also standing right here and can be talked to directly."

His eyebrows shot up with that sly smile making its way back, "Sorry, love. You got some fight. I like that."

Lou interjected by stepping in front of me again to repeat his earlier question, "Who's the new guy, Warrick?"

I looked around his shoulder as Warrick moved out of the way, "This is our new Director of Operations, Daryl."

Now more than ever I wished my poker face was firmly in place. The blood was starting to drain as my eyes met Daryl's. I subtly shook my head to tell him not to mention he knows me which only got me a confused look in return. After hearing what Lou was saying about how Warrick ran his pack, I knew this was not a good situation. The clock was ticking.

Chapter 6

Warrick and his crew, including Daryl, left the restaurant. Once they were out of there, I could see Lou's shoulders visibly relax. As he turned around, I took my hair down, "So, I have the job?"

His head whipped up, "What?"

"Are you looking at your new waitress or was that just a way to keep him from asking too many questions?"

"Oh, that," he grumbled. "Yeah, you have the job if you want it."

"You don't turn your employees, do you?"

Well, that was the wrong question to ask. Lou bristled and pointed at me, "Don't even joke about that."

His pointed finger moved over to the booth we were sitting in, "Sit."

I did as I was told with my head still spinning. I'm happy Daryl was here, but I wasn't happy about who he got himself entangled with and how that happened so quickly. I pulled out my phone wondering if the service worked here. There were full bars, so I sent Daryl a text letting him know to head back to the house tonight so we could talk about what happened. I got a thumbs up response and turned my attention back to Lou, "Sorry about the joke. That was insensitive. I was only trying to break the tension. Warrick's intense."

"Why didn't you just sit still and stay quiet?"

This question took me aback, "Hold on. You just told me to be quiet."

"I didn't want Warrick to see you because you're the type of woman he wants: easy on the eyes and feisty."

I rolled my eyes, "Oh here we go. I just can't escape this!"

"I want to take a step back for a second. What happened there with the new guy? You know him?"

I sighed and put my head in my hands, "Yes. He's one of my friends that disappeared on me. Actually, he's more than that. After everything you told me about Warrick, I'm sick to my stomach."

Realization dawned on Lou, "Ah, lover boy. Yeah, I can see why."

He started tapping on his chin making it obvious he was trying to come up with some sort of plan. I wasn't sure if I wanted to know what he was thinking, but I was coming up empty.

Lou leaned in, "You're not going to like this."

"Hit me."

"Warrick is clearly interested in you, and for the first time, I think his interest clouded the rest of his senses. He didn't pick up on the fact that you recognized Daryl and the other goons he had with him aren't smart enough to pick up on those subtle cues either. We could use that to our advantage."

"Hold on, we?"

"Yup, I'm going to help you get Daryl back. Hopefully before Warrick tries to turn him. The first step is to get Warrick's attention again."

"Wait, Daryl and I just started something. I can't just go and flirt with the next person I see," I said holding my hands up again.

"You may not have a lover boy for too long if Warrick can sink his claws in to him."

"I guess you have a point, but I don't like this. How do I go about getting Warrick's attention?"

Lou wasted no time jumping into business, "There's a summer solstice ball his company hosts. Super formal, everyone dressed to the nines. I can guarantee you're going to get an invite. I'll even bet dish duty he'll hand deliver the invite and lay the charm on thick. When he does, you flirt, but not too much. It drives him wild when he doesn't have your full attention."

"Okay, I'm already feeling slimy."

"We're going dress shopping this afternoon," he said not missing a beat.

"Wait, I don't have a lot of money on me. I don't even know if my money works here. I mean, my phone does, but that's not exactly the same. Also, do we have to do this now? Don't we have time?"

"Don't worry about the money. The ball is sooner than you'd think. As for the phone, did you text Daryl after he left?"

Lou asked that question too fast. "Was that not the right thing to do?" I asked slowly.

He gestured for me to hand the phone over to him, so I obeyed. He poked around on it before handing it back and telling me, "Your location is off. I don't want to give Warrick any upper hand. He can track your phone if Daryl says anything. What did you say to your boy?"

"I just told him to go by the house this evening so we could talk."

"Damn it. You better hope Daryl doesn't say anything. If anything, Warrick will just be watching him today, or if we're really lucky, he sent Daryl home for the day."

"What do I do?" I asked with panic starting to creep into my voice.

"When Daryl gets to your house, tell him to leave his phone out in the garage somewhere. Then, go to some part of the house that's on the opposite side of the garage. Turn on the TV in the room you're in at a higher volume so no mics can pick up your conversation. Take that time to warn Daryl and to let him know to play it safe – tell him to not go against Warrick no matter what he asks. He can't put up a fight either. That should keep Warrick from wanting to change him. The most important thing you need to tell him is that you can't see him after that."

I furrowed my brow trying to keep myself from shouting, "You're telling me I can't see the only person I know in this damn place?"

Lou closed his eyes, "I know. I know. That's the last thing you wanted to hear, but you have to stick to it. Warrick will track Daryl's phone the minute he starts his new job. He could get suspicious."

"Not if Daryl told him that's his house."

"You don't know if that's where Daryl woke up. I'm assuming he wasn't in the same place as you. He could've said something about not knowing where he was at and not having a place to go. Warrick knows there's something going on causing people to pop up here randomly, so he'll take care of Daryl by giving him a place to stay. What he'll also do is track Daryl's phone, so if Daryl isn't going to the place Warrick gave him –"

"He'll know something's up and will investigate," I said finishing his sentence.

Lou nodded his head, "Exactly, and that will ruin any upper-hand you have. Warrick will make you watch him torture and change Daryl."

I looked down at my lap trying to fight back the ache starting to take place in my heart again. I can't lose Daryl, especially with what happened the night before, but I needed to at least prep myself in case this plan of Lou's doesn't work out. I had to be ready to have him taken away from me. Man, I didn't want to think about that.

It was Lou's turn to put his hand on my arm as comfort, "We're going to get Daryl back, it's just not going to be easy. Trust me on this one. I'll be right here if anything happens. I won't let anything happen to you."

I took a double-take remembering Daryl saying those exact words to me before we fell asleep. *Great, that didn't help the ache in my heart.* Instead of letting my emotions get the best of me, I rolled my shoulders back, "Tell me what I need to do."

Lou smiled, "That's my girl."

After finishing our pizza and beer, Lou put up a Closed sign in the window and locked up. We headed out the back towards his car. I paused when we got there. He drove a black, luxury SUV, a brand I didn't know, but I could tell it was nice. Seeing me pause, he asked, "Is something wrong?"

"You know, for someone who has a dingy looking restaurant, you sure have a nice ride."

"There's more to me than what you think," Lou said getting into the car.

I guess there is. It was clean, too clean, and still had the new car smell. The seats were a soft black leather. When he started the vehicle, the engine emanated a low purr and a holographic screen came to life. Lou tapped in an address before easing out of the alley. I was so caught up in the tech in the car I didn't realize he was asking me a question, "Yoohoo, anyone home?"

"What?" I asked snapping back to attention.

"I was wondering if you had any issues with me picking out the dress?" he repeated the question I didn't hear.

"Oh, no, I guess not. I mean you know Warrick best and this is all part of a plan to distract him."

"Good answer."

I looked over at him to find him staring at me. Instead of startling and jumping his gaze back to the road, he casually shifted his eyes to the road in front of him. I asked, "Do I have something on my face?"

"No," he answered.

"Why were you looking at me?"

"No reason."

I scoffed, "You sure?"

"You sure like to ask a lot of questions," Lou said casually.

"Can I ask a couple more?" I asked figuring it wouldn't hurt to get as much information as I could.

"I guess."

I started twisting my hands together, feeling nervous, "Am I going to this ball myself?"

"I told you, I'll be here. I won't let you go into the lion's den alone."

"Okay," letting his words sink in and make me feel better, "is there anything I need to do to get his attention?"

"Your dress will do enough. I'll make sure you make a grand entrance and he'll come right over to you."

"On an unrelated note, what is my schedule for the restaurant?"

Not missing a beat, he answered, "I'll text you when I need you or you can just show up a half hour before you did today."

I nodded and sat back in my seat as he drove. I appreciated everything Lou was doing for me, but I was a nervous wreck. The thoughts of what Warrick might do to Daryl made me sick to my stomach, but the thought of what I was going to have to do made me sicker. I also couldn't figure out if there was something in this for Lou or if he was just being this nice. Hell, there's only one way to find out which means I just have to suck it up and do my best. I had to hope Daryl would be willing to keep things quiet and not be to upset by this plan. I had to get him back before trying to figure out where the rest of our friends were.

The car eased into a parking space in front of a high-end boutique with gorgeous dresses displayed in the front window.

I looked back over to Lou, "This is it? It looks really expensive."

He looked at me dead serious, "If you're going to woo the richest man in this city, you need to look like a million dollars. In other words, you have to look like something he wants."

"But I can't ask you to spend that kind of money on me," I said flustered.

"Don't worry about it," he said as he got out of the car. I started reaching for the car door when Lou grabbed the door for me.

"Oh, thank you."

He nodded then moved to open the store's door. I walked in and was greeted by a kind, smiling face of one of the ladies working the store, "Hi there, how can I help you? Oh, hi Louis!"

"Hey MaryAnn," he returned the friendly smile. "My friend here is looking for a gown for the ball on Wednesday."

"Perfect! Come this way."

Lou gestured for me to follow MaryAnn with him taking up the rear. She led us past rows upon rows of some of the most beautiful dresses I've ever seen until we landed at the dressing room. Her and Lou stood off to the side talking while I wandered over to a rack of dresses to admire the sparkles and soft fabric. Just out of curiosity, I searched for a price tag. After digging for a while, I found there was no price on the dress. That's the sign of an expensive item. This boutique was way out of my league and there's no way I could let Lou buy a dress for me, I don't care who I was trying to impress. I turned to Lou to let him know, but saw him sitting comfortably in a chair with MaryAnn nowhere in sight. I hastily walked up to him whispering, "You can't buy me a dress here."

He smirked, "Watch me."

"It's too expensive."

Lou shrugged, "You've never been here before, you don't know the pricing."

"But there's no price tag."

"And that's supposed to mean what?" he asked still smirking.

I heard MaryAnn's heels approaching, I rolled my eyes at him. This conversation was going to have to wait. The only way out of this was to say no to every dress I tried on. I turned back to MaryAnn to see her carrying five dresses and gesturing for me to head to the dressing room, "Ready?"

"Sure. Let's see what you have."

She placed the dresses on individual hangers. She looked over her shoulder as she stood at the exit of the dressing room, "I'll be around the store if you need anything. Let me know if you want to try on any additional dresses and I'll grab them for you."

I nodded and she shut the door. I heard Lou mumble thanks to her as she walked away. Turning back to the dresses, I cursed under my breath. These dresses were gorgeous, so it's going to be harder than I thought it would be to say no. *Oh well, I guess I can only go forward.*

The first dress I pulled was a pastel pink gown with a sweetheart neckline. The fabric was simple and there wasn't much to it in terms of design beyond it being form fitting. Once on, I took a second to admire myself in the mirror only to find this color didn't really match with my skin tone, so that made this decision easy. I couldn't contain the smug smile on my face as I opened the door to walk out to show Lou.

"Well, that's a no," he said before I even made it to the pedestal.

"Aw, but you didn't even let me get all the way out here," I jutted out my bottom lip to lean into my fake pouting.

He chuckled, "Just go back and try on the next one."

I smiled doing as I was told. Back in the dressing room, I reached for the next dress knowing this was also going to be a no. It was a pastel green. I'm not sure why so many pastels for a summer celebration. There were quite a few ruffles from the waistline down to the floor on the form fitting dress that didn't allow for a lot of movement. Rather than trying to make my way out to Lou, I said, "This one is also a no ... I can't move in it."

I didn't wait for a response as I got myself out of this monstrosity. That left three dresses remaining and it was going to be harder to convince myself they wouldn't work. Sighing, I reached for my third gown and slid it on. This one was by far the most comfortable. The fabric was stretchy which made it easy to move in while it hugged me like a glove. It was strapless with the neckline going straight across ending at points on either side of my chest with just enough push-up to make my breasts look a little extra perky. Starting from the point on my left side, there was a slit that crossed my torso just under my breasts, curving its way down to the waist where it met up with the slit starting at my hip bone. The dress itself was white and covered in crystals that gave it an iridescent effect so that when the light hit the dress just right, I lit up like a Christmas tree. With the slit on the leg going so high, I decided to do some quick movements to make sure I wouldn't flash anyone. It passed the test. Alright, now to show Lou.

I stepped out onto the platform and cleared my throat to get his attention. His eyes fell on me and all he could do was lean forward. He twirled his finger to tell me to do a slow spin. Once I completed my spin, I asked, "Well?"

Lou fell back into his chair smiling, "I think we have a winner."

MaryAnn poked her head around the corner, "You look stunning! And the size is perfect. Would you like me to ring you up?"

Lou nodded and started talking to MaryAnn again, so I made my way back to the dressing room to change back into my clothes. I took another look in the mirror cursing again. I wish I was wearing this to an event where Daryl was my date rather than trying to woo a slimeball in front of him. I sighed and slid out of the dress just in time for MaryAnn to knock on the door, "Can I please have your dress? I'll get it all wrapped up ready to go for you."

"Sure thing," I said as I handed the dress over the door to her. I finished getting back in my clothes then met Lou at the register. He had already paid so I had no chance of seeing what the dress cost. He knew what he was doing.

Looking over at me, Lou asked, "Ready?"

"Yup! Let's go."

B ack at the restaurant, Lou handed me the garment bag containing my dress, "You're a stunner, so you shouldn't have any problem getting Warrick's attention. Don't let that go to your head."

He was joking and trying to get a laugh out of me, but instead I gave a half-hearted chuckle while I turned away remembering how this wasn't going to be easy. I had told myself after Daryl and I had spent the night together I was going to change how I was when it came to the love side of my life. I wasn't going to be that woman who just slept around, but this felt like I was channeling my past relationships. With my back turned, I said, "Lou, I really don't know if I can do this."

I could hear the concern laced in his voice, "Are you okay?"

I turned back around, "This just isn't me, or at least who I want to be. I don't want to try and sleep with someone just to have the upper-hand."

"Woah," he said with his hands up. "No one said you were going to be sleeping with anyone. All you're going to be doing is flirting."

"With someone you said is dangerous."

"I won't let anything happen to you."

"How can you guarantee that? Are you going to be lurking in the shadows every time I'm in the same room as Warrick? What about the damage this is going to do to Daryl and I?"

Lou's face grew serious, "I'll be around more than you know. You won't always see me, but I'll be there. If we play our cards right, he'll never know what's going on. As for you and Daryl, I don't know what to tell you there, but this is our best option to minimize any harm that will come to him."

I nodded looking away, "Okay, but I still don't like this."

Lou came up to me and turned my face to his, "I never said this was going to be easy."

Chapter 7

I kept my garment bag in Lou's car since I didn't necessarily have the most storage in my chosen mode of transportation. The dinner shift started, and since this is my first time on the job, I got caught up in learning the ropes from Lou. Dinner was definitely the popular time which meant we were slammed until it was time to close down. The final customers left and I was cleaning up as Lou came over to me, "Let me know when you're ready to leave and I'll follow you."

"Sounds good, stalker."

At this point, we had quickly built a rapport that felt like we had been friends for years. We were efficient, but didn't hesitate to give each other a hard time when the moment arose. I was surprised with how easy it was for us to get past both of our barriers. It was nice to feel the tension from earlier ease, not to mention having some money in my pocket so I could start to take care of myself here.

Lou rested his chin on the end of the broomstick, "You're not too bad. The customers liked you, including some of the pack."

I kept sweeping as I responded, "It's not my first rodeo." I paused my cleaning for a moment, "Also, I didn't realize some of the pack came in."

"They like to hang low. There's not a lot of us here and we'd like to stay out of the way so our numbers don't get smaller."

"Makes sense," I said turning back to my work to wrap it up. "So, show up tomorrow for the lunch shift?"

"Yeah, same time. And be ready for your next interaction with Warrick," he tossed a couple of Lou's Pizza shirts my way, "Ready to head out?"

"Are we done cleaning?"

He looked around, "I would say so. Let's go."

I headed out to get on my bike then waited a second for his car to pull up next to me. I looked at Warrick's office building across the street to find all the lights were off except for the top floor where I could see the outline of a figure looking down at the street below, almost like the shadow was Warrick. I gave a little salute just to see if my suspicions were correct and he turned away. It makes sense for the CEO of a major company to be on the top floor with the best view. I was still looking up at the building when Lou idled next to me with his window down, "Something wrong with your neck?"

"Nope," I put my visor down, revved my engine, and shot out in front of him. I took the same path I trekked this morning back up the hill to the house thinking about the meetup I was supposed to have with Daryl. I was excited to see him again, but nervous at the same time. Lou's words repeated in my head to serve as a reminder for me to not get my hopes up too much, "This wasn't going to be easy."

Once at the house, I checked my phone to see if there were any messages from Daryl indicating he was on his way. There was nothing yet, so I invited Lou inside. If he was looking out for me, then the least I could do is give him the lay of the land so he knew where to go in case of emergency. Lou was onboard with a quick tour, telling me we were on the same page with making sure he knew everything about the house just in case. *Better safe than sorry.*

We were up in my room and I was hanging up my dress when I asked the question that had been plaguing me since we hatched this plan, "Do you really think this will work?"

Lou was casually leaning against the doorframe, "I sure hope so. I saw your salute by the way, nice touch."

"Something about me is that I don't half-ass things, even if I'm not the happiest about this situation. When's the next full moon?"

He had made his way into the room at this point and was looking outside at the city from the door that led to my balcony, "Friday."

I walked over to him so we were standing side by side, "What do you do for the restaurant when it's a full moon?"

"Find coverage."

"Do you think I'll be able to handle myself?"

"I think you can. I'll have everything prepped; the orders are usually pretty consistent."

"Makes my life easier. Where do you go for the change?"

Lou turned his attention back to me, "Calm yourself there, Val. You don't know me that well yet."

I was trying to come up with a quick retort when my phone buzzed. Daryl would be here in about five minutes. I sighed not completely wanting the conversation to be over, "Alright Lou, time for you to head out."

"Just remember to make sure he keeps his phone in the garage and to have a TV on."

I let him out the front door, "Got it, boss. See you tomorrow."

After Lou left, I grabbed a bowl and filled it with chips waiting on the couch for Daryl to get here. I had no idea how I was going to approach this conversation. Would I jump right into it or would I subtly hint at the idea? Would I start by talking about our relationship? Technically, we never said we were making it official or announced we were in a relationship. All that happened was that we talked about feelings and said we'd explore this a little more before having sex. Nothing official. I don't like that I'm trying to reason with myself right now, but I'm one of those women who likes to have clarity sooner rather than later.

There was a soft knock on the door. Opening it, Daryl reached out and gave me a hug, "Hi you. I didn't know what happened. I woke up with you gone and me in another spot entirely."

I returned the hug nodding. Pulling back, I pulled out my phone and started typing on it, playing it safe as Lou had instructed me, "You should leave any phone out in one of the cars in the garage. I've got some interesting developments to tell you about."

He gave me a funny look but shrugged his shoulders doing as I asked. Once he was back inside, I led him upstairs to my room and turned the TV on to a reasonable volume to where we could still hear each other. Gesturing for him to sit across from me on the floor, I confirmed how I was going to handle this conversation.

"Okay, thank you for dealing with the weirdness for two seconds."

"What's going on, Val?" Daryl asked looking at me confused.

"Clearly you know we're in someplace completely different than where we were, yet it feels the same. I was talking with Lou, the guy at the pizza place, and he told me a few things I wanted to pass along to you, but it's all probably going to sound like crazy talk. Bear with me. First, we aren't the only ones who basically popped out of the ground. There are others who have described similar scenarios and essentially woke up here starting from ground zero with no one they know, so consider ourselves lucky. Two, there are werewolves and you're apparently working for the most dangerous one, hence why I asked you to put your phone in the garage. He'll turn you if he gets the chance, and from what I heard, it's not a fun process. Don't cross him or that'll put the wrong kind of target on your back. He's a power-hungry person who likes to torture and I can tell you he's probably scoping you out now to see if you'd fit in with his pack. That brings me to my final point. I'm going to try to keep him from turning you so you can get out of there."

At this point Daryl's brows were furrowed even more than when we started the conversation, "What are you talking about? Werewolves don't exist, Val. Warrick is probably the best boss I've ever worked for. I believe you about the people who've popped out of the ground because I was hearing about that today too, but I think you're going off the rails about Warrick."

I cocked my head to the side, "You really think Warrick is a good guy? You didn't get a boy's club vibe off him in the pizza place earlier?"

He raked his hand through his hair starting to show his annoyance, "Val, that's just how guys like that are."

"Then how come you don't act that way?"

"Because I don't like to bring work home with me. I don't know how we got here or if we can even go back, so I'm happy to have found a solid job so I can make something of myself here in the meantime."

"Got it, I won't push that then. Do you at least have a place to stay?" I asked leaning back a bit. I could feel him pulling away from me, so I wanted to add some distance to keep him from getting even more distant.

He nodded his head, "Yeah, I'm all set up with an apartment near the office although I'm happy to see my car. I'll just take that when I head out tonight."

"So, you wouldn't stay?" I asked not hiding the hurt in my voice. This switch was starting to have an impact on me.

"Well, I have to work tomorrow," Daryl responded curtly, changing the subject as he did so.

I looked at my hands feeling lost. What happened to all the things he confessed to me just one night ago? How he wanted to be with me? He reached over and the familiar feel of his hand on mine took over, "Val, it seems like you're coming from a place of concern. I'll keep my eye out for anything fishy, but I'm going to do what I do best. I'll keep my head down and work without stepping on any toes. That's what made me successful before, I'm sure it'll work again. Don't get me wrong, I noticed how Warrick reacted to you and it didn't sit well with me, but I'm not going to let someone like him know what my weaknesses are. I think it's best we do our own thing for now"

"You can't let him know that we know each other," I said with my head down because I wasn't ready to address the last part of what he said. I felt if I looked at him right now the tears would start.

"Well, I might have already done that."

My head snapped back up, "Why?"

"He was saying something about how he'd never seen you around before and I chimed in saying that we know each other. That's all," Daryl said shrugging it off.

"I guess the cat's out of the bag, then."

"We'll be fine."

I shrugged, "Okay." Because I couldn't help myself, I asked, "Did you mean everything you said to me last night?"

Daryl looked me straight in the eyes, "I did."

"Then why are you acting so distant right now? Why are you wanting us to do our own thing?"

"One moment we were lying next to each other with bombs falling around us and the next we woke up in a completely new city with no idea if the other one was safe. I'm happy to see you here, but I also want to take a second to get my bearings before diving into a relationship."

Feeling like I had been slapped, "I'm over here worrying about you and your well-being while you're frolicking around being a kiss-ass to your new boss. Did you just say all of those things to sleep with me? Or did you just say those because you felt like the world was ending with the war? This is a completely different tone than last night."

"No!" He said holding up his hands in defense. "I'm just trying to process everything going on right now. You know I don't handle change well; it makes me distance myself from everyone."

"I'm well-aware," the anger starting to come through in my voice replacing the hurt that was there a moment ago. "You know I don't like to be played."

"Shit, Val, I know. Look, I'm going to go."

Before I could say anything more, he got up to leave. I stayed rooted to my spot until I heard the sound of his car driving away. There was a big part of me feeling like he just used me last night because he's been lonely. I feel so foolish thinking I could have something good with him, foolish thinking this time was going to be different. I know you're probably thinking I rushed to that decision, but if there's one thing I know about Daryl, it's that the moment he says anything about needing space, he cuts people off.

I curled my knees into my chest and let the tears fall. With everything that's happened in the last 24 hours, the flood gates opened consuming me with emotion. The love I had for Daryl, while I mostly viewed that as friendship, was always going to be there. I just didn't know if our friendship would remain intact. After what had been about ten minutes, I got up to close everything down so I could sleep. Tomorrow I was going to move on and focus on surviving.

Chapter 8

"Lou, you here?" I made my way into the restaurant after parking in the back. There was a lot I needed to catch him up on, so I showed up earlier than my scheduled time. I also gave my "uniform" my own spin on it because why not? Lou poked his head into the kitchen and stopped.

"What did you do to the shirt?"

I looked down at the shirt then back at him, batting my eyelashes, "Oh, this? I just made it a little more feminine."

All I had done was cut it so I could turn it into a V-neck shirt and show off my cleavage a little bit more. Might as well use what I have to my advantage. I walked closer as Lou responded, "Well, now you need to pay me for however many shirts you cut."

"Sure, no problem. Do you have a moment to chat?"

We made our way to the booth we occupied yesterday, "What's up, grasshopper?"

I scrunched my nose, "Grasshopper? We need to work on that nickname."

That got a smile out of him, "Not until you learn the ropes."

I waived him off as I jumped into my updates, "You know my friend we talked about yesterday?"

"Lover boy? The one we hatched a plan for? Yes. How did your talk go last night?"

"Long story short, he didn't believe a word I said and walked out of my life," I said, not making eye contact. The emotions were still too raw.

"Damn, I'm sorry, Val. Seems like a completely different guy than the one you told me about."

"That was the last thing I saw coming, but I guess we don't need the plan anymore."

"Wait, you're just giving up on him?"

I leaned back, "I don't like to be played and I felt like I just got walked all over. He insisted I back out of his business, so I'm going to give him the space he asked for and do my best to not think twice."

"Fair enough," Lou tapped on the table in front of me. "How are you holding up, though?"

My emotions hadn't quite cleared themselves out yet, so I took a steadying breath. Despite my best efforts, my shoulders dropped, "It hurts. A lot. Especially when I didn't think I was going to be alone anymore. And to have someone do a complete 180 always sucks the wind out of you."

"I get it. As for the plan, we'll drop it. I'll still have your back because you're going to need it. Warrick won't give up on you, you know."

I took a steadying breath before saying, "I was afraid you were going to say that, which is why I'll reject the invite to the ball and keep my head down."

"Ha!" he barked. "I hate to break it to you, but you rejecting him is only going to make him work harder. He won't stop until he gets what he wants."

"We'll see about that."

I stood up to make my way over to the bar and saw Lou sitting there shaking his head. Deciding not to continue this conversation, I made myself busy with getting things ready in order to open for lunch. All the condiments were in place, napkins restocked, cups and glasses cleaned and ready to be filled, Warrick's order ready to go. I gave Lou the thumbs up and he unlocked the door while he answered a phone call. He disappeared into the back just in time for Warrick to walk right in.

I held back the shivers that accompanied that icy blue gaze landing on me. I took a look at the back where Lou had disappeared hoping I could get some help. When there was no sign of him, I turned my attention back to Warrick, "Your usual?"

Warrick leaned on the bar, "I think I want to change it up today, love," he said as his eyes wandered down. *Gotcha.* My trap worked. I don't know what I was thinking I could accomplish, but I wasn't going to run away scared.

I pulled out my notepad to take his order, leaning on the bar as well to close the distance between us. I smiled and lowered my voice, "What'll it be?"

Might as well play into this a little bit ... good to know my reckless side is still intact.

His pupils dilated just a little bit giving away his pleasure in looking at me, "I'll take a beer and just a slice. Make that two beers and join me over there," he nodded his head towards a booth in the front.

I winked, "Coming right up."

I headed back into the kitchen to start working on getting the slice of pizza ready when Lou cornered me. He turned the radio up just enough and whispered through a clenched jaw, "What the hell are you doing?"

"Serving a customer."

"I thought you weren't going forward with the plan. Now you're over there flirting with him."

"You bought me an expensive dress, so I might as well make sure I can use it. I'll be careful, but let me do my thing."

Lou relaxed his jaw just enough so his teeth weren't clenched anymore, "You're making my life harder, but do what you have to I guess."

I squeezed his arm and left with the slice of pizza. As I was grabbing our beers, I looked over to see Warrick engrossed in his phone. *Ever the business man*. When I came over, he was quick to put his phone down and smile that same sly smile at me, "Thanks, love."

"Anytime," I said as I took my seat across from him. "You didn't get your usual."

Warrick wrapped his hands around his beer glass, "From what I understand, you haven't been here for long. How would you know my usual?"

"You got me there," I answered looking over his shoulder to see Lou watching us from the kitchen.

"Besides, if I got my usual order, I wouldn't be sitting here which brings me to why I came," he said leveling his icy blue stare on me.

He reached into his suit jacket pulling out a card. "Take this as my welcome," he said sliding it across the table.

I took the card knowing exactly what I was getting. I went through the motions for a second to pretend to read the plain black letters announcing the details of the summer solstice ball before responding, "Hm, a ball. Where I'm from, you don't see that very often."

"Up to you if you want to join."

I leaned forward a little bit to see him glance down my shirt for a split second, "Glad to know I have a welcoming committee."

Once again bringing his eyes back up to mine, he said, "Someone needs to welcome people around here. We all know Lou sits on his ass. And with someone like you, love, I couldn't just wait around for you to get snatched up."

I let out a soft laugh, "Laying it on thick, aren't we?"

"I'm not one to let something I want slip through my fingers."

I believed it, too. The way he was looking at me, there was a hunger in his eyes. Maybe I should've listened to Lou.

Warrick quickly chowed down his slice and chugged his beer before getting up. He buttoned his suit jacket and said, "Business calls, love. I hope to see you in two days."

Warrick left and I let out all the breath I didn't realize I was holding. I leaned back in my seat and covered my eyes with the heels of my hands. What was I doing?

"Like I said, I have my work cut out for me."

With my hands still over my eyes, "Shut up, Lou."

"In my defense, I did warn you," he reminded me.

I looked at him responding, "I know you did. You were right, though. He didn't waste any time giving me an invite."

"Are you going to go?" he asked.

"Depends. Will you be there?"

Lou joined me in the booth and I noticed he had some flour on his nose, "If you're there, I'm there. I made a promise and I intend to keep it. Plus, you can't let the dress I bought you go to waste. It'll be fun to see you mess with Warrick a little since you're about the only person I've seen who can hold their ground against him."

"Thanks," I said rolling my eyes.

"Anytime, grasshopper. Now, customers are coming in. Get back to work," he said while standing up.

And I did. I worked the rest of the day feeling excited and nervous about the ball. At least Lou was going to be there, so I wouldn't technically be alone, although I don't think Warrick would give me that chance.

I wasn't the only one who had the ball on their minds. Almost every customer who came in was talking about it – who they thought was going to be there, what they were wearing, if they should coordinate, what the food was going to be like, if there were going to be any fireworks or not. The conversations just went on and on about it even though everyone covered every imaginable topic there was. Of course, I got asked a million times if I would be there, and each time, I smiled and nodded mentioning how excited I was. I don't think I could've been any happier when it was time to close.

Lou was sitting at the bar pouring some beers when I turned around from locking the door. He patted the seat next to him. Thankful to get off my feet and have something to drink, I joined him with counting the money we brought in for the day.

Lou took a sip of beer then said, "You know, Val? I didn't like the change to the shirt, but I think that brought in more money."

"Believe it or not, I kind of know what I'm doing every now and then," I bumped him a little bit as a joke.

We went back and forth for a little bit with the banter, but spent most of the evening sitting there in silence winding down from the busy day. I set my glass down after taking another sip and asked, "Do you live around here?"

He raised his eyebrows and smiled, "Warrick not enough for you? Now you need to try to dig in to me too?"

Laughing, I responded, "You know that's not what I meant. You know where I live, I think it's only fair. Plus, I'll need a place to escape to if I ever need to run."

"I live here."

"No surprise there," still thinking he was joking.

His face stayed serious as he said, "No, I mean, I have an apartment above here. I keep that on the low, so you're sworn to secrecy now, too."

"Deal. Do you have anyone special in your life?"

Lou paused to think about his answer, "No, there's never really been anyone for me. I don't like to take risks because Warrick still likes to inflict pain whenever he has the chance, so the less weapons he has to use against me, the better."

I nodded. Warrick still had a hold over Lou, but I wasn't going to be the one to point that out. I reached over the bar and filled my glass, offering Lou the same. When he nodded, I filled his up and asked, "You have anything else to eat besides pizza?"

He didn't respond, but instead got up and headed back to the kitchen to bring out some garlic knots, "Will this do the trick?"

"Sure."

A few more moments of silence filled the space. I don't do well when its quiet for too long, so I drank my beer a little too fast. I had lost count of how many I had to drink and didn't realize it until I stood up to leave, stumbling over myself. Lou caught me, "Woah there. I guess I needed to bring out more substantial food."

I tried standing again. "It's fine," I mumbled as I stumbled.

Grunting as he caught me again, Lou said, "Nope. I'll take you home. Sit here for a couple of minutes while I park your bike in the garage."

I thought I felt fine, but I guess not. I was finally feeling good, truly good, and didn't want the feeling to go away. Maybe I could talk Lou into hanging out with me. I giggled thinking about Lou in his tight t-shirt and jeans that fit him just right flushing at the idea of seeing him out of his clothes. I was drunk …

Lou scooped me up not too long after he left and got me settled in his car.

"Where are we going?" I asked.

He turned the engine over and eased out of the alley, "I'm taking you home. I'm beginning to think you were trying to get into my apartment."

"What if I wanted to see the bat cave?" I asked while playing with the seatbelt.

"Bat cave?" he asked looking over at me with a cocked eyebrow.

"It's a comic book reference," I said waiving him off. "Forget about it."

"Okay," was all he said as he returned his attention back to the road.

When we got back to the house, he carried me in and settled me on the couch. Thinking he was about to leave, I called out, "Wait!"

He looked at me over his shoulder, "What?"

"Don't go. Please. I want to have some fun tonight."

"Val, not tonight."

I shook my head, "Not that. Let's play a boardgame or something."

"Fine," Lou sighed. "What do you have in mind?"

I beamed and did my best to walk over to where the games were stored. I picked out a few easy ones and we dived right into them. For acting like such a tough guy all the time, Lou sure liked to play boardgames. We were laughing the night away with everything feeling easy again. Like normal. I was starting to sober up and realized how late it was getting. We finished our game. I stood up, "I shouldn't keep you here any longer. Thank you for staying with me."

"Anytime. It was fun to just hang out. I haven't done that in a long time," he yawned.

I was standing there awkwardly still waiting for him to stand. When he didn't, I asked, "Are you stuck?"

"I might be," Lou yawned again. "I didn't realize how tired I was."

"Are you going to be okay to drive?"

"Would it be alright if I camped out here tonight?"

He looked about 10 years older and his eyes were half closed. I guess there wouldn't be any harm in bringing him a blanket and a pillow, or offering him a guest room.

"Sure, you can either sleep here, or there's a room upstairs you can use."

Lou looked at the couch for a second then back at me, "I think I'll use the room. While this couch is comfortable now, I don't know how well I'll fit."

I was thinking the same thing, so I gestured for him to follow me. I brought him to a room that was all ready to go reminding him he knows where to find me if he needs anything. We said goodnight and headed our separate ways to settle in for the night. By the time I laid my head on my pillow, I was grateful. Soon I was drifting off to dreamland and images of Warrick and Lou kept flashing through my mind. Funny how quickly my brain was moving on from Daryl.

Morning rolled around and I woke up feeling all the beer I had drank the previous day. I needed food. Greasy food. I made my way downstairs startled at Lou standing there in my kitchen prepping breakfast.

"Morning!"

"Woah, too loud," I said while rubbing the sleep out of my eyes.

"Here, drink this," he said as he slid a glass towards me on the island.

I gave him a suspicious look but still took a sip. Whatever fruit blend he made was delicious, so I kept drinking marveling at how my headache eased with every sip, "What is this magic juice?"

"Instant hangover cure. You sure put down a lot last night."

I winced, hoping I didn't do or say anything stupid, "Yeah, that'll happen."

Lou shrugged, "Sometimes we need it. Thanks for letting me stay over last night."

"Anytime. Glad to see you making yourself at home. You've been nice enough to take me under your wing."

"Eh, that's what I do," Lou shrugged. "So, want some actual food?"

"Yes, please," I said as I made my way over to the fridge.

Lou put his hand on the door, "There's nothing really in there. I checked already. I'll take you to one of my favorite places."

"You're starting to spoil me."

We got changed and headed out to this breakfast spot. I was pleasantly surprised when we pulled up to a little cottage on the outskirts of the city. It was a small, white cottage with green trim and ivy growing all over it. Once inside, I was greeted by a lot of natural light and friendly smiles. Everyone seemed to know who Lou was and was excited to meet the newcomer. It was a nice change of pace from being in the city. I started to think that if I couldn't get back to my world, I could at least be okay with staying here. It didn't take long for me to feel a little better about staying in my new home which is saying something for someone who also doesn't like change.

Chapter 9

Wednesday, the day of the summer solstice, arrived. The entire city shut down making me think it was Christmas with how everyone was acting. There was an excited electricity in the air as people buzzed around to get ready for the ball. Lou texted me telling me not to worry about coming in to the restaurant today and that he would be by later to pick me up for the ball. I finally had a moment to myself where shit wasn't hitting the fan, so I sat out by the fire pit sipping on my coffee enjoying the morning sun. It was a gorgeous day with a few fluffy white clouds rolling along in the sky. Birds were fluttering and singing as if they knew today was the mark of warmth and longer days.

I decided it wouldn't hurt to work my muscles and swim a few laps. I eased into the water delighted in the fact it wasn't too cold and started my routine. It had been a while since I had done any sort of workout, so it took a second for my muscles to wake up, but once they did, I felt rejuvenated. There's a certain feeling when you focus on you and this swim was melting away all of my concerns.

I swam until my fingers wrinkled, but not to the point of exhaustion. I did have a ball to go to after all. I checked my phone while I dried off to see another text from Lou saying he'd be by the house in a couple hours and that we should head out right after that. I spent more time in the pool than I meant to. Oops. I rushed upstairs to shower and start getting ready knowing I had a tight timeline.

The doorbell rang right when I expected it to. I paused what I was doing to yell, "Come in!"

I was still upstairs putting the final touches on my makeup when Lou stood in my doorway. I swiped my mascara over my false lashes one more time gaining a slow whistle from Lou.

"What do you think?" I asked giving a little spin.

Lou gave me one more look-over, "I think you aren't going to disappoint."

"Like you said, couldn't let this dress go to waste."

"I don't think you need to worry about that," he said with a shadow crossing over his features. It was gone before I noticed it too much, but I could've sworn it was a look reserved for intimate moments.

I smiled at him and held out my arm, "Shall we?"

Lou nodded. A man of many words. At least he was being a gentleman this evening, taking care of the doors on the way outside followed by making sure I was settled okay when we got in the car.

You could tell this was one of the biggest, if not the biggest, event. We pulled up to the venue, which to no surprise, is Warrick's massive skyscraper to see everyone dressed to the nines. Lou parked behind the pizza place no doubt because he couldn't trust the valet not to mess with his space car and we walked across the street. I looked around in awe at how everyone was dressed up – there was fabric and jewels everywhere, yet, everyone kept staring at me. All the attention was making me nervous making me tighten my grip on Lou's arm. I was wondering where exactly this ball was being held when we were ushered into an elevator since it wasn't in the big space on the first floor I saw off to the left. The doors shut whisking us away to the rooftop.

The doors opened revealing a scene that looked like it was right out of a fairy tale. A staircase led down to the dance floor where string lights traced the edges, massive leafy plants everywhere you could see with the occasional flower arch and water fountain. A live band was playing calm music that enticed people out on the dance floor. There was plenty of food and drinks to go around, but what really got me was the view. You could see everything from the top of this building, and with the sun just starting to set, you could get caught up in the beauty of the surroundings. I'm a sucker for a good golden hour. I looked up at Lou to find him looking down at me, "You didn't tell me how lavish this was going to be."

He raised an eyebrow, "Didn't you get the hint by the dresses you tried on?"

"Hmm, I guess I didn't piece together that puzzle. I was too busy trying to get my feet under me with everything changing in my life."

That got a chuckle out of him as we made our way out of the elevator. We paused again so I could soak in the view a little more when I saw Warrick staring right at me. He put down his drink and hastily made his way over. I felt Lou tense, drop my arm, and walk away leaving me alone.

"You look absolutely stunning, love," Warrick said as he kissed my hand. He led me down the stairs to the dance floor. The number of stares I was getting increased exponentially from the number I was getting on the way into the venue. I guess that's what happens when you're the focus of the host.

We got on the dance floor and Warrick pulled me in tight. We were quiet for a little while dancing, enjoying the music, until he whispered, "You are by far the most beautiful woman here."

"Thank you," I blushed.

"I persuaded you to come to this ball, how can I persuade you to go on a date? Somewhere we can be alone without so many eyes on us."

As he said that, he smoothly rotated me around so I could see Lou who nodded his head and raised his glass. Warrick knew the exact moment I would see Lou, and to show that, he slid is hand down lower on my waist. I stiffened just enough to let him know his hand wasn't allowed to go any further.

"Warrick, you sure are relentless, aren't you?"

"We've been over this. When I see someone I like, I go for them. I want you to be mine, but I'm not going to force your hand."

There was something about the possessiveness in his voice, the way his voice got husky that caused a jolt of electricity to work its way up from between my legs to my ears. *It has to be that damn accent.* The flirting went back and forth for a little while longer before the conversation shifted back to more substance.

He casually mentioned, "So, Daryl tells me you two arrived here at the same time?"

I felt myself stiffen again. Warrick picked up the response in no time. "Ah, he told the truth." Chuckling, he continued, "And there seems to be something there."

I clenched my teeth noticing the irony of being in a position where I couldn't look Daryl in the eyes, "Not anymore."

"Doesn't take much to get that fire lit in you, does it?" Warrick asked with his voice low, lips brushing against my ear.

"Are we going to keep dwelling on this topic?" I managed to get out between my still clenched teeth.

"All I wanted to say on that topic is I know how you got here. Did you arrive with a place to stay or are you holed up at Lou's?"

"Let's just say I was one of the lucky ones to arrive with my house."

"Interesting."

"Interesting?"

"I've noticed a trend with the newcomers here and you're just adding to my suspicions. I've been trying to dive into why so many new people are showing up here, not that I'm complaining. Enough about that though, I don't want to spoil being in good company."

I looked at him and gave him my best sexy smile. My mind got caught on his words. It sounded like he might have an inkling as to what may have caused us to show up here. Maybe he has the tools and resources to make headway on figuring out what has been transferring people to this specific spot. If he did know something, I knew I needed to try and figure it out. And as much as I'm having fun here, I would like to get back to my normal life if at all possible. I also knew I had to tell Lou to see if he thinks Warrick is bluffing.

It was like he knew I was trying to get him to come over. Lou walked up behind Warrick giving a little tap on his shoulder, "May I cut in?"

"Be my guest. The host needs to make his rounds anyways," Warrick said despite not looking like he wanted to leave.

You could feel the tension between the two in that quick interaction. Warrick wasted no time walking away giving Lou the chance to slip right into the spot Warrick just left, except he didn't pull me in as tightly. Thankfully. I looked over towards the direction Warrick walked off to see he was nowhere to be found. I was safe-ish to talk to Lou about what I had just heard.

To play it safe, I lowered my voice so that it was barely audible, "Lou, I think Warrick may be on to something."

"Yeah, he's trying to get on you."

I scrunched my nose in disgust and looked at him, "Stop. What I mean is I think he's on to something with why people are popping out of the ground here."

That got Lou's attention. He lowered his voice as he responded, "This is a conversation we need to have somewhere where there aren't so many ears. I've had my suspicions, but we need to compare notes before we take any hasty actions."

I wanted to protest so we could continue diving into this right here, but I just nodded my head in agreement since I knew Warrick's wolves were all around us and could hear just about anything they wanted to.

"Hey, let's just have a good time tonight, okay?" Lou said with his eyes lightening. "We'll have plenty of time to talk through this. Did I mention your dress looks like it was made for you?"

I rolled my eyes, "You've already given me a compliment. Don't feel obligated to keep going."

"I'm being serious. You clean up well although it helps that you're not half bad to begin with."

That got a laugh out of me and I leaned into him more. Something about his arms made me feel less exposed, made me feel safe. I said, "I do have to hand it to Warrick, though. He made this place feel magical. It's hard not to get caught up in the ambiance."

Looking me right in the eyes, Lou said, "I couldn't have said it better myself."

Uh-oh. I know that look. He was starting to get caught up in me. It was that damn Val effect Mark had brought up.

"Do you mind if I have a dance?"

I instantly recognized Daryl's voice. Lou looked at me again searching for any sign for what I wanted him to say. I gave a slight nod to indicate I would be okay. Lou stepped back and gestured for Daryl to step in. I wasn't sure how I felt about this given how the last conversation Daryl and I had went.

"Hi," I croaked.

"Hi. You sure have captured the attention of many admirers."

"Thank you."

"Val, I know I was harsh the other night. I think I was taking it out on you."

"I'm going to stop you there, Daryl," I said putting my hand on his chest. I knew where this conversating was headed and I didn't like it, "You've burned that bridge. You somehow made me question so much so quickly. I'm not ready to deal with that kind of heart break again. How can I trust you're not trying to sleep with me now?"

"That's fair, I guess."

I stopped dancing to put more distance between us, "You can't even answer my question which tells me all I need to know. You're getting all caught up in this atmosphere with the nice clothes and shit."

"You're jumping to conclusions," he said defensively with hurt crossing his face.

"I don't care if I am or not. I need to get some space," I said as I turned away and left the dance floor. Even though I was outside, I needed air. I grabbed a glass of champagne while heading to a secluded, quiet corner at the edge of the rooftop where no one else was. Finally, a moment where I'm not constantly surrounded by testosterone.

I took a sip of champagne and started to work on letting go of my frustrations. I wanted to enjoy this evening. It was a time for having fun, for getting lost in the moment.

I leaned on the railing soaking in the view and watching the sun make its final appearance for the day when I head harsh voices bickering. The voices were growing louder signaling their approach to where I was standing, so I hid behind the nearest bush hoping I couldn't be seen.

I was only able to make out the voices of two men to tell that they were getting into it. One of them turned and was facing in my direction – Warrick. I tensed up and tucked myself further behind the bush and willed myself to be as quiet as possible. It didn't take long for me to recognize who the other participant was. Just by what I could hear of the voice, I knew it was Lou. *Shit, this wasn't good.*

Warrick stepped closer to Lou, "You need to get your wolves under control." He jabbed his finger into Lou's chest continuing, "I can't have them gallivanting around here raising hell with my wolves and putting everyone at this ball at risk just because they get off on it."

Lou, trying to be nonchalant, just shrugged, "I don't see the problem here Warrick. I haven't seen them raising hell, and even if they were, I'm sure your guys started it. There are too many power-hungry assholes around here who can't stand when they feel the slightest bit threatened. That behavior starts at the top."

That set Warrick off. He responded, "I don't give a damn who started it. This is our territory, and if I remember correctly, our agreement states we'll leave each other alone and work to keep the peace at major events like this."

Lou stood his ground, "I also don't feel the need to micro-manage my people. As far as I can tell, the only people who are bringing this up are your guys. None of the other guests have mentioned anything. In fact, I think they're having a grand old time, chap."

Lou, you got to check the smart-ass comments.

If Warrick was mad before, he was steaming now. He snarled his lip and landed a swift punch knocking Lou's head back. Blood went everywhere.

Lou made a slight whimpering noise grabbing his nose. Lou wasn't paying attention to what Warrick was doing and he ended up on the ground with Warrick holding him down by his neck, pressing his leg into his back so Lou couldn't breathe. Warrick lowered his head to Lou's ear, "You forget, Louis, I still own you."

Lou was struggling and trying to get air while Warrick put more and more pressure on Lou's neck. I put my hands over my mouth to keep from saying anything and revealing my hiding spot. After a few more moments that felt like an eternity, Warrick got off of Lou, straightened out his suit, checked his hair, and walked back towards the ball. Lou got on all fours very slowly. *This really wasn't good.* There was a shift of electricity in the air making me afraid Warrick was coming back. I waited a hair longer to make sure the coast was clear before running over to Lou who was now struggling to get up. I knelt down and put my hands on his back. Every muscle in Lou's body went rigid ready for a fight, so I said, "Hey, it's just me. Let me help you. Are you okay?"

He relaxed a little and nodded his head, but didn't say anything. He wouldn't even look at me. I put a little more effort into guiding him onto his feet and made sure I didn't make eye contact. From what I could see, his eye color had changed which must mean his wolf was with us too. Lou breathed in deeply then said, "Meet me across the street. I need to gather everyone."

Not missing a beat, I started making my way towards the exit. I didn't want to be a rude guest, so I first found Warrick. You couldn't tell what had transpired moments ago.

"Hi Warrick, sorry to interrupt," I said placing my hand on his arm.

He turned around excusing himself from the conversation he was in before saying to me, "No worries, love."

"I just wanted to say thank you for the invite. This ball was lovely and the host sure knows how to throw a party."

That got him to smile as I knew it would. I didn't want to raise any suspicions, and so far, it seemed like it was working.

Warrick put his hand on my arm and said, "My pleasure. Although, it sounds like you're leaving?"

"I am. I'm feeling pretty tired. I need some rest."

"Well, that's a shame. I was hoping to get some more time on the dance floor with you. Thank you for sharing at least one dance with me."

He leaned in and kissed me on the cheek telling me I was free to go. I gave him a smile with a finger wave before walking away. I could feel his eyes following me as I headed towards the elevator.

I also noticed Daryl watching me, too, looking rejected, but not looking like he was going to make any move towards me.

I stood in the elevator waiting for the doors to close and saw Lou just now walking out from where the altercation took place. He was covered in blood, but no one seemed to notice. I looked over at Warrick to see if he was keeping a close eye on Lou. Thankfully, he wasn't, but he was still watching me. I winked at him to keep the game going and that was all he needed to turn back around to rejoin the conversation I pulled him from.

Once I was out of the building, I let go of all the air I had in me. What just happened up there? I didn't realize I had hardly been breathing until I was out here working on getting more air into my lungs. I went around the back to enter the pizza place busying myself with getting drinks and some quick bites ready for Lou and the pack. That was the least I could do with leaving ahead of him. I also unlocked the front door and it wasn't long before Lou made his way in. He quickly rearranged the space to make it easier for his wolves to pay attention to him.

"Lou," I started timidly. "Do you want me here or would it better if I made myself scarce?"

He replied without looking at me, "Stay."

I thought about joking with him if I should sit too, but this was not the time.

The pack started making their way into the restaurant and I noticed Lou stood a little straighter. I guess I get to see what it means to be the alpha. He waited a couple more minutes just in case there were any stragglers before starting.

"I'm going to keep this quick because I can't believe I'm even having to go over this. I know Warrick's guys may have been instigating, but either way, he wasn't a fan of how you all were trying to flex your muscles. He asked next time we're all out and about at a huge event like that to keep the peace. We don't need people to know who we are or see the tension. That's all, enjoy the rest of your evening."

One of the women in the back stood up to ask, "Since when do you take orders from Warrick?"

Lou put a growl in his voice to show he didn't appreciate the challenge, "I want to make sure everyone in the city has a *damn* good time and I can't do that when you all are bickering with the other wolves."

She quickly looked away and sat back down without another word.

Lou sighed, "This better be the last thing I have to say about this because remember, we have a physical agreement we have signed with Warrick's pack. Part of it states that we keep the peace at big events. If we break the agreement, all hell will break loose. I don't think any of us want to deal with that. Now, please, go enjoy the rest of your night."

Everyone nodded their understanding and left. Once the final person walked out of the restaurant, Lou collapsed in a chair putting his head in his hands. I could tell this evening was wearing on him which sucks because this was supposed to be a fun night.

I started working on cleaning everything up to save him the work later. I put the dishes in the kitchen to be washed tomorrow, I wiped the tables and rearranged the dining room, then locked the door. When I finished, I walked back over to Lou and knelt in front of him, "Hey, I'm going to head out. I'll take care of all the cleanup tomorrow when I get here."

I stood up and went to leave out the back door. Lou grabbed my wrist and mumbled, "Stay."

"But then I'll see the bat cave."

He didn't say anything, only tightened his grip on my wrist. He must really be going through a lot if he was asking me to stay with him. I think I'm marching into territory no other person has before.

"I'll be right by your side as long as you need me."

Lou pulled me closer to him. His voice cracked a little showing the emotion he's carrying, "Please, stay."

"I'm not going anywhere except maybe upstairs."

He didn't make any movements or say anything for a little while longer. I broke the silence, "Come on, Lou, it'll be better upstairs. We'll get you cleaned up."

With that, he got up and led the way to his apartment still holding on to my wrist. Warrick must have a strong hold over him with how torn up this interaction made him. It made me wonder what really happened in those early stages of him becoming a wolf and the torture Warrick put him through. It definitely wasn't a challenge for Warrick to take him down today, so that must also be eating at him.

We got into his apartment and Lou immediately flopped on the couch. I stood there for a little bit to take in my surroundings. He kept his apartment neat and didn't have too many furnishings. Despite that, it still felt cozy. The apartment was decorated with a rustic, modern, mountain cabin kind of feel. You could tell everything was organized and in its place. There wasn't a lot of color in the décor, but where there was, it was deep shades of blue. He had a fireplace and even though it wasn't cold, I still went over to light it to try to bring some sense of comfort. I needed to get him out of whatever dark place he went to.

Once the fire was lit, I kicked off my heels finally realizing how tired my feet were. I wandered into the kitchen and dampened some towels so I could start cleaning the blood off his face.

Lou's eyes were closed when I got back over to the couch. I spoke in a low tone so I didn't startle him, "Ready to get that blood off your face?"

He opened his eyes with his wolf at the surface again. Lou just nodded his head signaling me to start. The second I touched his nose, he winced.

"Sorry," I said pulling back. "I'll be gentle. It looks like it needs to be set back in place. Are you okay if I take care of that really quick?"

I again got a silent yes from him and placed my hands on his nose. I counted down from three then made quick work of getting his nose back to where it needed to be. There was a low grumble emanating from his chest making me wait a few seconds before getting back to cleaning up the blood.

"You know, I would've thought you wouldn't be feeling any pain by now. Don't werewolves heal fast?"

The warm feeling I got as he responded caught me off-guard. I didn't realize I was wanting to hear his voice so badly. And not the authoritative, alpha wolf voice, but his normal, easy-going voice.

"We normally do," he said as he closed his eyes again. "Somehow Warrick has found a way around that, though. I'm not sure how he figures these things out, but it doesn't surprise me."

"Must mean he's involved in more than what he lets on."

"Would make sense. I guess I never put two and two together."

I nodded, letting the conversation take a little pause while I looked for any more blood needing to be wiped up. After finding some more spots, I resumed the conversation, "Did you grow up around here?"

"Yeah, I was born and raised here," he said. Lou opened his eyes again and I was relieved to see them back to normal.

"So, do you know how the werewolves got started around here, then?"

"Not really. I don't think anyone does, but there's a rumor amongst us that it started with one person who was born as a wolf, or got sick then became a wolf. I can never remember the way it goes. No one knows how that just happened, but it seems like the whole werewolf line here gets traced back to that one person a long time ago."

"But no one knows who it is?"

"Not that I'm aware of. We just know about this through the stories being passed down between generations of werewolves. I think a lot of us have been trying to find a name or any other indication as to who that person was, but everyone keeps coming to a dead end."

"Interesting. Do you ever wonder if there are werewolves in other worlds?"

Lou thought for a moment, "Maybe a little, but I only just started considering that when new people started showing up here. I didn't think there could be more than one world."

"To be honest, I feel like I'm in the same boat as you. I would've never imagined that other places like this exist."

I took one last look at his face then smiled when I didn't see any more traces of blood. I got back up and deposited the dirty towels in the kitchen sink.

"Lou, do you want anything while I'm up?"

"No. I just want you back over here."

I headed back over to the couch and angled myself so that I was looking at him more while sitting right next to him, "Can we circle back to what Warrick had mentioned to me tonight?"

Lou closed his eyes at the mention of Warrick's name, "I guess."

I didn't want to lose my chance at this conversation, so I responded quickly, "He had said he's starting to look into why people are showing up here. Could that mean he has some information on what's happening and how to reverse it?"

Lou thought before responding. "Potentially."

"So that means I could go back home and find my friends?"

He sighed, "Look, if he has any information, you'll want to get in to where he holds important research and that's going to require you to get close to him."

I didn't hesitate with my response, "I would do it. I would do whatever it takes just to even know how this all happened."

"You'll have to do the whole flirting thing with him. It wasn't too long ago when you said you wouldn't. Although, after your whole thing with lover boy, you kind of flipped on that."

I looked him straight in the eyes and said, "Lou, I'll do whatever it takes."

"Famous last words. Anyways, you know what you need to do. Get close to him and work on getting the information out. Shouldn't be hard, you've already got his attention."

Seeing how much he was straining to make it through this conversation, I nodded to end it. Talking about the man who rattled Lou wasn't going to help him calm down and feel better. Plus, we were at a point where we were going to be heading in circles without more information.

Lou closed his eyes and laid his head back on the couch. I sat there a moment watching him.

"Val?"

"Mmm?"

"Your staring isn't helping."

I blushed, "Oh, sorry." I looked away deciding it was time to get out of this dress, but I didn't have anything with me since I was planning on going home when we were done.

"Lou?"

He opened one eye to look at me, "Yes?"

"Do you have anything I can change into?"

Lou didn't say anything. Instead, he got up to head down the hallway towards what I'm assuming is his room. I heard him ruffling around for a little bit before he came back out. He had clearly changed and was now just wearing pajama pants leaving his scars on full display. They were worse than I had imagined. You could tell they covered the majority of his torso and some were deep judging by how much scar tissue had built up.

I found myself making my way over to him. I reached out starting to trace Lou's scars. Even though he didn't stop me, Lou tensed and his breathing became ragged. I looked up at him to see the wolf starting to show again in his eyes as I asked, "Did he really do all of this to you?"

Lou gently grabbed my hand stopping it, but not removing it from his chest. He replied, "Yes."

"I didn't know it was this bad," I said looking back at all the scars. I have never seen so much scarring.

We stood there a moment longer with Lou still holding on to my hand. I was once again reminded how hard this evening has been on him. I looked back up to him to find his looking down at me. He said, "Are you disgusted by this? Most can't handle seeing what he did."

"I'm anything but disgusted. I'm angry he did this to you and that he could be doing this to whoever he pleases. I'm scared because of how quickly he can take you down when you're not a small guy. I'm sad because of how much pain this must have caused and is still causing. And I'm appreciative you weren't afraid to share something so personal despite not knowing me for very long. Do I need to continue?"

That must have released something because Lou's face softened and his eyes returned to normal. He handed me the clothes I could change into, "Feel free to change in my room." Lou pointed to the doorway at the very end of the hallway.

"Can you unzip me?" I asked before grabbing the clothes. I turned around and had to wait a moment before I felt a slight tug on the dress followed by the sound of the zipper going down. Lou's hand lingered when he reached the end.

I muttered my thanks and headed towards his room to change before anything happened. When I turned to close the door for more privacy, Lou was still just standing there, staring towards a window.

It didn't take long for me to get out of my dress. Honestly, it felt really good to be in more comfortable clothes even though I was swimming in the shirt he gave me and the shorts weren't really doing anything to stay up either. I looked in a mirror and giggled. The size of the clothes on me made me look like a little kid. I made my way back out to the main room and held my arms up, "Ta-da!"

Without holding on to the shorts, they instantly fell down around my ankles. Lou raised his eyebrows and the corners of his lips started twitching. At least I was getting somewhere, but I was thankful the shirt was like a dress on me in this moment. I bent down to pull the shorts back up to see if they at least tied so I didn't have to worry about losing them every time I tried to do something. After I finished tying them, I looked back at Lou, "There, now you don't have to worry about seeing my ass. Do you want anything to drink?"

He was back to laying his head on the back of the couch with his eyes closed, "There's tea in the drawer by the sink. Cups are above it."

I headed over to his kitchen to start looking for a tea kettle or anything else to warm the water. Hearing me search, Lou said, "Just put the water in the mugs and warm them up in the microwave."

I did as I was told and grabbed some calming tea. When I got back to the couch with our mugs, Lou didn't move a muscle. I was sitting with my body angled towards him again and started to sip on my tea. As I put the mug down, Lou's arm swept me into him. Startled by the movement, I tensed. He noticed I tensed up, "I don't know what it is about your presence right now, but it's helping. Feeling you against my skin is keeping the wolf down."

I nodded, honestly feeling a little flustered. It took me a moment to calm my breathing to be able to relax into him. Lou smelt faintly of pizza and his cologne. His body heat was a comforting warm starting to make my eye lids droop. Lou leaned forward, waking me back up, and grabbed his tea only to gulp it down in one sip. No wonder he didn't have a tea kettle ...

I turned myself so I could look back up at him and asked, "How are you feeling?"

Lou tucked some of my hair behind my ear, "Better."

I gave him a kind smile before leading into another question that's been playing in the back of my mind for a little bit, "Have you ever been romantically involved with anyone?"

I knew the answer currently was no. He kept most people at an arm's length and I'm assuming that's because of Warrick. Lou confirmed my assumption when he responded, "Yes, once, but Warrick took that away from me too."

By the way his face tried to contort with pain, I knew what had happened had been bad. I didn't want to press any further, so instead I sat back up and cupped his check with my hand. Lou leaned into my touch and breathed deeply.

"Lou?"

"Yes?"

"Do you have any music?"

"There's a record player over there. Feel free to put on whatever."

I went over to the shelf he pointed at. Flipping through the records, I didn't recognize any of these artists, so I took at shot in the dark hoping I could find some slower music. The record started playing and I had guessed correctly. I went back over to Lou offering him my hand, "May I have this dance?"

That got a little smile out of him as he stood up. Instead of joining me right away, he closed the blinds shutting us out from the outside world. He then went over to his front door to lock it and finally joined me. Instead of the more formal slow dancing we were doing at the ball, Lou wrapped his arms around me and hugged me to him. We swayed back and forth, slow dancing to the music for a while. The next song to play was a little more upbeat, so we pulled away from each other. Lou looked at me with a face full of tenderness. I looked away from him and went to grab a sip of my tea thankful for the distraction. I turned back towards him, "Sleep is trying to take over. Where can I crash?"

Again, he didn't say much. Instead, he walked towards me, took my mug out of my hands to place it back on the coffee table, and scooped me in his arms. I tried to protest a little, but didn't want to. Lou took me into his room and gently sat me on the bed. He headed back out of his room to turn off all the lights and the music.

Lou went to his dresser on the wall opposite of his bed. I didn't realize until I heard the slow notes of music that he had another record player in here. He moved so he was in front of me and kneeled down on the floor so we were able to look each other in the eyes as he said, "It would mean a lot if you stayed in here with me tonight. Sleep is the hardest when shit like this happens."

I reached out putting my hands on his shoulders, daring myself to lean in closer, "I'll keep those demons at bay."

Lou gave me a little smile and gently wrapped his arms around me enveloping me in a hug. I wrapped my arms around him returning the gesture. When we separated, I said, "Lou, I just want you to know I'm happy to help you through this time, but I don't want anything more to develop between us. It's not a good idea right now."

He paused before responding, "Have you thought about staying here, in this world?"

"I have, but I'm just trying to figure out what's going on right now. There's been a ton of change. We've grown pretty close in the short amount of time I've been here, but I worry it may grow into something more when I'm trying to get close to Warrick to get information. The last thing I want to do is cause you any more pain than what you've been through."

Lou looked away moving to his side of the bed still not making any move to look in my direction. He sighed sitting on his bed, "I understand and will keep that in mind. Thank you for everything you're doing."

I reach out to touch his shoulder, "You're doing so much for me, it's the least I can do."

I took my hand back and worked my way under the covers. Lou did the same so we're laying with our backs to each other. I'm on the edge of the bed to give as much space as possible between us reminding myself I'm just here to provide comfort. I started to drift off into my deep sleep, but just before I was gone, Lou rolled over and draped his arm across me before pulling me in closer to him. I kept reminding myself I'm helping Lou through a hard time and keeping those nightmares at bay. I'm not going to let anything romantic happen between us, we're going to keep our relationship at a platonic level. Although, I can see us being happy here and this would give me a fresh start in a completely new area. I wouldn't have to worry about wooing Warrick. But no, I can do this. I can stay strong and get things back to normal.

Chapter 10

This time I woke up before Lou. I rolled over to see him sleeping soundly in the same position he had been the night before. He looked so peaceful in this moment. I did my best to move as carefully as I could so I didn't disturb him. I headed to the kitchen and started making coffee while looking for food. I found some oatmeal, bread, and jelly. *Good enough for me.* I got the water boiling when Lou came out of his room. I smiled at him, "Good morning sunshine."

He was rubbing the sleep from his eyes when he looked at me through one squinted eye and grumbled, "I smell coffee."

I poured a cup then handed it to him, "Here. I'm going to need to get a ride back to my place so I can get ready for the day."

Lou didn't respond. Instead, he went back to his room with coffee in hand. I heard him rummaging around, so I turned back to the stove to keep the oatmeal going. Lou was sitting at the counter sipping on his coffee by the time I turned around to serve up the oatmeal. In front of him were some clothes and I laughed, "I don't think your clothes are going to fit me."

"Hold them up."

I did as I was told to find the shirt and jeans to be woman's sizes, and even better, they were my size. I looked at him a little confused as to why he would have clothes that were my size.

Holding up his hands, Lou said, "Before you jump to conclusions, I didn't buy these for you. I just had some spares."

Our conversation from last night flashed through my head. These were the clothes from the one Warrick took away from him. I almost felt like I still shouldn't wear these, but I knew Lou wouldn't have brought them out for me if it wasn't okay. I looked back at him to find him watching me. I said, "Thanks. I'll make sure to get these back to you soon."

"No rush."

I put them back on the counter and we ate in silence. The weight in the air was heavy and I felt even more for Lou. This guy has had a lot ripped away from him by one person. If I did decide to stay, I would make sure nothing else would get taken away from him, ever. Not with all the kind gestures he's done for everyone else in his life.

Once done with breakfast, we both worked on getting ready for the day. I gathered the few things I had with me and headed down to his car so they were ready for when I went home. Lou was already in the kitchen working on getting some pizzas ready for the lunch crowd, including Warrick's usual order, and I started working on getting the dining area ready. I went back into the kitchen and leaned against the counter next to Lou as I asked, "You really think Warrick is coming in today?" I gestured to the whole pizza on the counter and the two slices next to it that were ready to go into the oven.

Lou looked at me with a cocked eyebrow while he continued kneading some pizza dough, "Is that really a question?"

I stopped for a second to give him a look, "What do you mean?"

He stopped what he was doing and turned to me, "You had his undivided attention yesterday. He's been stopping in daily since you've been here where he would only stop in once a week before. I can almost guarantee you that he's coming in again today and I'll even bet he'll ask you on a date. I'd even go as far as predicting that he'll give you a gift."

I stuck my hand out and said, "Shake on it. If you're right, then I have to do whatever you want. If you're wrong, you give me a day off."

"Bet," he said as he shook my hand. Lou's smile told me everything I needed to know – he was 110% confident in his prediction and I was probably going to end up doing something ridiculous.

We went back to getting everything ready. We had the pizzas in the oven and were working in the kitchen when I heard the front door open, "Be there in a second. Grab a seat."

"No rush, love."

I froze looking at Lou who was doing everything he could to hold back some laughter. I knew that voice and I wasn't sure if I wanted to go out there to see if he had a present in his hand. Lou pointed at Warrick's order that was hanging out under the heat lamps. *Ugh, no point in pushing this off.* I rolled my eyes and grabbed the food plastering a smile on my face as I headed out into the dining area.

"Warrick! What a surprise. What'll it be today? Slices or a whole one?" I asked as I held up the food in my hands.

He paused with a shadow of a cloud on his face before returning the smile as he said, "Slices, and I was hoping to get my lunch partner."

"Sure thing."

I headed over to the booth to set down the slices and started to get drinks when Lou was beating me to it. *Damn him for encouraging this.* Warrick was right behind me and placed his hand on the small of my back, "Please, take a load off. Lou's finally doing some work around here."

"Okay," I said. I slid into the booth noticing a gift bag in Warrick's other hand. *Damn it.* I should know better than to place bets against someone Lou learned so well.

"What's in the bag?" I asked pointing to the gift bag.

Warrick looked down at the bag and then back to me, "I was hoping to talk to you a little bit before bringing it up."

"I guess I can wait."

"How did you like the ball?"

I took a bite before answering, "It was beautiful. And I had a wonderful time. I appreciated having a little bit of a distraction and something to make me feel like I belong here."

"Good, mission accomplished."

Lou set down our drinks and I noticed he set Warrick's down just hard enough to make it splash back on Warrick. I had never seen a death stare quite like that one, but Lou played it off like it didn't affect him. As Lou was turning away, he said, "You kids don't have too much fun now."

Warrick scoffed and turned his attention back to me, "I couldn't help but notice you're wearing a familiar set of clothing. Did you and Lou end the night together?"

I didn't know how much Warrick knew about what had happened after the altercation between him and Lou, so I decided to omit as many details as I could. To play it safe and all.

"We did, but not in that way. The champagne got to me and I ended up falling asleep here before Lou could take me back home."

"Ah, good. I don't like sharing with others which brings me to my next question and this gift bag. I'd like to follow up on what I mentioned last night about getting together in a more private setting. Would your boss be willing to let you have the night off?"

"Hmm, you might have to give him something in return for his best employee," I said in what I hoped was a super flirtatious tone.

He winked at me then turned towards the kitchen, "Lou, your waitress is feeling a little ill and needs the night off."

Lou leaned against the doorway leading into the kitchen with some pizza dough in his hands, "You could just say you're taking her on a date. I can hear every word of your conversation, and honestly Val, if you try any harder, I think I'll be sick."

Thank goodness for Lou leaning into this, too.

"So, boss man? Can I have a night off so I can be wined and dined?"

That got a little grin out of him and I couldn't tell if he enjoyed being called boss man or if he was keeping up the charade. Lou looked at me, "Sure. I got it covered."

Warrick turned back around to me, "I'll pick you up here at 9 tonight."

He got up to leave taking the rest of his pizza with him. I stayed in the booth long after he was gone trying to convince myself this was still a good idea. Lou joined me since the lunch rush wasn't living up to its normal hype.

"You haven't touched your pizza since he left, or your beer," Lou said while he took a swig of my beer.

"Is this still a good idea?" I asked in a serious tone.

"Well, it's all up to what you want to do. You could back out on this and just get into the rhythm of a new life here, or you could continue to work on finding a way back to your old life and to your friends."

I pondered that for a moment, "I'm sure they would do this for me, right?"

Lou leaned in and took a bite of my slice. With a full mouth, he said, "The fact that you had to ask that should tell you all you need to know."

I stared him down, annoyed he pointed that out and annoyed at the fact that I wasn't even sure I could count on my friends to find a way to fix whatever happened. I didn't necessarily want to date Warrick for the sake of getting information, but I also don't know if I'd be okay with not trying to solve this either.

Lou looked over at the gift bag, "You didn't even open your gift."

I shrugged, "Go ahead. I don't even know if I want to see what's in there."

He started to dig in the bag and his eyebrows shot up. Now my curiosity was piqued, "Lou, what is it?"

Lou looked at me and pushed the bag across the table, "All I got to say is when a man has money and wants someone, he makes sure to go all out."

He got up to go back to prepping pizzas while I stared down the gift bag trying to talk myself into going through with this. When I finally pulled the bag towards me and peered inside, all I could see was a pile of black fabric. There was a note on top saying everything Warrick had just talked to me about, so I put that on the table and pulled out a classic little black dress. From what I could tell, it was made of satin and looked like it would hug my body in all the right places. I stood up to see what the length was with it coming halfway down my thighs, so at least I didn't have to worry about flashing anyone.

Lou mentioned, "He has a good eye."

I jumped not realizing he was there. He had a serious expression reminding me of how he looked at me last night. I put the dress back in the bag and said, "Lou, I don't have to go through with this. It's not too late for me to change my mind."

"I never said don't do this. I also said this wouldn't be easy. Have some fun with it though. You're going to be eating at some fancy restaurant and not scarfing down on some pizza."

It was like a switch flipped in him in that last part turning into his joking self again. I didn't want to press it too much longer, so I gave him a joke back then got back to helping him prep for the dinner rush since I wasn't going to be there. It was easy to push down all of the doubt and other feelings from earlier to go on with my day.

6 o'clock rolled around and I had a moment to catch my breath in the kitchen. Lou was still working away moving his prepped pizzas from earlier in and out of the oven. He glanced at me, "What are you doing? Shouldn't you be getting ready?"

"You have everything handled in here?"

"Yeah, get out of here. You have a date," he said in a mocking way.

I turned to leave and Lou whipped a towel at me.

"Hey now! I'm getting out of here. Can I use your place to get ready?"

"Yeah, I figured you would. It's unlocked."

I gave him a thumbs up, grabbed the bag from Warrick, and headed up there. The only thing I didn't have was makeup and I didn't think Lou would be the one to have makeup lying around.

I slipped into the dress and took a look at myself in the mirror. Damn, I hated to admit it, but this dress fit perfectly. After twirling in front of the mirror for a few minutes, I got back to work. Now, just to figure out what to do with my hair. While I was playing around with a couple of styles, Lou popped in really quick once again making me jump.

"Will you stop doing that?"

"Why? It's fun," he said with a smile growing across his face. "Anyways, I figured this was going to happen today, so I had one my pack members grab some supplies."

I put my hands on my hips, "Do you two plan these things?"

That got a bark of laughter from Lou, "Warrick uses the same playbook. I've just learned all of his moves."

"Gee, thanks. Glad to know this isn't original."

I grabbed the bag of makeup and hair styling supplies from him and continued, "You should get back to work anyways. Sounds like it's popping down there. You don't want to leave people waiting."

Lou winked at me and headed back down to take care of his customers. I looked in the bag of makeup seeing it had everything I needed. *Impressive.*

It didn't take me much longer to get ready. I popped on the heels that were at the bottom of Warrick's gift bag and headed back downstairs. It was 8:40 pm so I had a little bit of time before Warrick said he'd be there.

Lou let out a low whistle when I got into the kitchen, "You clean up nice."

"You think so?" I asked as I looked down to make sure I was put together.

"It's going to be hard for Warrick to not rip off that dress."

I winked at him, "That's the goal. Get him wrapped around my little finger."

Lou smiled, "There's my girl."

Lou looked over my shoulder out into the dining room and gestured with a nod. I followed his stare and saw Warrick walking in. He was still in his signature look of a suit, but instead of being all buttoned up with a tie and a crisp white shirt, he loosened up a bit. Warrick was wearing a black shirt with several buttons undone to show off the beginnings of his sculpted chest. His hair was slicked back in his usual fashion, but I couldn't help staring. He looked hot, there was no denying that.

I looked back at Lou, nervous, "Well, I guess it's time."

He put a reassuring hand on my shoulder, "You got this. I'll head out there with you. Gotta check on some tables."

I took a steadying breath then headed out there. The minute I walked into the dining room caused Warrick to level his piercing ice blue gaze on me. It was like Jack Frost was in the room. He wasn't the only one staring, but he was the only one I was paying attention to. I have to lean into this, right?

"Hi you," I said.

Warrick grabbed my hand and kissed it, "You look better than I could've imagined, love."

Lou stepped in really quick, "Okay you two love-birds. Have her back by 11, alright?"

Warrick put his hand on my lower back starting to usher me out of the pizza shop, "Don't worry, dad. I'll bring her back in one piece."

I didn't get a chance to look back at Lou before we were outside getting into Warrick's car. *It's game-time and I needed to enjoy myself.* As much as I loved pizza, I was looking forward to switching it up.

"Where are we eating?"

"It's the best restaurant in town. You'll be eating at the top of the world."

"Sounds exciting."

I focused my attention on the road ahead of me while Warrick took us to our destination. It was hard to ignore how nice his car was. The seats were made of leather so soft it felt like I was sitting on a cloud. Every surface was the color of dark oak and the screen was holographic with so many apps and images flying across it.

"You're a popular guy." I mentioned as I saw the never-ending stream of email notifications.

He glanced over at me before returning his attention to the road, "When you run the biggest company, everyone wants a second of your attention."

"And yet, here you are, choosing to spend at least a couple hours of your attention on me."

"I wouldn't have it any other way, love."

I blushed a little bit as we pulled into the valet. Maybe this wouldn't be so hard to fake it.

We made our way into the restaurant with Warrick positioning himself in a way to be able to protect me if anything were to happen. I could appreciate that, although I think the most dangerous person in the room is him.

We got to our seats and Warrick held out my chair for me waiting for me to get settled before he moved to his side of the table. I wasn't sure if he really was this gentleman-like or if this was an act to get me in bed. Either way, I'm going to enjoy this for now.

Warrick took charge, no surprise there, and ordered us a bottle of the finest red wine. Once the waiter walked away, we dived into conversation.

"I have to know, Warrick, what got you into tech?" I asked.

He chuckled, "I've been curious about things and want to be the best while providing solutions to my community, so you do the math. You're no slouch yourself, though. I saw you have an MBA and were pretty high-ranking with the job you have."

That caught me off-guard a little bit. I wasn't expecting someone here to know anything about me.

"I work hard. How do you kno - ?"

Before I could finish that question, Warrick finished my question, "Know so much about you? I was so intrigued when I first met you, I had to make sure you weren't a serial killer in your previous life."

"That's a little much, but wasn't quite my question."

"I can't divulge all my secrets, love. All I'll say is that I have been able to uncover technology that allows me to research all the newcomers who've made their way here. Enough about that, though." He waved me off as the waiter came up with our wine.

We both took this second to take a long drink. I have to know more about this technology he's talking about, but I can't laser focus on that. Too obvious, but at least the plan was starting to work.

Warrick broke my train of thought by asking, "What do you think of the wine?"

"It's very smooth. Just the right mix of flavors for me right now."

That got a smile out of him. "Good, I was hoping you enjoyed a glass of wine."

"What makes you say that?"

"I've only ever seen you drink beer."

"You've also only ever seen me eat pizza, but here we are."

Our waiter made his way back to take our orders. Warrick, still being the gentleman, gestured for me to order first.

"I'll take the surf and turf, please. Can you make sure my steak is cooked more on the rare side?"

Our waiter nodded then prompted Warrick for his order. He ended up ordering the same thing as myself and placed our dessert order, too. A dark chocolate slice of cake and a bottle of dessert wine.

I reached across the table placing my hand on his arm gently running my fingers up and down his arm. "I see you have great taste."

"I can say the same about you," he said in response. I noticed his pupils were a little more dilated. Apparently, it didn't take much to get under his skin. That'll make things easier for me later on.

"How many women have you taken on this date?"

He placed his hand over mine as he responded, "Contrary to popular belief, I haven't dated all that much."

I raised an eyebrow, "Really? Because of work or?"

Warrick chuckled, "A mix of things. Mostly work. Running a huge company takes the majority of my time. As you know, I also lead a large pack which sucks up just about any remaining time I have. I guess at the end of the day, there haven't been too many ladies who have caught my eye quite like you."

"And we're back to you choosing to take time out of your busy schedule and spend it with me."

"And again, I wouldn't have it any other way."

Our conversation kept going back and forth in a flirty way. The food arrived which gave us the opportunity to take a break in getting to know one another, and I have to say, this food is about the best I've ever had. A little moan escaped that any normal human wouldn't have heard. Warrick, however, had no problem with hearing and looked up at me, "If you think the food is that good, just imagine what the sex would be like."

He was so forward with that statement I immediately felt the heat of a blush rushing to my cheeks. That was the last thing I was expecting him to say. I also wasn't expecting, or appreciating, the heat building between my thighs.

"Don't worry, love. You have a curfew, remember?"

"I'm surprised you're respecting what Lou said even though he was joking," I said, finally able to get control of myself.

"Believe it or not, I have a lot of respect for Louis. Also, you and I both have work tomorrow and need our rest."

Warrick didn't have to say anything else. Tomorrow was Friday and that meant a full moon. Of course, he'd need the energy to change and do whatever it was he did in wolf form. That also meant Lou would be changing, too.

We made our way through the rest of the meal. Dessert was quickly brought out with the dark chocolate cake taunting me. It smelled and looked so good I was afraid another moan would escape again. Warrick must've had the same thing on his mind because a smirk slowly crept across his face, "If you moan again, I may not be able to keep true to my word."

"Stay tuned," I joked diving in for the first bite of cake. *Don't moan, don't moan.* Thankfully, no sound escaped me, but it was hard to resist. I don't know what was in this food tonight, but I don't think I've had anything better. The two bottles of wine helped with that, of course.

We talked a little longer before making our exit from the restaurant. I'm sure he was getting tired of me saying how delicious everything was, but Warrick didn't show any signs of annoyance. He resumed the protective posturing now placing his hand on the small of my back. Clearly, the night went well for him since he's more willing to touch me now.

Warrick pulled back up to Lou's restaurant and turned his car off. He looked over to me smiling a genuine smile, not the cocky grin he wore leading up to this date. It fit him, made him seem a little bit more on the same playing field.

"You look really good when you smile like that."

"Well, I had a really nice evening with you."

I returned the smile, "Me too. And I appreciate the dress. You didn't have to get me something this nice." I smoothed it out a little because I wasn't sure what else to do with my hands.

"I'm glad I got it. It looks like it was made for you," Warrick softly mentioned while brushing a loose strand of hair out of my face.

He got out of the car and opened my door for me, extending a hand to help me out.

"Thank you again, Warrick. I had a wonderful time."

He kissed my hand, "I'm looking forward to the next one, love."

I smiled again, "Thank you. Goodnight."

I turned to go, but Warrick pulled me close to him. He tilted my chin up and he kissed me. Gently at first to see if I would reciprocate, and when I did, he turned up the passion. Warrick hugged me tighter to him as his tongue grazed my lower lip. *Damn, he was good.* I started getting lost in this moment. His hand slowly made its way down my back and rested underneath my ass with his other hand behind my head loosely gripping my hair. One of my hands started to drift towards his ass, too, while the other worked its way through his soft hair. We turned slightly so he could push me against the side of his car as his kissing became deeper, more wanting. Warrick's hand was now working its way back up towards my chest. Before he reached my breast, I pulled away. It was very easy to get caught up in him, but I couldn't do that quite yet. I had to leave him wanting more.

"I should get going. It's starting to get late." It was only five after 11, but still.

"You're right," Warrick said standing up straight. "Early morning tomorrow. Goodnight, love."

He straightened his suit jacket and turned to let me have a clear path the to door. I reached the handle looking over my shoulder at him. Warrick nodded and turned to get in his car. I pushed open the door, blushing and smiling like a high school girl.

The restaurant was empty, but not completely cleaned up. Lou was sitting at a table counting tonight's earnings when he looked up. He didn't look the happiest which made me wonder how the night went. Maybe I shouldn't have skipped work.

"Have a good time?"

"Yeah, it wasn't too bad."

"I could tell. I enjoyed the show," he said as he jerked his thumb towards the window.

"Hey, I at least got more confirmation he has technology to learn about the newcomers."

"I'm surprised it didn't take you being naked to get any information out of him."

There was an edge to his tone I didn't like. I clenched my fist frustrated at how he was handling this. Lou was the one who told me to go forward with this when I gave him the option of me backing out.

"Normally I would storm out at this point, but seeing as how I have no way of getting home, I have no other option."

Lou heaved himself out of the seat he was in, not responding. He locked the front door and turned the lights off. As he walked past me, our shoulders brushed giving me the chance to feel the lightening coming off him.

He grabbed his keys and continued to walk towards the kitchen. This just frustrated me more.

"Lou!"

"What?"

His back was to me, but I could see how tense he was.

"Do I need to remind you this was as much your plan as mine? We both knew how this might develop, the risks involved. And I did give you the chance to tell me this was stupid."

Lou turned his head so he wasn't quite looking at me, but gave me a view of half his face. "I did also say this wasn't going to be easy. That didn't mean just for you."

He continued heading out the back door to get his car and I finally convinced myself to follow.

Chapter 11

I woke up laying in bed for a while thinking through the events of last night. There was a side of me who wasn't happy with the fact I enjoyed the date, but the other side was happy I got the confirmation I needed to keep figuring out what Warrick knew. I also wasn't happy with how Lou responded. He was the one who originally hatched this idea and pushed me towards it. The least he could do was keep his feelings in check. But, I reminded myself, he did deal with a lot of emotions from his interaction with Warrick at the ball.

I ran my hands over my face sitting at the edge of my bed. I checked my phone seeing a text from Lou telling me to come in for the lunch shift. *Shit, I needed to get ready now!* I ran around getting dressed then grabbed a Pop Tart for breakfast. I hopped on my bike and sped my way into the city parking behind the restaurant. I checked the time on my phone again to see I was five minutes late. *Great, something else to make Lou even more cranky.*

I burst into the kitchen to see him doing his usual prep work. He didn't even look at me as he said, "I didn't think giving you the dinner shift off would mean you get the next day off, too."

Pure ice in his tone. I can see his frustration from last night still there.

"I'm sorry. I know I'm late, but I'm here now. I'll go ahead and start getting the dining room ready."

I started to make my way out of the kitchen when Lou put his arm out to stop me, "No need. Everything's ready to go. I do need to talk to you, though, and we don't have long before your best customer pops in."

I slowly turned towards him, "Okay, what's up?"

Lou finally looked at me frustration etched in his brow, "Today's Friday, which means it's also the full moon. I'll be closing down for the night, so you have the night off again. I don't want you hanging around here. Go back home and lock yourself in."

"You're acting like I'm in danger."

"I don't trust what my wolf will do. This last week has been putting me on edge."

"Clearly," I said rolling my eyes and crossing my arms.

That got Lou to stop. He hung his head and looked back up at me. There was some hurt behind his eyes as he said, "I'm sorry. All I can ask is for your patience."

I dropped my arms and any frustrations I was feeling, "It's okay. I'm human and react to emotions without really thinking about what you may be going through."

"Either way, I'm dead serious, Val. I don't trust myself and I don't know what Warrick will do."

I completely forgot about Warrick also being a wolf for a second. It wouldn't surprise me if he tried to track me down and I still wasn't ready for him to know where I lived.

"I'll be careful, I promise," I said, nodding my head.

"Good. The other thing is that the restaurant will be closed tomorrow so I can have some recovery time. Use that to explore a little bit rather than staying cooped up for even longer, okay?"

I gave him a thumb's up. The door opened, and guessing by the time, it would be Warrick. I headed out armed with slices and a full pizza to see what he would choose today. I pasted a smile on my face as I greeted him, "Hi handsome."

Warrick leaned in to kiss me on the cheek. He responded, "Not the greeting I was expecting, but one I'll take. I'm afraid I have to run and get back at it, so I'll take the pizza." He pointed to the box I had in my hand.

I handed over the to-go box, "No worries, I'm slammed today, too."

I gestured to the empty dining room getting a laugh out of him. A sweet sound considering the person it was coming from. There was a small part of me starting to actually like him and I hated that.

"I'm looking forward to the next time I can see you, love, but until then," Warrick leaned over to give me a quick, but passionate kiss before making his way back out onto the street.

I was relieved I didn't have to sit through another lunch with him. I don't know how much longer my body could handle the daily intake of pizza. Lou must've been picking up on that because he came up to me at the bar and slid a smoothie over. I don't think I've been happier to see a cup of blended fruit in my life.

"Thank you. You have no idea how much I've been wanting something healthy."

Lou shrugged and leaned against the bar, "No problem. I figured you loved pizza, but not enough to have it every day."

I took a big gulp savoring the refreshing flavor before asking, "Does everyone around the city know about the wolves?"

"We've been over this before, no. People do have enough sense for the most part to lay low, though. There's enough superstition about the full moon making people crazy that they do what they can to avoid having to go outside."

"This might be pushing it, but can you tell me anything about the previous love of your life?"

Lou let out a slow whistle, "That was a quick change in topic. And, no. I don't want to open the door on that. I'll just be even more on edge."

"Understood."

I took another sip.

There hadn't been any more customers for the remainder of the lunch shift, so Lou and I started shutting things down earlier than normal. He locked everything back up and shooed me out the door to head home. Being the good person I was, I headed straight home then got things ready for a night in. Grabbed some movies, cleaned the house, prepped my dinner, and settled in under a blanket on the couch.

During the second movie, I started to get antsy. Things have been going non-stop since before I got here and I wasn't doing well not having something occupying my mind. It was only 7, so I paused the movie and decided to go for a quick swim to work my muscles a little bit.

Outside was quiet. There were no sounds of birds, bugs, or anything else. There was hardly any traffic. I listened to see if I could hear a wolf howling and there was nothing. Maybe Lou was overreacting a little bit. I shrugged and dived into the pool to start my laps. Loosening up my muscles felt great. It had only been about a week, but it felt like a lifetime since the last time I did any sort of workout. I was feeling all the tension and nerves wash away so I took a break to float on my back. I had only been out there for an hour and was feeling bored again, so I got out, showered, and dressed in some riding clothes. I decided I was going to explore a little bit.

I hopped on my bike and headed for the top of the mountain. I wanted to get a good view of the city and just think for a second. Try to sort through all my emotions and what I really wanted to do, as well as piece together what information Warrick may have. I found a spot to pull off that gave me a great view point of the city. I took my helmet off and leaned forward on my handlebars, resting my head on my arms.

Let's start with the feelings. Daryl played me, that I was completely sure of. Warrick made me feel uneasy, but there was a part of me starting to develop feelings, very small, but they were there. He was definitely a gentleman on dates, but that didn't hide the fact he was a power-hungry monster who wasn't afraid to do whatever it takes to eliminate the competition. Which brought me to Lou. Lou definitely liked to pretend he had a hard outer shell, but he's really a teddy bear. The night in his apartment had been difficult to not give in to the butterflies wreaking havoc in my stomach. I could see staying here with him and running the pizza shop living as normal a life as you could with werewolves running around. At the end of the day, I still couldn't convince myself not to try to get out of here and determine what really happened. To do that, I needed to stifle any feelings I may have for Lou and focus my energy on getting Warrick to hand over anything he has.

All I knew so far was that Warrick has access to some technology to be able to look into each newcomer's information from wherever they came from. He also is well aware of people having their houses come with them if they didn't get bombed. Warrick was still keeping things at a high level and I needed to get that to change. That meant only one thing – .

My thought stream was interrupted by a branch snapping. I slowly turned around to see if there was anything behind me. At first, all I saw were the infinite number of trees stretching behind me with some bushes here and there. Just as I was getting ready to turn back around, I caught a slight movement out of the corner of my eye. The movement stopped for a moment before beginning again and my eyes began to understand what was before me. A massive black wolf was heading in my direction and I couldn't tell if it was stalking me or just approaching. One look at the eyes told me everything I needed to know. They were a piercing ice blue and I was so familiar with that gaze at this point. Warrick.

I wasn't quite sure what to do in this situation, so I got off my bike slowly and turned around so I was facing him not losing sight of him at any point.

"Hi Warrick."

The fact I acknowledged him slowed his movements to a stop. It was almost as if he wasn't sure what to do.

"I can leave if you want me to."

Apparently, he didn't like that suggestion. Warrick came right up to me and nipped at my hands.

"Got it. I'll stay."

I couldn't get over the sheer size of him. His head was level with mine. His muscles didn't go away in wolf form either with the outlines of them clearly visible under his thick fur. I could also feel Warrick's power. This is what it must mean to be alpha. No wonder Lou had a hard time against him.

There was a low rumble emanating from Warrick's chest. I had no idea what I did to cause this. I was starting to feel the panic rise in my throat when Warrick turned so he was facing the forest. *It wasn't me, then, thank goodness.* I looked out from behind him to see if there was anything coming towards us. This time didn't take me as long to see another wolf making its way toward us. The wolf approaching was another large one. His fur was a sandy color with silver eyes staring directly at me. Lou. *Great, I was going to be hearing about this.*

Lou's lips curled as he snarled at Warrick. I looked over at Warrick to see his body rippling. These two weren't going to be civil for very long. I also couldn't help but wonder if this is what Lou meant when he said he would need tomorrow to recover. Was his intention to look for a fight?

"I can see you two are busy. I'm going to get out of here to give you both some space."

I moved to put on my helmet and get on my bike. I didn't want to take my chances here. I shot out into the darkness to put some distance between myself and the two wolves. I'm sure there were more lurking in the trees, but I took a second to stop and look back on the scene I was leaving. Warrick and Lou were now circling each other looking ready to fight. I didn't stay around too much longer because if I did, I would've probably done something stupid and gotten myself between the two. To do what? I have no idea, but I didn't like the idea of either of them fighting.

I got back home and finally let out the air I didn't know I was holding in. That was a close call. I went back to my movie and did my best to focus on it. I couldn't get the images of their wolves out of my mind, though. They were massive, intimidating, but beautiful. Feeling the power those two had was intense.

I was feeling antsy again, so I grabbed my laptop to finish my movie outside in the hot tub. Before I pressed play, I listened again to see if I could hear anything and it was still dead quiet. I looked towards the mountain I just came from and wondered if everything was okay. *I'll check on Lou tomorrow. I'll get yelled at, but at least I'd have the reassurance he was okay.*

That quieted my mind enough for me to get back to the movie. It didn't take long for my nerves to get rattled again ... I heard rustling in the bushes behind me. I paused the movie and looked around for anything I could use to defend myself. Nothing. Absolutely nothing. *Shit.* With nothing to protect me, I just turned and stared down the spot I heard the noise come from. I didn't know what I was expecting, but I was a little surprised to see two eyes staring back at me. I couldn't tell who it was, but once I made eye contact, the eyes slowly retreated and went away.

Chapter 12

Last night was eventful and I had been stupid. Looking back on it now, I realized I should've listened to Lou. Speaking of Lou, I should go check on him.

I grabbed all my things, including an overnight bag. If something happened after I left that made him rattled, I wanted to at least be prepared this time if he asked me to stay. Or maybe, I was hoping I didn't have to spend the evening alone again.

I made it to his apartment and knocked on the door. It was pretty quiet so I wondered if he was even home. Then I heard some signs of life. The door cracked open as far as it could with the security chain engaged and I saw the same silver eyes from last night looking back at me.

"What are you doing here?" Lou growled. There was definitely a different edge to his voice I hadn't heard before making me wonder if it was taking a while to transition back.

"I wanted to check on you. Can I come in?"

Instead of saying anything, Lou closed the door. I started to turn to go, but I heard the chain slide out and the door open again. He was looking at the ground when he said, "I thought you wanted to come in. Leaving so soon?"

"I wasn't sure if I pissed you off enough to just shut me out."

I stepped into his apartment. The clean living area I had seen the other night was a disaster. Books and trinkets from

149

his shelves were scattered. His kitchen was also a mess with everything strewn about.

I panned my eyes back over to Lou asking, "What happened?"

Lou finally looked up at me and the half of his face I hadn't seen before was a bloody mess. One of his eyes were swollen shut and there were cuts all over. My eyes traced the cuts down his neck and his arm which was also covered in quite a few bruises. I forced myself to look back at his face.

"What the hell happened, Lou?"

"I should ask you the same thing. I thought you were going to stay in for the night."

I held up a finger to stop him, "No, I promised that I would be careful. Which I was. Nothing happened to me, but clearly something happened to you after I left."

I dropped my bags and the container holding a hearty breakfast at the island to grab a washcloth. Here I was cleaning the blood off him again. The second I touched his face, he winced.

"You're going to need to suck it up for a second."

That got a growl in response from Lou making me pause. It was obvious he wasn't fully human yet.

"Why is it taking you so long to change back and heal?"

"I don't know," he said through a clenched jaw. "I've never had this issue before. Warrick has something figured out and it felt like he was testing it out on me last night."

"What do you mean?" I asked as I kept gently wiping.

Lou reached up and pulled my hand away from his face. "Let me show you." He winced as he started to take his shirt off revealing even more damage. There was a large slice that went across his abs that looked like it was starting to heal. I was surprised there wasn't more blood showing on his shirt with how much the wound was still open. There were a lot of other cuts, bruises, and dried blood all over him.

My eyes were widening, "Lou, I'm going to need more than this little washcloth."

He chuckled ever so slightly, "Val, as mad as I am for you putting yourself at risk last night, I'm sure glad you're here."

"Something told me to check on you and I'm glad I did. Why don't you go to a doctor?"

"They aren't going to be able to do anything for me."

"Okay," I said slowly. "What can I do to help you out the most?"

"Can you help me wash off? I don't have the strength to do it myself and I feel a hell of a lot worse than I look."

"Sure. I'm going to need more wash cloths though," I said holding up the very dirty wash cloth I had been using.

Lou closed his eyes and shook his head. He grabbed my hand then led me to his bathroom.

I blushed. *So, this is what he meant.*

"I don't think we know each other well enough to hop in a shower together."

The corners of his lips twitched, "No, Val."

Lou moved to turn on the water to let it warm up. He took off his shorts, but left on his briefs. This is certainly not helping any of the thoughts I was wrestling with last night. I have to be more careful.

Once the water was warm enough, he started to let the tub fill up and eased his way in. There was a lot of hissing as the water worked its way over the numerous cuts covering his body.

"You're not going to like me."

"Don't worry, I know what's about to happen."

"Is your wolf going to do anything about it?" I asked with my hand hovering over him waiting to get to work.

"No," Lou replied gruffly.

I got started with washing him. As I was running over his abs and chest, I couldn't help but notice how firm his muscles were. A shiver shot down my spine and I had to do everything in my power to get rid of the butterflies having a party. Thankfully, it didn't take long to get to a point where I could start working on his face. I cradled his chin with one hand forcing him to look at me while the other kept working on getting the blood and dirt cleaned off. I had finished, but still held his face in my hand.

"Val, why are you looking at me like that?"

"Just checking to see if the wolf is still here or if you're fully back."

"He's long gone at this point," Lou said closing his eyes.

"I can see that," I said, but still made no move to let go of his face. We sat there in silence for a little while longer before Lou reached up and pulled my hand away to break what we were sharing.

"I don't need any other reason for Warrick to go after me more than he already has been."

I looked down at the wash cloth in my hand and tried to hide the hurt in my voice, "Sorry."

It's only fair considering I was the one to push him away first.

I helped Lou get back to his feet and handed him a towel to dry off. I started to look for whatever first aid he had, and after finding a large roll of gauze, I wrapped up the large slash. Not wanting to linger any more than I already had, I headed back out to the kitchen to start warming up the steak and eggs to have it ready for Lou once he got back out here.

He came out drying his face, "Whatever that is, it smells delicious."

It seemed like whatever had happened in the bathroom moments ago was gone. *Thank goodness.*

I smiled at him, "Steak and eggs. Figured you could use a hearty breakfast."

The timer beeped and I pulled everything off the heat then served it. I poured some juice and we sat at the island. Lou devoured everything he had in front of him in no time.

"I should've brought more food," I said as I looked over at his now empty plate in surprise.

He chuckled, "That was plenty, thank you. I do appreciate you coming over to help out."

I looked around the room, "Anytime. Although, I think I have more work cut out for me than I thought."

Lou looked at me, "Sorry about that. You don't have to clean up after me."

I waved him off as I finished up my breakfast, "It's no big deal. You need to rest anyways."

I wasted no time getting to work and any time Lou tried to help out, I ordered him to sit on the couch. There were a couple of times he dozed off into a nap making me stop to admire the peace that came over his face. When I was done, I turned on the fire place and joined him on the couch.

I rested my head on his shoulder, "Lou, how are you really doing right now?"

He placed his head on top of mine answering, "I'm doing a lot better than I was this morning. Seeing you last night stirred up a lot of emotions in me I wasn't entirely expecting. I couldn't trust that Warrick wouldn't do anything and I didn't want to risk anything. I was a mess this morning. I couldn't stop wondering if you made it home safely or not." Lou gestured at the now-clean apartment.

I moved my head off his shoulder to look at him, "Wait, what do you mean you didn't know if I made it home safely? Didn't you stop by?"

He furrowed his brow, "No. I got my ass kicked then headed home. Did you see something?"

"I was sitting in my hot tub after I got back and there was a wolf hiding out in my bushes. Once I looked at it, it went away and wasn't there for long, but I couldn't tell who it was."

Lou cursed under his breath before looking back at me, "I bet you anything that was Warrick. Do you have a security system?"

I had been thinking that too, but hearing Lou say it sent a chill down my spine. "I do, and I'll keep checking the cameras," I said as I was rubbing my arms trying to warm back up.

"Stay here a few days. I don't know that I trust Warrick to not try anything. He might be feeling cocky now."

Lou got up slowly.

"Good thing I packed some clothes, then."

Lou nodded then headed back to his room. It was only then I realized he was only wearing a towel. *I really needed to stop focusing on those things or I'm going to get in trouble.* When he came back out, he was back in shorts and had a blanket with him. I appreciated the change of wardrobe and was even more appreciative when he tossed the blanket my way.

We spent the rest of the day just hanging out and helping each other ease the negative emotions from last night. Lou started cooking a dinner that consisted of salmon and roasted broccoli. While he was cooking, I came up to him and started examining the cuts from this morning. Everything looked to be mostly healed, especially his eye that he could now open more than what he could earlier. I reached for the gauze forcing him to pause, "May I?"

"Be my guest."

I unwrapped the gauze from this morning to see the slash minimized to a small line finally scabbing over. I ran my fingers along the edge smiling, "I'm happy to see you don't have a gaping hole anymore."

Lou pulled away from my touch to continue prepping the food, "I'm happy, too. It's not very often I spend a long time hurt anymore."

Changing the subject, I asked, "Do you have any wine?"

He pointed his spatula to the fridge, "There's some white wine in there. Glasses are above the sink."

I prepped our glasses and moved to the couch. Before settling in back under my blanket, I turned on the record player and selected a jazz record. I turned back as Lou was setting our plates down. He looked over at me with a raised eyebrow, "Don't get any ideas."

I held up my hands in defense, "Just keeping the relaxed vibe going, nothing more."

Lou grunted but couldn't hide the small smile fixing itself on his face.

We sat down and enjoyed our dinner with jokes splashed in our casual conversation. Thankfully, there was a good amount of laughter keeping the mood light. Lou mentioned he was going to move my bike into his garage so Warrick's goons couldn't find me and told me to get some ice cream ready. I served both of us some big bowls because we more than earned it at this point and I refilled our glasses. I was grabbing the second bottle of wine when Lou got back up here.

"You know? I was expecting a little bit more than just ice cream." I said teasing him.

He joined me at the fridge to grab a can of whipped cream. Shaking it, Lou said, "You forgot the best part."

We returned to the couch for him to drown our ice cream in whipped cream making it look like a little mountain.

"I wouldn't have taken you as a sweets guy."

Lou had just taken the first bite and said, "I'm a sucker for ice cream."

I laughed, maybe a little too hard, and took a long sip of wine. The conversation from earlier continued while we kept making our way through the wine. Before I knew it, we were two and a half bottles deep, way more than what I would normally drink at this point. Lou took some whipped cream and dabbed it on my nose. I responded by doing the same to him, and next thing I know, we were having a whipped cream war. I leaned over to lick some off his cheek not having a care in the world if I was crossing a line. *Damn this wine, it's making me feel too good.*

Lou rolled me over and pinned me down. He leaned in so he was inches away from my face, "You have something on your face."

He leaned down and traced my bottom lip with his tongue, getting the whipped cream. I took in all of his scent of pine knowing it would be so easy to get lost in this moment. I almost lifted my head up to kiss him, but something clicked reminding me not to go there.

"Lou, I don't think this is the best idea."

He paused releasing his grip on me. I sat up and wiped my face off with a napkin, Lou doing to the same.

"I know I'm being a buzz kill again. I just don't know if I'm ready to cross that boundary," I said not being able to bring myself to look him in the eyes.

A dark shadow clouded his face and he turned his head away from me, "You're right."

I reached for him, but I was too slow. He got up and started cleaning everything. I watched him for a moment before turning my head to look out the window. Maybe this wasn't the best idea coming here, but now I was staying here a few days. *I'll make sure to sleep on the couch.*

I grabbed my overnight bag and headed to the bathroom to get ready for bed without saying anything else to him. I opened the bathroom door to find Lou on the other side ready to knock.

"Sorry," I said as I walked past him without being able to look at him.

If he was going to say anything, I didn't give him the chance. I walked out to the living area and finished any cleanup. I shut off the record player and lights then crawled back under the blanket I had been using all day. If I hadn't had a lot of wine, it would've been hard to fall asleep, but I wasted no time drifting off.

The sun started poking through the blinds waking me up. While I didn't feel the best, I decided to go for a jog. I needed to get out of here for a moment to clear my head. Last night was too close and I reminded myself to stay focused.

I got outside to find it was a beautiful day for a run. There wasn't a cloud in the sky and it wasn't too hot yet. After stretching, I got into a nice rhythm for a run and found my way to a park to run some laps. I found I wasn't the only taking advantage of a beautiful morning. I heard someone coming up behind me, so I moved more to my right to allow them plenty of space to pass. Rather than passing, the person behind me slowed their pace and matched my rhythm.

"Hi love," said a familiar voice. An electric chill settled into the air around us and I dared myself to look over at the person next to me.

"Hi Warrick. I'm surprised to see you out here. Don't you have a high-tech gym or something?"

"Couldn't pass up a run on a day like this."

His familiar smug grin was back in place making me feel uneasy. It seemed like something had changed since I ran into him in the forest and there was a shield back in place.

"I don't blame you," I said.

"Look, I won't take too much of your time, but I just wanted to say good morning."

I didn't get a chance to respond as he picked his pace back up pulling away from me taking the chill air with him. It was almost as if he was trying to mess with me a little bit. A reminder that he's there. *Does he know something?*

I ended one of my laps early then headed back towards Lou's, not wanting to give Warrick another chance to make his presence known.

I got back into the apartment after making sure no one had followed me to find a smoothie sitting on the island. I looked around and found Lou sitting on the couch with a book.

"Good morning. Thank you for the breakfast."

Lou glanced over at me before returning to his book, "I had to return the favor. Did you enjoy your jog?"

"It was shorter than I wanted, but for the most part, yes."

He nodded his head while taking a sip of coffee. I downed my smoothie without saying anything else to him then made my way to the shower. I noticed he kept all the makeup and styling tools from the other day which was much appreciated since I was camping out here for a little while.

I hopped into the shower letting the warm water run over me for a moment then dived right in to getting cleaned up. Nothing beats a nice warm shower after a jog to loosen up the muscles and clean the sweat off. My moment of peace was interrupted by the sound of the door opening.

"Lou, can't you hold it?!"

He closed the door behind him, "I don't need to go."

I poked my head out from behind the shower curtain, "Then why are you in here?"

"I wanted to apologize for my actions last night."

Lou sounded really formal, making my heart lurch the tiniest bit. I didn't want him to feel like he had to be formal around me.

"Can the apology wait until I'm done?" I asked in a softer tone.

He took a step closer to me, "No."

Here come the butterflies again. "Lou."

"I'm apologizing for what I did, but I'm also apologizing for what I'm about to do."

I stuck my hand out to stop him, "Don't. I'm serious Lou. I don't want to hurt you and I'm not ready for that hurt either."

Words escaped me as Lou continued to close the distance between us clearly not caring about what I had just said. He grabbed my face and kissed me. Everything exploded in me. There was heat, fireworks, passion, you name it. I had to stop this before it went any further. I pulled away knowing I was hurting him as much as I was hurting myself. There had been some feelings growing for a while between us that have been kept beneath the surface. I guess I've been better at keeping those feelings there than Lou. Another reminder that this whole process of getting info from Warrick won't be easy on either of us. I just shook my head and that was all he needed to turn away, leaving me alone.

Chapter 13

A few weeks had passed. I made sure I didn't find myself staying over at Lou's anymore since I didn't want to make things harder between us with me still having to get close to Warrick. Speaking of Warrick, I went on a few more dates with him working little bits of information out piece by piece while still keeping him at a distance without being too suspicious. If he wanted to kiss me, I made sure it wasn't where Lou could see so I can avoid seeing the hurt on his face. Now, it was time to start turning up the heat and getting a little more aggressive to get into the nitty gritty details from Warrick.

I was swiping mascara on my eyelashes getting ready for the day. I packed my waitress uniform to change into later since I had other things I needed to attend to first. I was wearing one of my favorite business casual outfits so I could pop in and deliver Warrick's lunch. I wanted his attention. Lou and I had talked about doing this eventually, but that was a while ago. He prepped me with a blank flash drive he programmed to discreetly pull information from Warrick's computer so all I had to do was get into his office and get a moment where I could plug it in.

I got into the pizza shop with my bag and dropped my stuff in a rarely used locker. I walked over to Lou asking, "Got the pizza ready?"

He hadn't even looked over at me when he said, "Yup. I have a bottle of wine, too. Hopefully he's not too busy to sit down and enjoy some food with you. Are you read - ?"

As he was asking that question, he looked up from what he was doing and stopped. I saw his pupils dilate. *Did I really look that good?*

I was wearing a lightweight white blazer with the sleeves rolled up to just under my elbows. I was wearing a black satin tank top that dipped perfectly in the middle of my chest to show the right amount of cleavage. To match the blazer, I was wearing white shorts made of the same material showing off my legs, which in my opinion was my best asset. I topped the look off with black pumps, a simple silver necklace and diamond studs. My face was made up with a natural look and I had spritzed myself with my most expensive perfume.

"Earth to Lou?"

"S-sorry. Not what I was expecting this morning. I take it today is the day?"

"Yup, I don't want him to think I'm pushing him away and I'm hitting roadblocks with getting any more information. You sure this flash drive won't trip anything on his side?"

"Positive. It should fly under the radar especially with you walking in there looking like that. He has a weakness for business."

"That's what I'm hoping for," I said as I turned to grab the boxed pizza. "This feels like a spy movie or something."

That earned me a bark of laughter out of Lou, "You better go over there before he starts making his way here, agent."

I saluted him then headed out to go across the street. I walked in and winked at the receptionist when I walked into the building. She was dealing with a disgruntled delivery man so she waived me through. I made my way up to the top floor where the higher ups all sat and sauntered my way towards Warrick's office oozing confidence. Right before I got to the door, I saw Daryl working in his office and we locked eyes for what felt like forever. A sad look took over his face but I didn't want to deal with it any more so I refocused on what I came here for. I wasn't letting him toy with my emotions.

I pushed my way into Warrick's office. He was sitting at his desk completely absorbed with what he was working on. Without looking up, he said, "I'm in the middle of something. Come back later."

"I guess I'll share this pizza and wine with someone else then." I stood there holding up the wine and the pizza box popping my hip out ever so slightly to be as sexy as I could.

He whipped his head up and laid those icy eyes on me. *That got his attention.* That chilly electricity filled the air again sending a small shiver down my back. A slow smile made its way on his face solidifying my appearance did the trick.

He leaned over speaking into his phone, letting his admin know to reschedule his next couple of meetings and to make sure no one came into his office. While he did that, I sashayed over to his desk, sat on the edge placing the pizza and wine down next to me.

Warrick leaned back into his chair, his eyes tracing every inch of my body, "To what do I owe this pleasure, love?"

I leaned forward giving him a better view of my cleavage, "I must've done something to offend you because you've stopped having lunch dates with me."

He got out of his chair closing the distance between me. His eyes flicked from my breasts to my eyes, "If I would've known I could've had my lunch delivered to me, I would've stopped having lunch dates a while ago."

Warrick's hand came up to trace my jaw line. He leaned in for a kiss wasting no time with getting passionate. He picked me up and moved me to be in front of where he was sitting just moments ago. Warrick pushed papers out of his way in one swoop and quickly got back to me, both hands getting tangled in my hair.

There was some shuffling and noise just outside his office, but we ignored it until someone burst through his doors. We heard the shouting between this individual and Warrick's admin taking our focus off each other and on to the commotion.

Warrick pulled away quickly and I hopped off his desk. He was livid, "What the *fuck* is going on?"

I turned around to see Daryl who looked at me before looking back at Warrick stammering, "S-sorry, sir. I got the figures you asked for."

He held up some papers with a panicked look on his pale face. I looked back at Warrick to see one of his jaw muscles twitching. This wasn't good. I busied myself with opening the wine while watching the situation unfold.

Warrick leaned on both of his hands on his desk, "Did you not listen to my admin when she said not to come in?"

He asked that in a scary calm way, voice on the quieter side. I looked back at Daryl screaming in my head for him to get out. *Just turn around!*

"You told me this was urgent and to bring you the figures as soon as I had them completed."

Warrick stood straight and walked over to where Daryl was standing. He repeated the question, "Did you not listen to my admin when she said not to come in?"

"I-I didn't know you had someone in here," Daryl said looking down. His voice sounded shaky and I didn't blame him.

"Bullshit!" Warrick yelled. Daryl flinched and I looked away. I glanced over at Warrick's computer then back at the pair realizing this was my chance to plug in the flash drive. I leaned over the desk and popped it in one of the drives on the computer, standing back up just as Warrick gestured towards me, "You can't expect me to believe you didn't see this magnificent creature walking past your office, especially when you *know* her."

Those words made me pause. Daryl continued staring at his feet while Warrick continued.

"My office is off-limits for the next hour and a half. You make sure everyone else knows that and apologize to my admin for your behavior. I can't stand this sense of entitlement. Do you have anything to say?"

"No, sir."

"Then get out of my fucking office. Don't think I'll forget about this."

Warrick was in Daryl's face as he pointed to the door. As Daryl turned, Warrick yanked the papers out of his hand. Once he was out of the office, Warrick locked the office and placed the papers on the table next to the door. I could feel the anger coming off him in waves.

Warrick loosened his tie making his way back over to me, "Apologies you had to see that, love. Where were we?"

There was still an edge to his voice. He raked his hand through this hair letting out a sigh to try to gain some composure.

I picked up the pizza and wine hoping I could cool his temper a little bit, "About to enjoy lunch."

He wiped everything else off his desk in one swipe, took the pizza and wine to place them on another surface, took a big gulp of wine, then picked me back up and laid me on his desk.

"I think we were about to enjoy a hell of a lot more than lunch. You ready for this?"

I nodded my head giving my consent.

And he crashed down on to me, kissing me with such passion and such aggressiveness. He was angry, very angry and I didn't want to be his outlet, but I needed to make sure I killed enough time to allow for the transfer of all his files which Lou said would take an hour.

I put my hand on his chest signaling him to pause, "Warrick, you going to share the wine?"

"Apologies, love," he sighed as he stood up and grabbed the bottle. I stood back up graciously accepting the bottle and took a *long* swig. I needed this wine to help me loosen up a little bit with feeling on edge. While I was drinking, he was busy nibbling at my neck. I took a look at the clock as I finished my drink to see only ten minutes had passed. *Damn it.* It felt like more time had passed since I got the flash drive plugged in.

Warrick took the bottle from me to put it back next to the pizza. He said nothing as he came back over and laid me back down on his desk again. He went back to nibbling on my neck as he was working a hand under my shirt.

"I love the outfit, but you don't like to make things easy, do you?"

I let out a sultry laugh, "That would take the fun out of it. I like to see you work."

That got a growl of approval out of him. He finally found a way in and his hand made a quick journey up to my breast. When he felt the lace of my bra, he looked at me with a hint of his wolf poking out in his eyes, "You didn't skimp on anything today."

"I dress to impress."

I pulled his face back down to mine trying to take some control of the situation. He pushed my bra aside so he could fondle me more freely. He occasionally pinched and twisted my nipple which I hated to admit I liked. A moan escaped my lips only encouraging him more. This continued for a little while longer before I sat back up and adjusted my bra and shirt. Warrick let out an impatient grunt.

"I have to keep the theme going. I can't make this too easy."

I stood up and we were pressed against each other. I could feel how attracted he was to me by the bulge in his pants.

"If I didn't know better, I would say you *want* me right now," I whispered in his ear as I traced my fingertips along his pants. It was my turn to get a shiver out of him.

I slid my way out from between him and the desk to make my way back over to the wine. Another ten minutes passed by which meant I still had another 40, minimum.

I looked back over towards Warrick to see he was breathing hard. This was my only chance to take control of the pace we took this at. I slowly walked back over to him, gripped his tie, and pulled him close to me so our lips were barely touching.

"You may run a company, but I'm running this show now."

I took his tie off and used it to tie his hands together. I pushed him on his desk and crawled on top of him.

"You're on the clock, love. You can only keep me pinned down for so long."

I started grinding my hips against him as I started to unbutton his shirt. He closed his eyes enjoying every second of this. I took his hands above his head and tied the tie to one of the drawers. I took a second to adjust my hair only looking away for a brief moment, and when I looked back down, he wiggled his fingers at me in a teasing wave. Warrick had gotten out of the tie and I knew my time was up.

He placed his hands on my hip and before I knew it, I was back on the desk and he was tying me up.

"I told you I couldn't be pinned down for long."

He wasted no time untucking my shirt and hiking it up so he could admire me. Warrick untied me from the drawer and pulled me up so he could take off my blazer and shirt.

"Absolutely beautiful."

He then made his way to unbutton my shorts pulling them off, noticing my matching bra and thong moaning in appreciation. There I was in my bra, thong, and heels tied to his desk. Now it was his turn to drink some more wine, finishing it.

Warrick came back over, his shirt still unbuttoned revealing his hard muscles. I took a sharp inhale.

"We're a little uneven here, Warrick."

"Patience."

And he crashed back down on me. His hands were working my breasts out of my bra, playing with my nipples as he did so.

He finally decided he no longer wanted my bra on and I watched as the pile of my clothes grew.

Warrick untied the tie restraint from the desk and motioned for me to stand up and turn around. I did as I was told standing at the edge of the desk. Warrick bent me over and tied me back to the desk.

"Enjoying the view?" I asked as I turned my head to the side.

"You have no idea," he said as he caressed my ass. I felt his hands lift off me and saw him move to a drawer. He pulled out a couple more ties and got to work tying them around my ankles. *Shit.* I took a look at the clock. 30 minutes to go. I looked at the computer wondering if there was any way I could see the progress, feeling some sense of relief when I found a little status bar in the corner and there was about 15% complete. I willed the flash drive to work faster.

Warrick spanked me, catching me off-guard. I let out a small yelp.

"Did you like that?"

I let out a breathy yes as I felt him caressing me again. He propped me up so I wasn't completely against the desk. He walked back over to his door pulling the blinds to give us more privacy.

Warrick was back behind me wasting no time getting to work. He groaned when he felt how wet I was and it was his turn to grind against me. He didn't take too long to get his pants off, put a condom on, and work his way inside me. He started thrusting grabbing my breasts to steady himself. As his thrusts became harder, he pinched my nipples harder. I couldn't hold back anymore and both our moans soon rang throughout the office in a chorus.

I could feel the orgasm building and Warrick must've sensed it because he slowed. He leaned back over so his lips brushed my ear while staying inside me, "Not yet, love. I've been waiting a while for this day."

I let out a frustrated moan much to his enjoyment. To my relief, he untied me and laid me back down on my back on his desk. His mouth found its way to my nipples and he started to suck with the occasional nibble making my back arch. His fingers were in me working slowly.

"That's it," he mumbled into me.

He slowly worked himself back inside and I couldn't keep myself from wrapping my legs and arms around him. *Damn, this is good.* I arched my back so I was pressing my breasts in him feeling the orgasm getting closer. I whispered into his ear, "If you're not careful, I'm going to come."

"Then do it. Come for me, love."

I reached my climax the second he finished talking causing him to lose himself too.

We were lying there on the desk breathless for a few moments. Warrick stood up and excused himself after kissing me on the forehead. I propped myself up on my elbows taking a quick look at his laptop. The flash drive was at 99%. *Finally.* I watched as it clicked over to 100% and quickly took it out of the laptop tucking it into my shorts pocket still on the ground. It sounded like Warrick was about to come back out, so I laid back on the desk.

He rounded the corner stopping when he saw me, "Love, you're wrecking me."

I looked over at him putting a little arch in my back, "I don't know what you're talking about."

He chuckled moving to help me off his desk. I slowly worked my clothes back on continuing the show while he sat in his chair and admired. I turned so I was facing him again after getting dressed, "Your pizza is probably cold by now."

"Cold pizza never hurt anybody," he said as he rolled over to where the pizza was. He offered me a slice and I gladly took it now feeling how hungry I was. I was pretty buzzed, too, considering how much I drank on an empty stomach.

"There's a restroom around the corner if you need it."

I nodded and went to make sure I was put back together. I didn't want Lou to know what happened over here even though I'm sure he would have an idea. I found some of Warrick's cologne to cover up the smell of sex that may be lingering. Looking in the mirror, I didn't look too bad. My hair was a little disheveled, so I ran my fingers through it to straighten it back out. Beyond that, everything else was good.

I made my way back out to Warrick and he was back working on his computer. I searched his face for any sign of him knowing the true reason behind my visit today, but there weren't any hints. He looked back up to me, a genuine smile forming on his face this time.

"You can deliver my pizza anytime, love."

"Hmm," I said as I sat back on the corner of his desk. "Don't get used to this."

Warrick leaned back smoothing his black hair back in place and adjusting his tie, "When's the next time I can see you?"

I stood up and headed towards the door, "When I say you can." And I left.

I got back into the restaurant going straight back into the kitchen. I started to get changed and had my shirt off when Lou popped in. I jumped holding my blazer to cover myself up as much as I could, "A little warning would have been nice."

He blushed looking away, "Sorry. Did you get the flash drive connected?"

"Yup," I fished it out of my pocket and held it out for Lou to take. "Next time, can you make it work faster?"

Lou gave me a look, "You know that's not how it works."

I slumped my shoulders, "I know. Turn around."

He looked away and I finished getting changed.

"You can look now. How long do you think it'll take to get through the data?"

Lou shrugged, "Could take a while. You'll need to hold tight."

I didn't like his answer, but knew it wasn't going to be overnight, "Patience isn't my strong suit, but I'll do my best not to bug you."

I had to get myself through the rest of my shift without thinking of the events that transpired earlier. Thankfully I had the next two days off and could lay low for a while.

"I don't know if I really want to know the answer, but how did you keep him distracted for that long?"

I gave Lou a look, "Why ask the question if you don't want the answer?"

That got another shrug, "I guess I like to know the weaknesses of my enemy so I could use that in the future."

I chuckled, "This may not be a method you necessarily want to use."

Lou stopped what he was doing turning to face me, "There's very few methods I don't like to use. What do you mean?"

I looked away from Lou and felt myself blushing, "Let's just say the relationship went to the next level."

"Leveling up? Eas – oh," he trailed off as realization dawned over him.

Lou got quiet and went back to work. With the tension in the air increasing, I left the kitchen heading to the dining area ready to take care of any customers who came in. There were some trickling in for a later lunch which thankfully kept me busy enough to stay away from Lou. Dinner was where it really picked up, and before I knew it, it was time to go home.

"See you later, Lou, I'm headed out for the night," I said poking my head in the kitchen.

He didn't look up as he responded, "Enjoy your next two days. I'll let you know if I make any progress on the flash drive."

I went in to the kitchen and put my hand on his shoulder, "Hey, everything good? You've been on edge for a good chunk of the day."

"I'm fine."

"Not if you're saying that with your jaw muscles twitching. Be honest with me."

Lou sighed, "Just processing everything. I still don't like the idea of you two dating and the thought of him putting his hands on you ..."

He trailed off, but didn't need to say anything else. Lou has hinted at something more developing without acting on it since that day in his apartment. Seeing him like this made something in me hurt.

"Lou, I'm only doing what we agreed upon to get this information out of him. I'm not his biggest fan, but I couldn't have kept the conversation interesting enough for him to not look at his computer. I'm not saying I feel good about what I did, I honestly don't, but at the end of the day, I got the information. Let's just move on from this and see what we can find out, okay?"

He nodded turning away from me, "See you in a couple of days."

Chapter 14

It had been a few weeks since the flash drive mission was successful. Lou didn't have any updates yet, and the worst part? He put more distance between us. No matter how much I joked around or suggested we hang out after work to just catch up, Lou would keep it business and minimize his time around me.

It was my first night off for the week and I was taking advantage of the clear night. Swimming laps in the pool again, I took a break to lay on my back looking at the stars. They were all out tonight, twinkling in a rhythm that made me get caught up in their dance. I got back to swimming a few more laps and rested again at the far edge of the pool, pausing to look at the city. Maybe I could stay here and start a new life. I've already got a job, have a house, and have been working on a new friend group here. I didn't want to dive too much into those thoughts, so I turned around to get back at it.

I stopped, feeling my breath catch in my throat as I laid eyes upon Warrick. We hadn't seen each other since the time we spent together in his office and I had been ghosting him. Probably not my brightest move considering he's a loose cannon.

I floated there, suddenly remembering I was naked. Also, not my brightest move, but in all fairness, I wasn't expecting company.

"Do you like what you see?"

Warrick was sitting on the opposite end of the pool swinging his feet in the water. He had a lazy grin on his face as he said, "How could I not, love?"

"Are you going to sit there watching or are you going to join me?"

He didn't hesitate with stripping down and getting in the pool. He swam over so gracefully I hardly heard the water move. No wonder I didn't know anyone else was here, he moved as silently as a snake.

"It's been a while, love. I've started to think you've been avoiding me."

I wrapped my arms loosely around his neck allowing myself to be closer to him, "I wanted to leave you wanting more."

His pupils dilated with that response and he closed the distance between our bodies. "Mission accomplished, then."

I didn't get a chance to respond before he gently kissed me. Those kisses became more passionate. Warrick was gentle this round, taking his time and exploring much to my relief.

We were laying in a lounge chair when we had finished with him tracing his fingers along my back.

"Warrick?"

"Yes, love?"

"Have you always been a wolf?"

His fingers paused momentarily before he continued, "No, I was changed about 15 years ago."

I could feel some of his muscles flexing with tension underneath me, so I didn't keep pressing.

"How did you become alpha?"

"The company I run – I started in the lower ranks and worked my way up. I knew about the pack and was part of it, but I didn't have a true role there and that lit a fire in me. Once I learned about what was going on behind the scenes with the higher ranks, I knew I had to be a part of that."

I could feel the tension from earlier slowly dripping away. Good, I could at least stay on this topic without ruffling too many feathers.

"I cut out the middleman and went straight to the CEO to see how I could solidify a higher ranking position in the pack. I wanted to feel more powerful, earn more respect. I knew I had the strength in me, I just needed the right avenues to prove it."

Ah, double checkmark in the box next to power-hungry. It all started in his early wolf days. I kept quiet to let him continue.

"I figured out the formula for what our alpha was looking for. Didn't take me long to make my move. He was ruthless, but I liked how he ran things. It took maybe a year before I was CTO."

I looked up at him with wide eyes, "A year?! To go from lower-level to C-suite? That's unheard of!"

A smile started crawling across his face, "It was hard, taxing, but that's what made me want it even more. I wasn't afraid to do whatever it took."

"How were you able to jump pack ranking so quickly?"

"Our alpha scheduled fights. He put me against the next higher-ranking wolf, and if I won, I moved into their spot and they moved down a notch if they survived. I went for blood and made it known I wasn't afraid to fight dirty," Warrick said with a faraway look in his eyes. It was like he was going through the fights again enjoying every moment of it. He was also starting to sound more intense, more unhinged.

"Were the pack members people from the company?"

"Yes, it was structured very much the same way then as it is now. When I got to the CTO position, I was our alpha's right-hand man. I did all of his dirty work and started bringing in more profits to the company. We were a dynamic duo, but that wasn't enough. I wanted more, so I started paying attention to his habits."

"You wanted to be alpha," I said looking out into the yard.

"Exactly. I wanted to be alpha and the only way to do that was to take down the current alpha. This wasn't something that happened quickly. I took my time building my strength and figuring out his weaknesses, which weren't a lot mind you. When the time came, I walked into his office and told him exactly what I wanted. He wasn't very surprised, and he refused, at first. That didn't stop me, though. As you know, I can be very persuasive. By the time I convinced him, news traveled quickly. The same day I had walked into his office was the same day we were going to be fighting. I had recovered fully from the previous fights at this point and was stronger than ever, so I knew nothing could stop me. We got into the fighting ring that night with everyone in the pack placing bets. When the bell rung, everyone else went away."

Warrick was completely consumed with retelling the memory. I looked back up at him and saw his eyes were distant, focusing on something I couldn't quite see. There was a fire in them, though, telling me he was at his favorite part – the part where he became the most powerful wolf in the pack.

The smile from earlier turning more sinister as he continued, "It wasn't an easy fight and there were times where I thought about submitting, but the thought of doing that disgusted me. There were times where I knew I had the upper hand which pushed me harder. The fight went on for over an hour, and when it finally ended, I stood up covered in blood, but I was alpha."

"Did the other alpha just give up?"

"Love, I killed him. I stood over his body triumphant. There was no way he would be okay with just stepping aside. He wasn't that kind of person and he definitely wasn't that kind of wolf."

Another reminder of how Warrick wasn't afraid to do what he had to. It sent chills down my spine how easily he confessed the result of his fight.

Warrick continued, "The pack was unsure of what to do for a while, but I ran things the same way. I was promoted to CEO of the company and now ran the largest pack in the city, but I wanted to keep the pack growing."

"How were you going to do that?" I asked. With the way his story was going, I might be able to get the information Lou was taking his sweet time looking for. I was hoping I could anyways, I was getting tired of waiting and Lou was still being distant.

"I continued to up the profits of the company to justify hiring new people. I bought other companies, like research-based ones and tech firms so I could get my hands on the latest and greatest technology to keep that edge. It worked. The pack numbers started to have a steady increase for many, many years after that until the pack's growth started to plateau. Then, I started to notice a lot of new people were showing up around here with no idea how they got to where they were. Another idea hit me. I could find a way to bring some of the newcomers into the company and eventually in the pack."

It was now or never if I was ever going to get information out of him.

"Weren't you even curious about where they were coming from and how they were getting here?"

He chuckled, "I was very curious. I tapped into the other companies I had bought to see if they would be able to find some solution and they found a gold mine. The war tearing apart your world was a gift to me. It turns out someone was able to find a way to create a bomb that transports people to alternate worlds. Once I knew that, I had to find a way to contact this person to see if we could form an agreement."

"Wait, how could you contact someone in a different world?"

"I'm not giving away all my secrets, love, but I will tell you it took a lot of time, money, and smarts for us to figure that out. When we did, it was like the floodgates had opened. There are other packs around this world, so I want to have the largest and strongest pack. Same goes for my company."

Again with the power. At least I got some new information with him being able to contact the world I came from. I didn't want to keep pressing this in case I blew my cover, so I changed the topic.

"Warrick, have you ever been in love?"

That got his hand to still again as he asked, "Why do you want to know?"

I looked back up at him hopefully giving the most innocent look I could think of, "Your story sounds lonely. You must have wanted someone to share that with."

He resumed tracing his fingers along my back and I laid my head back down on his chest. *Phew.*

"There was one woman who managed to teach me how to love."

"Was she the only woman you had been with?"

Warrick let out a small sigh with a laugh at the end, "No. I had been with plenty of women, but no one captured my attention enough for me to want to be in a relationship."

"Tell me about her."

I was very curious now. Was this the woman who was also in Lou's life? He made no mention of Lou in his story at all and I wonder if he purposely omitted him. Either way, I wasn't going to mention him in case that would derail this conversation. I was getting some juicy details I didn't want to miss out on.

"She was stunning, much like you. We actually met in a similar way, except she grew up just outside the city and wasn't working at the pizza place. I happened to walk in for my lunch order the same day she was there. It was just her and I in the dining area so we struck up a conversation. She was so easy to talk to. And her laugh. Her laugh just took away all the bad things in the world. I could get lost in her blue eyes and she had the softest, long, thick caramel colored hair. That first day talking to her, I easily let my guard down. I wasn't trying to make her feel intimidated by my power or woo her with my money. It was nice to be able to take away all the exterior and just show her my true self that I had tucked away a long time ago."

"Sounds like love at first sight," I said.

"Yes, it very much was. I wasn't happy to find out she was already in a relationship, but I didn't let that stop me. I eventually persuaded her to go on a date with me and I knew I would get her hooked. It didn't take long for her to leave the guy she was with. I truly felt on top of the world and unstoppable then."

His voice had trailed at this point and I wasn't sure if I should keep asking on this topic or not. I didn't know if I was going to like what I heard. I didn't have to ask, though, Warrick kept going almost as if he were in a trance and the only way to break it was to finish the story.

"All of that came crashing down on me so quickly. She came to visit me at work one day. Everyone knew who she was, so no one thought to stop her when she headed into my office. I was in the middle of disciplining one of my wolves who disobeyed my orders. I'm sure you've heard by now I'm not afraid to use violence to get my way. Well, she didn't know that about me and I had kept it that way for a reason because I didn't want to do anything to jeopardize what we had. Anyways, she came into my office as I was on top of this guy beating him senseless. He was unconscious at this point getting closer to death. I had no idea anyone had come through my door until I heard the sound of glass breaking. She had brought me a vase of flowers because she thought my office needed a little bit more color, but she wasn't expecting to see some other color being added at that moment."

"That must have been hard for her."

"It was, especially since she had never seen that side of me before. I couldn't stop her before she ran out, so I rushed cleaning up before following her. I asked my admin if she could make sure the cleaning crew knew they were going to be dealing with blood as I ran out of the office building. I knew exactly where she was going, so I wasn't too worried. I headed over to the pizza shop to find her sobbing in her ex's arms."

Anger was starting to creep into his voice at that point. I put my hand on his stomach to try to help keep that in check, but it was only a temporary solution.

"I begged her to walk with me so we could talk in a more private setting. I didn't want to give him the chance to intervene any more than he already had. Thankfully, she agreed and we set out. I explained to her how that was the way I ran my pack to keep them in check. It was the way things had always been done and those methods had worked. Why change something if there's been a lot of success?"

I piped in, "If it's not broken, don't fix it."

"Exactly," Warrick agreed, tapping his fingers in the same rhythm. "She didn't like that answer and tried to reason with me that I could still be the most powerful alpha while not beating people to the brink of death when they stepped out of line. That was when she told me she feared I wouldn't hold back against her if she did something wrong. I tried to plead with her, but there was something in me that knew this was the last time I could call her mine. She finally walked away from me causing everything to shatter. My defenses came right back up and I was filled with a rage I never experienced before."

He paused for a moment either for effect or to gather his emotions. I'm sure this wasn't easy reliving all this pain, but I wasn't going to stop him if he was willing to be so open.

"The first thing that crossed my mind was that if I can't have her, no one can. I followed her around when I wasn't working to keep tabs. I sent some of my most trusted wolves to follow her when I couldn't be there. I had eyes all around the city and reporting back to me. I wasn't ready to let her go. Then, I saw her sitting across the street in that damn pizza shop flirting and having the best time with her ex. She was on a date. I wanted to kill him right then and there, but I had to wait. I hatched a plan and struck at the right moment. She was walking in a park one night by herself as she often did. We control the level of crime around here and that was a place where there was virtually nothing."

"That explains why I've noticed people walking in some parks at night. Not something you see a lot where I came from."

"Hard to commit a crime when a wolf can take you down at any second. Anyways, something came over me and threw my plan out the window. I grabbed her and let the rage take over. Before I knew it, she was no longer there. I couldn't believe what I had done and this was the only time I felt anything after I killed someone. Remorse didn't consume me too long, though, because I left clues for her ex to find. My way of saying not to mess with me."

I stilled. Any words I had escaped me and I didn't know if I wanted the answers to the questions running around in my head.

"From then on, I vowed I wouldn't love again. Then, I walked into that pizza place for my lunch order and saw you. Except, I thought my eyes were playing tricks on me because you're almost the spitting image of her."

I didn't like being compared to the love he had killed. What would stop me from seeing the same fate?

Warrick chuckled again as he continued, "Except there are quite a few differences. You don't have those same blue eyes that looks like an ocean. And you have a lot of fire in you. She was nothing but a saint. I could go on, but you get the picture."

I was hoping this picture included me being safe from murder.

"It was hard that day when you were wearing her clothes, though."

"That explains the weird face you made before smiling."

"Yeah, I wasn't expecting that and it took a second before I realized you weren't her. I guess ghosts really can come back to haunt you."

That was the confirmation I didn't realize I needed to hear until now. Warrick had killed Lou's love and left her for him to find. No wonder. And looking so similar to her explains Lou trying to make moves on me and getting jealous so fast.

I sat up and turned to Warrick so I was looking him in the eyes. I asked, "Do you want anything to eat or drink?"

"Yes, please."

I wanted to get away for a moment because I was worried about how that conversation was going. The last thing I needed right now was for Warrick to express any sort of feelings towards me. If he did, it would be the mark of death especially since I wouldn't be able to reciprocate those feelings. I steadied myself on the kitchen island taking a few deep breaths for a moment. This was starting to be a bit much and my head was spinning.

"Everything okay, love?"

I jumped. I hadn't even heard the door open or him come in, but there he was standing in front of me.

I smiled, "I'm fine, just startled me. That's all."

Warrick started to slowly walk towards me as if he were stalking prey. Maybe this was it. This was why Lou had always warned me to lock up everything and keep a low profile. Yet, I couldn't help but admire Warrick. Even though he wasn't the best person, he was easy on the eyes. His prominent muscles, those piercing eyes.

Before I knew it, his hand was cupping the side of my face. There was something soft in his expression as he said, "Sorry, I didn't mean to startle you."

Warrick leaned in and gave me a long slow kiss, tracing my bottom lip with his tongue every now and then. I had to remind myself that I couldn't, and wouldn't, get lost in this.

When we pulled apart, he rested his forehead on mine, "You let me do a lot of talking. It's your turn."

I pulled away from him and turned so my back was facing him. I needed to keep busy and find us some food.

"Help yourself to any of the drinks in the fridge. I'll grab us some snacks."

"Wait, I have a better idea. Let's go out."

"Okay," I said slowly, silently thanking the stars he wasn't pressing to know more about me at this moment. "What were you thinking?"

He turned me back around, wrapping his arms around my waist, and leaned me against the counter, "How do you feel about seafood?"

"Let's go. Only question is do I have to dress up for this one?"

"No, we'll keep it casual."

I smiled, "Well, let me go get dressed."

We pulled up to a little shack of a bar next to the ocean. It took about an hour to get here, so it was pretty late. I was surprised to see it still open with a few people there. When we walked in, we grabbed a seat outside to listen to the steady rhythm of the tide pushing and pulling the water from the shore. The lighting was low and even though the bar looked like it was one windstorm from falling over, it felt like the most romantic spot.

I brought my gaze back to Warrick, "How did you find this place?"

"It's a place I often come to when I need to be alone and away from it all. You're the first person I brought with me."

Our waitress came up and Warrick placed our order. I continued to take in the scene. Warrick actually dressed in casual clothes joking with the waitress. The ocean twinkling with the light of the moon that was only showing half of itself. The slight breeze carrying the smell of the ocean salt. The occasional house or building further up the shore. There really wasn't a lot out here enhancing the appeal for needing to escape.

Warrick brought my attention back to our table when he asked, "So, are you going to let me be the only one to share tonight or do I get to learn more about you?"

I cocked my head a little bit and grinned, "Who would have thought I would have seen the more personable side to you? But, I guess I can't leave you hanging since you so graciously let me in. What do you want to know?"

"Have you ever been in love?"

Right, this wasn't going to be easy since he admitted to doing some research on me.

"I have, once before. His name was Gabriel, my angel."

"And? What happened?"

I looked down into my water glass. *Was I ready to relive this all over again?*

I sighed. Here goes nothing, "It clearly didn't work out. He was someone I met in college. We really hit it off and were always called the golden couple, everyone wanted a piece of what we had. It wasn't a show when we were out in public either, we really loved each other and were consumed with one another. He had proposed and there was no one else I really saw spending my life with, so of course I said yes. There were so many times when we would just sit there in the small hours of the morning in bed just looking at each other, not believing what we had was real because it was so amazing. But, then this stupid war started. We had just graduated from grad school, bought a house, and were planning our wedding. He got a draft notice in the mail making our world stop. He only had a few days before he had to go, so we locked up our house, turned off our phones, and spent those days completely wrapped up in each other to savor every moment. We didn't talk about what could happen, we only focused on staying in the present."

Warrick reached across the table to place a comforting hand on my arm without saying anything. I was still looking down in my water glass as I continued.

"The day finally came for him to go. I had no idea that would be the last time I would see him, but I remember every detail, every small movement he would make, the twinkle he would get in his eyes when he was up to no good."

I had to stop for a moment. Emotion was starting to creep into my voice and I could feel the tears starting to form. *Breathe in, breathe out.*

I dived back into the story, "I tried to go about my day-to-day life without him there. We wrote a lot of letters and I sent him as many care packages as I could. The house was so empty without him though, and a lot of nights were hard. It had been half a year when I got the knock on our door. I opened it to find someone from the military holding a folded-up flag with his dog tags. It was like the floor fell out from underneath me. There was nothing in my life that had matched that level of pain. I couldn't get out of bed, couldn't breathe. My life was over, but my close friends did everything they could to get me functioning again. So, I worked up the courage to sell our house, move into a tiny apartment, and try to get back on the dating scene because that's what he would've wanted, right?"

Warrick just nodded his head, still not saying anything, but encouraging me to continue.

"I filled my life with useless relationships, if that's what you want to call them. I spent my time mostly sleeping around with guys and breaking it off before anything got too serious because I thought that would fill the hole in my heart. My friends knew I was slowly destroying myself, but they never got in the way to stop it. I've always had a hard time thinking of committing to someone else since I was so convinced there would be no one else I wanted to spend the rest of my life with."

I stopped again, this time having a harder time fighting back the tears. Finally, Warrick said something.

"I can't imagine going through something like that."

I couldn't hold myself back, "Well, you appreciated the war for being able to give you more people to add to your circle. Meanwhile, it was starting to take everything away from me. You killed the woman you loved out of spite. I had my one love ripped away from me with no say in the matter."

I was expecting him to get angry with me for saying that considering his short fuse, but all he did was squeeze my hand.

"Let's change the topic, love. I'm sorry for making you relive that."

I shook my head, not able to meet his eyes. He was the only person I had told that too and I never intended to tell another soul. I still had a box of Gabriel's things in the back of my closet at my parent's house that I was happy at least made it to this new world.

Our food arrived and we dug in. A heavy silence was still hanging over our table, but I was glad I didn't have to talk too much.

Once we were done, we went for a walk on the beach. Warrick had to run to the restroom giving me my first real moment alone since he had come over to my house earlier. I sat on the beach, staring out to the ocean. Could Gabriel see me in this new world? *Could he still be with me?* The tears came all at once and there was no stopping them this time. I should have known better than to open that door by asking Warrick if he'd been in love.

It didn't take long for Warrick to come back finding me silently sobbing. He just sat down and put his arms around me. Who would've thought the person I viewed as my enemy is now someone who knows enough about me to be in my inner circle? I guess it is true what they say about keeping your enemies closer.

The next morning, I woke up in my bed alone. There was a small ache in my heart in the spot that was ripped open that fateful day I got the news. Thank goodness I had today off, too. I don't know if I could muster up the energy to deal with people. Maybe I'll just have a day where I stay in bed ignoring the world.

My phone started ringing. *Of course.* I groaned as I rolled over to look at the caller ID. Lou. I answered it.

"Val, I thought you were going to let me talk to your voicemail."

"Thought about it."

"Did you just wake up? It's one in the afternoon."

"Late night. What's up?"

Sleep was still in my voice, tinged with sadness. I was hoping he didn't pick up on the sadness.

"I finally got through everything and I think you're going to want to see this."

That at least snapped the sleep out of me, "Did you find something good?"

"I don't know if you can call it that, but I think it'll answer a lot of your questions."

"I'll be down there in ten minutes."

I hung up springing out of bed. I threw on some shorts and a light sweater. I paused and grabbed the box out of my closet to get the necklace with my engagement ring on it. I needed something to provide me comfort.

I rushed down to the pizza place and let myself in. It only took Lou forever to get anything useful and I didn't want to wait any longer than I already had.

"Lou?"

"In here!"

His voice carried from the dining area, so I made my way out there. Everything was still closed down from the night before.

"Are you not opening today?"

"Not planning on it."

"But it's not a full moon."

Lou leaned back in his chair crossing his arms over his chest, "Do you want to know what I just found or do you want to focus on me choosing to have a day off?"

"Right, sorry," I said as I made my way over to where he was sitting. "What did you find?"

He looked back at his laptop before looking at me, "I found out who was behind the bombs."

Lou turned the laptop towards me so I could start looking at what he had loaded on the screen. There was an email pulled up sent from Warrick verifying what he had mentioned last night about being able to contact people in another world. When I read who the email was addressed to, everything stopped.

Chapter 15

I couldn't breathe, couldn't think, couldn't do anything except read the email over and over again. *This can't mean what I think it does.* There's no way this email pinpoints who created the bombs. On the other hand, if this does, this would rock the entire world and shift the dynamic within the war. Either way, my dad has a hand in this ... he was the one who sent it to Warrick.

I looked back up at Lou and he just nodded his head, neither of us feeling the need to exchange any words. My eyes trailed back down to the computer to read the email for what had to be the 50th time: "I have the next bomb ready to go for Saturday night. Be ready."

I was finally able to let out a sigh looking back at Lou, "Am I reading this right?"

Lou leaned back, "It hasn't been edited or changed in any way. This is its original form sent to Warrick's private email. It took me a while to break into those files."

I looked back at Lou, "Well, I'm sure it wasn't going to be easy getting in to something like this. Sorry for rushing you on this. Why would Warrick make it easy to expose what he's doing?"

"No worries. I wanted to make sure we had access to everything."

"So, we know my dad is involved with these bombs and seems to be partnering with Warrick."

"Yeah, there's more solidifying that."

I shook my head, "I can't believe this. My dad is a high-ranking military official. The bombings have been happening on our turf and they've said it's from the enemy."

"I know," he said as he took the laptop back. "There's more. Your dad may have been updating Warrick of the timeline of the bombings, but he's also involved with their creation."

"Hold on," I held my hands up. "You mean to tell me my dad is creating these weapons of destruction against his own country? That's treason. I can't see someone doing this when they would do anything for their country."

"He's at least a part of the team who makes these. And somehow Warrick has figured out a way to partner with him. There's no wonder his pack numbers have been jumping."

"Does Warrick have any information about why these were being created to transport people? And has he been using me as much as I have been using him? Why is he doing this? Was Warrick the one who came up with this idea of a bomb that transports people?"

It was Lou's turn to hold up a hand, signaling me to wait, "We'll answer one question at a time. Let's start with the easy one – he's doing this because he wants more power, and in his mind, having more people in his pack is more power. For the second question, Warrick definitely knew who you were before you got here, but I'm not sure if he was using you. I think it's a perk of being with you, but not the entire reason he pursued you. Your last two questions go hand-in-hand. He wasn't the one who came up with this idea. New people started popping up randomly and we had no idea what was causing this, so he took matters into his own hands and found a way to capitalize."

I rested my head in my hands on the table, "This is too much. I still can't get over the fact my dad is involved in this. I can't go back now."

"Can't go back?"

"I can't go back to the world I started in. I'm furious. How much of my life has been a lie because my dad decided to sneak around and commit serious crimes? Was any of my life real or was it just a cover for him?"

Lou started to reach across the table and stopped, "I don't know how to answer those questions."

"Never mind that, those were more rhetorical. Do you think Warrick has any idea we have this information?"

"If he does, he hasn't showed anything."

"That's good," I said fidgeting with my necklace. Lou looked, eyes lingering for a second before looking back down at the laptop. I knew I needed to get back home. I bet it wasn't a part of my dad's plan for his own house to be transported away from him and I was going to take full advantage of that. I needed to get back so I could start digging around his office.

"Val, has Warrick been over to your house?"

I stopped, "Yes, why?"

"Shit," Lou muttered under his breath. "Has he been inside?"

"Yeah, just briefly and only in one spot."

His fists clenched a muscle started twitching in his jaw. I reached across and put my hands over his fists to try and calm him down.

"Lou, what's wrong?"

"He knows who you are. He knows that's your parent's house. Starting to do the math?"

I paused trying to see what he was getting at. Once it clicked, the blood drained from my face, "You don't think he would try to break in, do you?"

"We need to go there. Now."

Lou wasted no time getting up to head out the door. I followed suit and hopped on my bike. Before speeding off, I took a look up towards Warrick's office hoping to see the outline I've seen before. Thankfully, he was there, so now I needed to play it cool. I gave a little wave and got one in return. Instead of peeling out, I eased out of my parking spot so I didn't give him any reason to worry about me running off so quickly. If he was in his office, there's no way he could be at my house. Something was holding him back, and whatever that was, I was thankful.

Lou had beaten me to the house, leaning against his car as I pulled into the garage. He followed me into the house up to my dad's office. As I sat behind the desk, he asked, "Why did you take so long?"

"I checked to see if Warrick was in his office. Thankfully he was, so that gives us plenty of time before he even attempts to get in here."

"If he hasn't been here already."

I gave him a look while I started opening drawers. Lou got to work looking through the various bookshelves. A lot of time was passing where we weren't finding anything and I was starting to think my dad had taken everything with him. Lou must've started thinking the same thing because things were starting to be slammed.

I looked up, "Nothing is going to be found if you break – "

I stopped. I was lifting up papers in one of the drawers when I found a ribbon. I pulled up on it, revealing a secret compartment. I don't know what I was expecting, but there was only a flash drive. I held it up for Lou. He quickly made his way over producing his laptop. I held up my hand and pointed to the computer at the desk, "We'll use this. I don't know if he'll be able to see that this has been plugged in, so I'd rather it be traced back to his own computer rather than yours."

Lou just nodded.

I plugged in the flash drive waiting for the computer to recognize it. Once we were in, there were so many folders and files I had no idea where to start. I started clicking into each one to see if there was anything that would offer any more information than what we already found. Schedules, blackmail on our government reps, war plans. Nothing that would tell us something new. I was losing hope as I got to the last folder.

Clicking in that folder, there was only one document that had no name. I opened this document to find it was password protected. *It has to be something good if it's locked down.* I had no clue what the password would be, so I just started to type in random guesses. I finally got in after guessing the date the war began.

"Lou, come here."

I felt him put his hand on the chair and he leaned in, "I've been here. What did you find?"

"Oops, sorry. Anyways, this looks like it's a formulation," I kept scrolling through slowly, but only to skim. "It's more than the formulation. This is everything to create the bomb. All the technology that went into it, how it works, what triggers it, who's involved in this from the team to the investors. Everything."

We both became very quiet as I kept scrolling through. This document was the one thing that proved my dad was not only involved with this technology, but he was the one behind it all. I had to stop. I abruptly pushed myself away from the desk and left the room.

"Val, wait!"

I heard Lou scrambling to grab what I assumed was the flash drive and clean our messes up. I was making my way to my room when he finally caught up with me.

"What's going on?"

"I can't handle this right now. I need to get out of this house. I can't breathe."

Lou placed a hand on my shoulder stopping me, "I know this is a lot, but it should help us with at least figuring out a way to travel between worlds."

"Don't!" I yelled, brushing his hand from my shoulder. "Can we please just take a second to pause all of this?"

Lou kept trying to reason with me as we got into my room and I kept ignoring him. I was grabbing clothes and other items needed to stay away from here for a while. I turned ready to head downstairs when I saw Lou looking through the box I had pulled down earlier. He looked up at me holding on to a picture of Gabriel and I. "What is this?"

"What do you mean?" I asked feeling my voice catch with emotion.

"What is this box, Val?" Lou asked, his brow furrowing with concern.

I looked away, "It's nothing."

"Just like that ring around your neck is nothing?"

"Yeah." I responded, suddenly feeling very small.

"You don't have to talk about it if you don't want to."

Lou started to put things back in the box carefully sensing how much it means to me. Emotions flooded me and I couldn't stop the tears again. I stood in the middle of my room, crying. Lou looked unsure of what to do, so he stood there momentarily before coming over and grabbing me in a soft embrace. He let me have my moment and when I finally calmed down enough to catch my breath, he lifted my head from his shoulder so I was looking him right in the eyes, "You know you soaked my shirt."

That got a small chuckle from me, "I'm sorry."

His thumbs wiped away any remaining tears, "No need to be sorry, just happy I got some semblance of a laugh out of you. There's been a lot going on, let's just try to relax a little tonight."

I nodded my head and separated myself from him. Between going down memory lane and learning about my father, my brain was spinning. I was glad to have Lou here where I didn't need to pretend to be something I'm not.

We made our way downstairs and Lou started to pull out food to cook. With his back to me, he asked, "You good if I stay here for a little bit?"

"Please. I don't want to be here alone, especially if Warrick tries to do anything."

Lou paused, "Speaking of, we should probably close everything down. Do you have room in your garage for my car?"

"Let me check," I said as I made my way towards the garage. It would be tight, but there would be space if I moved a few things around. I got to work, appreciating the distraction. When I was done, I grabbed his keys and got his car and my bike safely hidden from street view. I came back in and closed all the blinds. Lou was still cooking when I got back to the island.

"Val, you don't have to answer this if you don't want to. Were you engaged once?"

I instinctively pulled out my necklace playing with my ring. I zoned out for a second before responding, "Yeah, but it was a while ago."

"Did you guys split up?"

"Not necessarily. You aren't the only one who lost someone they loved. You haven't been the most open about your love life, why dive into mine?"

He put down his spatula and slowly turned to me. I could see the hurt in his eyes and I immediately regretted what I just said, "I-I'm sorry. I shouldn't have said that."

"No, you don't need to apologize. I just assumed you broke it off or something."

I could tell he was being sensitive about this topic which was much appreciated. He knew what it was like to have lost someone near and dear to his heart while also knowing how hard it is to talk about it. Talking with Lou felt a lot easier than talking with Warrick because Lou knew what it was like to have someone ripped away so quickly and so uncontrollably whereas Warrick was the one who made that choice.

I openly talked about what had happened in more detail than what I provided last night. I had now told two people a very secret part of my life. I guess it helped talking more about it, but the feelings still ran deep. When I was done with my story, Lou sat there looking at me with something along the lines of admiration.

Lou said, "You've been through a lot, especially here. Yet, you're still standing, tackling each day and owning it."

I shrugged, "You have to. Letting things like that consume you is only going to lead to hate. I don't want to be filled with that. As cliché as this is going to sound, Gabriel wouldn't want me to live that way either. He probably wouldn't want me sleeping around like I have been, but I'm trying to get better."

Lou nodded and finished cooking. He put everything on plates and jerked his head towards the back door, "Let's go enjoy this outside."

"What if Warrick is out there?"

"Fuck him. We can still enjoy the little things."

So, we went outside and enjoyed our meal. I was happy my diet was no longer consisting only of pizza. I was also happy Lou redirected the conversation to something lighter. We were laughing, not having a care in the world and life felt normal. As we kept bouncing from topic to topic, joke to joke, my heart starting warming to Lou in a way it hadn't in a while. I excused myself for a moment and went to my room. I took my necklace off, gave the ring a kiss, and tucked it safely in the box that I put back away. It wasn't going to help me move on if I was still clinging to my memories, and while it was nice to have a moment, I needed to be open to new relationships that lasted longer than a few months. I wasn't wanting to completely forget, but I didn't want the lingering sadness to threaten me anymore.

On my way back outside, I grabbed the supplies needed for s'mores. When I got out there, Lou looked confused at what I was holding.

"Have you never had s'mores before?" I asked while I got back in my spot.

"No, that's not something we typically have around here."

"Follow my lead," I said as I handed him a marshmallow ready for roasting.

I hadn't expected I would need to teach someone how to make one of the best snacks, but here I was. We were enjoying the ooey gooeyness and I was seeing the inner kid in Lou come out.

"What's the verdict?" I asked with a big smile on my face.

"This is delicious."

He had some melted marshmallow on the corner of his mouth, so I reached up to wipe it away. My thumb lingered and Lou brought his hand up to mine. We stayed like that for a moment longer before I pulled my hand away, blushing. I looked down into the fire, "They make a mess, too."

Lou was still looking at me, "Yeah, I can see that."

I shifted uncomfortably still looking at the fire as I said, "Lou, Warrick told me I look a lot like her."

"You do."

"Is that the reason you've tried making a move on me?"

"No."

I looked at him when I asked, "Are you sure?"

Lou sighed, "Yes. While you look a lot like her, you also have a lot of differences that set you a part."

Somehow that reassured me a little bit, but I still couldn't get it out of my head.

Lou went back to looking over the fire. I leaned back and looked up at the stars watching them wink back at me. Silence enveloped us and it was oddly comforting with neither of us feeling the need to talk. I started shivering a little bit and Lou moved his way closer to try to help me stay warm. The amount of body heat surprised me. I warmed right back up in no time, but

I wasn't ready for him to move away from me. I leaned my head on his shoulder.

"It sure is a nice night," he said now trying to fill the silence with small talk.

"Mm-hmm."

"Are you getting tired?"

"Maybe."

Lou patted my leg, "Let's go inside, then."

I didn't argue. I got up and turned off the fire pit while Lou grabbed everything else we brought out. We made quick work of getting the house cleaned up and headed up to my room. Lou started to head towards another room, but I grabbed his sleeve silently asking him to stay with me. It was a nice feeling to have someone else here.

We started working our way through our nighttime routines to get ready to sleep. Lou wanted to make one more check around the house to make sure all the doors and windows were locked up before finally calling it a night. When he got back up to the room, I was already in bed with the covers up to my nose.

"Cold?"

I nodded my head patting the spot next to me. He picked up on the signal getting in next to me and I started to warm back up. *It's nice to have a personal heater.* His warmth drew me in and he didn't back away when I laid my head on his chest.

"Lou?"

"Yeah?"

"We have to find a way to stop Warrick. It would be nice to find a way to travel between worlds, too. I'd like to know if my friends are okay, but I don't want Warrick to get more of an upper-hand than he already has."

He squeezed me tighter, "We will. Let that be something we figure out tomorrow."

With that, I drifted off into one of the most restful sleeps I've had in a long time.

In the morning, Lou and I took our time getting up. Apparently, I wasn't the only one who slept really well.

"Lou, what are we going to do about Warrick?" I asked as we finally got around to making breakfast.

"I've been trying to figure that one out. I think the best thing we can do is try to get ahead of him and start working on a device that'll allow us to jump between worlds."

I paused, "Us?"

He looked at me, "Yeah. I'm not letting you do this on your own."

"What about your pack?"

"They'll be fine. I'll talk with my second and let him know what's going on. He's more than capable of leading them in my absence."

"Okay. Well, let's do this, then."

I got a thumbs up from Lou. He pulled out his phone to call his second to debrief him with everything going on. The loyalty runs deep since I heard Lou asking his second to take care of the pizza place for him. Once he got off the phone, he smiled at me, "We're all good to go. For Warrick, try to keep your distance as much as possible. No need to keep up the act since we got what we needed. I don't want to put you at risk of him doing something irrational any more than we already have."

We both knew what he was referencing giving our previous conversations. I gave him a thumbs up in return and continued working on breakfast.

In between bites of food, Lou started throwing out some ideas, "We could make this device handheld or see if we can integrate it into our phones somehow. Oh! We would need to make it untraceable, too. We don't want anyone being able to figure out what we're up to."

"Hold on, Lou. Great ideas, but the problem is that we need the components, software, skills, and a place to put this together. Plus, we need something to help us get started. Just because I'm related to the man who created something to transport people doesn't mean I instantly know what to do."

If I hadn't interjected, he would've kept going. I don't think I've seen him this energized since we met.

"True," he said tapping his fork against his chin thinking. "Maybe if your dad had a secret compartment, he has a lab tucked away somewhere in this house? And you forget, we found his documentation that practically spells everything out."

I rolled my eyes, but nodded my head, "I think that could be a stretch. A secret lab is a lot bigger than a compartment in a drawer."

He was about to respond when there was a knock on the door. We paused, looking at each other. There was only two people who would know I was here and my money was on one of them. I motioned for Lou to take his food with him and hide. I got up to answer the door sending a silent thank you to him for moving so silently.

I opened the door, not surprised to see Warrick standing there, "Good morning."

"You feeling okay, love?" Warrick asked with some concern.

"Yeah, why?"

"You're not looking the greatest this morning and I hadn't heard from you."

"All is good, just wanting to lay low," I looked away. "Just a lot of things running through my mind and I need some time to myself."

"Understood," he said. Even though he said it, I couldn't help but get the feeling there wasn't a lot of meaning behind that. I looked back up at Warrick to see he was no longer looking at me, but around the house instead.

"Are you looking for something?"

"Hmm?"

"You're looking around. Is there something you're trying to find?"

That got his attention back on me, "No. I was just wanting to check on you. The pizza place has been closed longer than normal."

"Yeah, all I know is that Lou told me not to come in. I don't know much beyond that. You need Lou for something or you missing your pizza that much?"

Warrick shook his head turning to go, "I'll head out. Let me know if you need anything. I know our conversation the other night wasn't exactly the easiest."

I squeezed his arm, "Thanks, Warrick."

I closed the door, but still had the feeling there was more to his visit than a wellness check. He definitely seemed to be looking for something, but what? Was he looking for something that would help him continue his plan for ultimate power? Or was he actually looking for Lou?

His car drove off and Lou reappeared.

"Lou, something isn't sitting right with me about that conversation."

Considering he was frowning, he must've felt the same. Lou said, "I agree. Something's up and I don't like it. It was almost like he didn't trust you."

That made something click and I snapped my fingers, "That's it! Warrick wasn't looking for something, he was looking for someone. You were gone and I was laying low, so he was wanting to see if you were here. Warrick was trying to see if I was cheating."

Lou whistled, "You must've been doing a really good job at selling your relationship to him. It would make sense, though. All the lunch dates in the pizza place right in front of me, the kissing after the first date, him all of a sudden attacking me more than he ever did."

"I just figured that was part of his personality."

"It is, to an extent. He was essentially trying to mark his territory and he didn't like that you were still so close to me."

Some of the tension went out of my shoulders, "At least he's not trying to use me to get more info about my dad. Let's get back to work."

We made our way back up to the office. I was doing the best I could to keep a level head despite all the curve balls that had been thrown my way. I pulled up the document Lou reminded me of a little earlier and gestured for him to pull up a seat across from me.

"I think if we use a lot of the same science that's here, we can get a device up and running. Do you have any experience creating a device from scratch?"

Lou shook his head, "No, but I do have some engineering experience. Not the most. You're asking someone who runs a pizza joint, remember?"

"Right, right. What was I thinking?"

I leaned back in the chair and scrolled through the document more. The only thing in there that could give us a starting point was the dimensions of the bomb. I looked back at Lou and jokingly said, "We could make the device the same shape as the bomb."

He paused before responding with, "Actually, we could do something like that, but just try to scale it down to whatever size we want."

"We could except there's one thing we're missing."

"What?"

"A lab. Well, there's actually more than one thing missing. We also need all the components that are the right size for the scale we're working with."

Lou grabbed the computer and found some paper. He held up a finger to me making me stop from asking what he was doing and started scribbling with a pencil.

I watched him for a moment before chiming in, "I thought you said you don't have engineering experience. Now you're scribbling away like you know the exact answer."

He kept writing as he said, "I didn't say that I don't have any engineering experience. I said I didn't have the most. I did pick up on some things while working for Warrick, though. If you work for him and are successful, you learn to be sneaky to pick up a few more tools. I can't forget the engineering degree either."

I just nodded, feeling confused. Here Lou was saying he didn't have a lot of engineering experience, but he's knocking this out like it's no problem. The rescaling, the drawings, what needs to go into this device. In all fairness, the document contains a grocery list of what will do the trick for transporting people, but smaller size doesn't necessarily mean we'll be able to find the exact same things.

Lou finally finished, proudly looking up from his work, "I think I got it."

I held out my hand, "Let me see."

He handed over the papers. I didn't know exactly what I was looking at, but I got the gist of it. I looked back up at Lou, "How were you able to do this so quickly?"

Lou shrugged his shoulders, "Math has always been a strong suit of mine. Besides, I've been messing with you. Graduated top of my class and ran circles around the other engineers at Warrick's company."

"That's right. You were able to go from lower level to CTO in no time. Okay, next step is to figure out if there's a secret lab somehow hidden in here or we need to find a space where Warrick won't be able to track us down."

Lou stood up and started looking around. He was pulling books out of the shelves, looking for switches on the book cases, moving chairs and the rug to see if there was a trap door. Meanwhile, I was standing back, watching him to see if he made any progress while also thinking of what my dad would do if he were going to hide something.

I remember him and I always watching *Young Frankenstein*. I don't know why that memory was coming to mind in this moment, but I couldn't help but think of the scene where they hear the violin playing from somewhere behind the wall. *Hold on, there's no way.*

I moved toward one of the light fixtures in between the bookcases. This would be wild. I looked at the light to see if there was anything odd about it that might give it away. When I didn't see anything, I pulled on it. It gave just enough to tell me I could keep pulling. I pulled down on it waiting to hear a click, something that would tell me it was hiding a room. There was nothing. I stood there for a moment, the hope not fully leaving me. I looked over my shoulder at Lou and shrugged. He was watching me expectantly, too.

After a couple more minutes of waiting, I turned to head back over to the desk, "I guess we need to find a lab. Any ideas of where we could go?"

I was met with silence. I turned back to where Lou was standing and he was just staring at the spot I was just at, "Hello? Earth to Lou?"

He pointed to the spot where he was staring. I followed his finger to lay my eyes on an open doorway, "Hold on, what?!" Apparently, my mom and I have been oblivious to everything my dad was doing. I shook my head, "This is something out of a movie."

"Either way, we have a secret room."

"Lead the way."

Lou gave me a confused look for a second before heading through the door. I don't know why, but I wasn't feeling like being the first of us to head in there. I wasn't sure what to expect and I didn't want to see anything that would freak me out.

We descended the stairs in silence. After reaching a certain point on the stairs, the door closed behind us. Lou and I paused for half a second before continuing our journey. We finally reached the bottom of the stairs to be met with a dark room.

"Lou, are you going to turn on the lights?"

"I would if I knew how."

"Start smacking the wall or something."

He grunted. I could hear his hand feeling around on the wall. He took a step out to try to extend his reach and the lights flipped on, "Huh, must have a motion sensor."

I was too busy taking in the scene before me to respond. Everything was shiny and new and it was most definitely a lab. *Problem solved.* It wasn't the most spacious room, which isn't surprising considering it was hidden in the house, but it had state-of-the-art equipment. It was something out of a futuristic movie.

Lou let out a low whistle, "I think we'll have everything we need."

"I guess so," I said in disbelief. How my dad had hid this, I will never understand, but I was thankful in the moment. I stepped further into the room noticing there was a camera feed looking out the front door. I pointed at it, "At least we'll know when we have company."

"Yeah, and it looks like company hasn't left."

I squinted at the feed seeing a car parked on the street with someone watching the house, "Shit. You've got to be kidding me."

"Nope. He knows something's up and he doesn't like it."

I moved to lean against one of the counters crossing my arms as I did so, "You know this means we're going to have to find ways to go to the pizza shop and work, right? If we stay hidden too long, it'll only be a matter of time before he breaks down this door."

"Already ten steps ahead of you. I'm going to bet he's thinking you're holing up with me which is eating him alive."

"I'm hoping that's the case. If it were him trying to get answers to the tech we just discovered, we'd be in a lot more trouble."

We quickly turned our attention back to the lab and started exploring. I don't know what Lou has up his sleeve, but I'm going to trust him entirely on this one. There's not enough room for me to think about anything else.

It didn't take us long to start finding the parts we needed to make our device. We decided to call it quits for the day and start fresh in the morning so we didn't work ourselves too much. We checked the camera feed and saw Warrick had finally left for the evening which made both of us breathe a sigh of relief. We made our way back out to the kitchen, closing everything up.

Leaning on the island, Lou asked, "So, want to make our way to the pizza place after we eat here?"

I shrugged, "Sure. I'll stay over for tonight only. Then, I'll be coming back here."

When Lou gave me a skeptical look, I rolled my eyes and said, "It's only going to add to suspicion if all of a sudden I was spending all my time at the pizza place and not coming back here. He's definitely going to check on this place and it won't help if my house is locked up and dark 24/7."

Lou only held up his hands in defense as he started gathering ingredients for dinner, "Here I thought I'd be getting a couple of days off."

That got a chuckle out of me, "No one's stopping you."

We got to work on dinner and the banter continued back and forth. My mind would occasionally drift to Warrick – *what was I going to do now?* I knew for certain I was going to have to keep up the gimmick of dating him and find a way to break it off easy. It didn't take long before my mind decided to focus on what Warrick's intentions were, though. Did he want to be with me for me? To get to Lou? To try and get the answers he needed to get ultimate power?

Lou and I headed over to his place after getting everything cleaned and locked up. We got in and Lou instantly turned on music. He put his stuff back in his room, grabbing my bag in the process, then came back out to make tea. I decided it would be best for me to stay out of the way, so I made my way over to the couch and sat down to look out the windows. A storm was rolling in, and by the looks of it, it was going to be a big one. Lou joined me, handing me a mug. We sat listening to the music for a little while longer enjoying the small amount of peace we were feeling with the progress we made.

I looked over at Lou and asked, "How strong is your smell?"

He paused before looking at me, "Pretty strong. Why?"

"I was just thinking," I started as I set my mug down on the coffee table. "Can Warrick catch your scent on me with all this extra time we're spending together?"

"Probably," Lou said as he looked away. I could see the gears turning in his mind as he was trying to piece together the reasoning behind my questions. The moment everything clicked into place, Lou whipped his head back around to me, "We need to make sure the normal scents he's used to smelling on you come back."

"That's what I was thinking, but I was also thinking this might help build the story that you and I are becoming closer which may give us more time to build on our head start. It's probably distracting him from continuing his mission."

"Not a bad idea. You should go on another date with him, too."

I looked down into my mug, "Again, I was thinking that, too."

"What's wrong?"

"I wasn't necessarily wanting to continue this façade. It's starting to wear on me. I mean, I told two guys something I very purposefully kept tucked away. Who knows what I might do next?"

Lou reached over to put a comforting hand on my knee, "Hey, I know I appreciated you opening up to me and maybe it'll help you later on even if it doesn't seem like it will now. Don't be afraid to let your walls come down. I'm here for you. I said it from the beginning and I'm not going back on my word now."

I gave him a quick reassuring smile before working on finishing my tea. We didn't say anything more until we got up to put our mugs away. I leaned against the counter as Lou was closing the dishwasher, "I'll stay out here tonight."

"No, you're coming with me."

"That's not going to help with the whole scent thing."

Lou was busying himself with getting everything ready for the night, "You're right, but I'm not letting you sleep on the couch. Trust me, it'll leave your back jacked up for weeks."

I looked at the couch before bringing my gaze back to Lou, "It doesn't look that uncomfortable. Plus, I've slept on it before."

"Well, it is, I know, and I don't want you sleeping on it again."

Before I knew it, or could respond, Lou picked me up and threw me over his shoulder in a fireman's carry. I let out a squeal while I poked his back, "Put me down!"

"Nope."

I knew this was a battle I was going to lose, so I gave up my small protest to let him carry me into his room and plop me on his bed. I let out a sigh shaking my head. When I got up, Lou paused to watch me to make sure I wasn't leaving the room. I held up my hands as I said, "I'm just going to the bathroom to get ready. Calm yourself."

That seemed to do the trick and he let me pass. I went through my nighttime routine then crawled under the covers with Lou not too far behind me. It didn't take long for us to succumb to sleep.

The next morning Lou was already busying himself with breakfast by the time I rolled out of bed. I yawned as I walked down the hallway rubbing sleep out of my eyes.

"Good morning, sunshine."

A rumble of thunder slightly shook the windows. I looked outside to see rain pelting the windows and not an ounce of sun poking its cheery face through the clouds, "There's no sun."

"And?"

"Don't call me sunshine."

He laughed a little pushing a plate towards me with bacon and eggs, "Eat up."

"Thanks," I mumbled as I started to chow down.

Lou grabbed his plate and joined me. We were eating in silence for a little while before Lou broke it, "Don't be late. I'm sure there will be a line of customers waiting out the door and the boss doesn't like tardiness."

I gave him a little salute and headed back to the bathroom to get ready. I wasn't sure how effective the shower was going to be at getting rid of Lou's scent, but I'd at least give it a try.

The pizza place was open and we had a few more customers than usual for the lunch rush. I kept checking the clock as the minutes passed wondering if Warrick would actually make an appearance. I started to head back into the kitchen for a quick break when the door opened and I heard, "Long time, love."

I plastered a smile on my face I hoped was convincing enough to make it seem like I was happy, "I was just beginning to worry I'd have to eat by myself."

Warrick closed the distance enveloping me in a hug, something he didn't normally do. He pulled away but kept his hands on my arms. There was nothing different in his facial expression or body language which told me the shower did enough to squash any of the concerns he had about Lou and I. Warrick let a genuine smile tug at the corner of his lips, "Sorry, love. My calendar won't let me enjoy your company until this evening. Would you join me for dinner?"

"Sure. Is there a dress code?"

He shook his head, "No, we're keeping it casual tonight."

Before I could respond, Lou came up and handed over Warrick's to-go order. Warrick nodded his thanks as he left. I turned to follow Lou back in the kitchen. Once we returned to the kitchen, Lou looked at me with raised eyebrows asking a silent question.

I busied myself as I said, "It worked. I'll be having dinner with him tonight."

"Be careful, Val," Lou said causing me to look up. "Don't let this be a false sense of security."

The dinner rush was more delivery orders than anything which Lou's pack helps out with. I took my cue to get ready and headed over to Warrick's office building. Heading up to his office, I couldn't help but feel a little uneasy remembering the last time I was here and how he treated Daryl. *Was I going to see Daryl still working tonight?*

It didn't take long for my question to get answered. Daryl was busy typing away engrossed in his work. I looked towards Warrick's door for a second to see it was closed, so I didn't want to let myself in quite yet in case I would interrupt something important. I know how much he *loves* that.

I tapped on the door frame of Daryl's office, "Hey, stranger."

He looked up startled before the shock melted into relief, "Hey."

"May I sit or are you running up against a deadline?"

Daryl gestured to the chair on the opposite side of the desk, "By all means."

"How have you been?" I asked, making myself comfortable.

"Good. Job can be stressful, but I don't have too much to complain about. You?"

I looked around a little bit, "I'm happy it seems like you're doing well. I'm doing good. Just trying to get the lay of the land, sort through some things."

As I finished that sentence, I saw him wince. I could tell he was trying to piece together the words he was going to say next, so I waited.

"Look, Val. I'm sorry. I should've never said what I did," he sighed while running a hand through his hair.

I shook my head, "Nothing to be sorry about. We got thrust into a new world trying to figure out what we needed to do to survive. You got the better end of the deal."

"You don't seem to be doing so bad yourself with your boyfriend."

I cut a dangerous look to Daryl warning him to not cross a line. He got the signal and started fidgeting with his mouse to make himself look occupied. He cleared his throat, "Why'd you take a job at the pizza joint across the street instead of something here?"

"Change of pace. I figured that would help me learn where I want to be. Plus, it wouldn't look so good if I was involved with the boss. How is it working for him anyways?"

Daryl shrugged and brought his full attention back to me, "Not bad. Warrick's tough, don't get me wrong, but he's successful for a reason. I figured if I want to see success in this new life, I might as well buckle down and take some notes."

I chuckled a little at that, "Nothing's changed with you, Daryl."

"Sorry for making you wait, love."

Warrick's voice directly behind me made me jump. He had the same effect on Daryl because Daryl wasted no time getting back to work and didn't even try to look in my direction. Warrick placed a protective hand on my shoulder causing me to look up at him, "And sorry for making you jump. Was I interrupting something?"

Chapter 16

There was no reason for me to feel nervous, but every part of me was on edge. Warrick had something dangerous behind his eyes looking at Daryl and the last thing I wanted was for any jealousy to come into play.

I looked at Warrick placing my hand over his, "Did I get here too early?"

I felt some of the tension melt away as Warrick brought his gaze to mine. His eyes softened as he answered, "Right on time. I had a call run a little long, but I think we should be good to go."

I nodded and stood up giving Daryl a quick wave without saying anything else. Warrick moved his hand from my shoulder to the small of my back. He directed me to his office and started working on cleaning everything up. I ran my hand along the back of one of the chairs that sat opposite of him asking, "What's the plan for tonight?"

He was putting the final touches on cleaning up his desk, "I thought I could cook for you giving us a more private venue considering how our last conversation went."

I appreciated the effort because I really didn't want to cry in public again or have anyone hear the questions I was planning on asking him tonight. I may not have been the most enthusiastic about Warrick, but I didn't want to have any negative impacts on his image.

I gave him a warm smile, "I didn't realize you cook."

He leaned into the jab, "I gave my cooks the night off."

We made our way out of the office down to his car to make the trek to his apartment. We pulled into a garage belonging to another tall skyscraper and got into the elevator. Warrick punched the button for the top floor and swiped a badge. *Why am I not surprised?*

The doors opened revealing a modern penthouse with floor to ceiling windows along the outer walls. All the furnishings, artwork, everything was of varying shades of black and gray. The place was immaculate with everything in its place. Where Lou's apartment felt warm and homey, Warrick's was cold and corporate fitting his personality to a tee.

"So, this is what the bat cave looks like?" I asked bringing my attention to Warrick behind me.

His mouth twitched, "Alfred has the night off too."

I wasn't entirely surprised he caught my reference giving his connection to the world I came from, but I was more surprised I used the same reference I had with Lou's apartment. *I need to work on new material.*

Warrick dropped his keys in a dish, "Make yourself at home. I'll get started on dinner."

I nodded and ventured in to his apartment careful not to touch anything in case I knocked something out of place. I started wandering to get more familiar with the layout. The main area was open concept with the kitchen on the opposite side of the windows. There was a giant black leather couch facing a large flat screen TV. A long glass dining room table was behind it with a grand piano in the corner where the windows met. I headed towards the hallway next to the TV to find a large guest bathroom with lots of marble. There were several bedrooms and an office along the hallway leading to the primary. Two of the walls were more windows overlooking the other side of the city and eventually the ocean. There was a large bed facing the windows. To the left of the bed was a door leading into the giant master bath with more windows, a large walk-in shower, a large tub, and the walk-in closet.

I let the smell of food lead me out to the kitchen where Warrick had his sleeves rolled up a little and was getting into his cooking. He looked completely relaxed, the exact opposite of what I had seen back at the office.

I grabbed a seat at the island, "What's for dinner?"

"A specialty of mine, love. We're having some burgers with some flare. Did you enjoy your tour?"

"You have an impressive place here."

"Thanks," he said looking over his shoulder. "You look good in here."

I blushed, not able to bring myself to say anything else for a while.

"Where have you been hiding?"

I looked down at my hands fidgeting a little bit, "I wanted to have some time to myself. Relax a little at home."

"Well, I missed you," he paused waiting for me to respond. When I didn't, he added, "Corny, I know, but surprisingly true."

I got back up and started looking more closely at some of the things he had on his shelves, "Surprisingly?"

"Believe it or not, you do have some sort of hold on me."

That made me pause. "Careful, you're showing some emotions," I said jokingly.

He chuckled and I went back to looking at his shelves. I came across a framed picture of him handing over a giant check,

"Warrick, your charity work. Is that something you do because you need to or because you enjoy it?"

He threw a towel over his shoulder and leaned against the island letting the food do its thing, "I care about my image, but I care more that this community is taken care of. I do a lot more around here than people realize and I like to keep it that way. There's only one thing I do that's super public."

"What's that?" I asked heading back over to the island to take up my seat across from him.

"The summer solstice ball."

"What about it?"

"It's a fundraiser to give back to the organizations around town that help out families in need. We do a silent auction and all ticket sales for the ball contribute, too."

I was genuinely impressed, "Wow, so there is a human behind that cold, hard exterior."

He turned back to check on the food, "I do care, Val. About a lot of things."

"Well, I'm glad you invited me here so I could see more of the human side of you. I'm not the biggest fan of your business side."

"Join the club."

His response made me wonder if he didn't like who he was when he was working, when he was being the alpha.

Before the conversation could continue, he plated our food and took them to the coffee table in front of the couch rather than the dining room. I followed him and took my seat while he grabbed us a couple glasses of wine. I waited to start eating until he returned to his seat next to me.

The moment I took a bite of the burger, flavor exploded in my mouth causing a moan to escape, "There's no way you made this. You must have ordered it from somewhere and made it look like it was from scratch."

"If I would've known my cooking got this kind of response from you, I'd have invited you over sooner."

I gave him a look that got a bark of laughter. In this light, there was a kindness, a gentleness quickly drawing me in. Butterflies started to stir in my stomach and I was finding it very hard to calm them down.

"Thank you for dinner, Warrick. This is nice to be away from everything."

"Anytime, love. This place is my safe haven. It's quiet, no one knows I'm up here because everyone thinks I live in the office, and I can look out to an amazing view."

I nodded my head in agreement letting a comfortable silence fill the space. We stayed there while we finished our meal. Warrick didn't let my wine glass empty making me feel light.

When I finished my plate, I rested my head on his shoulder, "Can werewolves get drunk?"

Warrick placed a hand on my knee, "Don't worry, you're not the only one feeling it. Just takes a little more than normal."

"Good," I said softly lifting my head to look at him. He was very handsome with blue eyes that sucked you in. He was returning my gaze, causing heat to rise to my cheeks and my lips to part. Warrick leaned in bringing his hand up to my cheek. His lips met mine and I wasn't sure if it was mostly the wine or something else, but all the butterflies took flight.

Warrick was the first one to pull away. He rested his forehead against mine, "Love."

I could tell he was trying to hold himself back.

"I have to be careful around you. You're dangerous."

That caught me off-guard. *Me? Dangerous?* That's something coming from him.

"How am *I* dangerous?"

He laid back on the couch with his eyes closed, "You're making me feel things I haven't ever felt."

I playfully punched him in the arm, "You're saying that to get laid."

It didn't take long for him to move so that he was on top of me. A little playful growl escaped his lips, "Is it working?"

I tapped my cheek with my finger before responding, "No."

He nipped at my neck, "That's too bad."

Warrick returned back to how he was sitting before and grabbed his wine. I sat back up taking another long drink. I got up to go find my way to a bathroom to put some space between us and to calm down the butterflies. I ended up venturing to his home office letting curiosity get the best of me and I moved to look at the papers on his desk. There were printed articles about me, magazine covers featuring my face, all things I hadn't seen before. *Why the hell was I plastered all over these?*

There were headlines claiming I was missing and highlighting my relations with a high-ranking military official who was crucial to our progress in the war. I scoffed reading that knowing the real truth behind it. In the articles, Warrick had the date I disappeared circled along with the company I worked for. Before I could read too much more of these, I heard Warrick approaching.

"Val?"

"In here."

I turned so I faced the door and made sure I was holding the papers. When Warrick appeared and saw what I was holding, the color in his face drained.

"What the hell are these?"

"It's nothing," he said slowly walking towards me.

"You're saying me being plastered over all these magazines and articles from where I came from is nothing? How did you get these?"

Warrick carefully took the papers from my hand setting them on the desk, "Love, I don't know if I want to get into this now. Please," he pleaded. "Let's go back out there."

I didn't press the issue any further because I knew all the answers to my questions. There was just a small part of me wanting to hear him confess everything, but I'd let this pass for now.

"Fine. This isn't over, though," I said making my way out to the main room letting the fight drop from my shoulders.

I made my way back to my glass and threw rest of the wine back. Warrick was back in the kitchen prepping more food showing no signs of frustration or anger from me snooping around. While he did that, I wandered over to the piano and started to trace the keys occasionally letting myself put more pressure to let the soothing sound of music dance in the air. To distract me from my emotions.

Warrick glanced up at me, "Do you play?"

"Not for a while. What are you making?"

"Something I hope will get you to forget what you saw in my office."

Curiosity moved my legs toward the kitchen island where there was a wonderful dessert waiting. I had no idea what it was, but I could tell it was a type of chocolate cake with homemade whipped cream. Warrick met me so we were on the same side and fed me a bite.

Damn him and his good cooking. Another moan escaped despite my best efforts to hold it back, getting a smile from Warrick. He put down the fork and grabbed his own dish to join me in devouring this dessert, sliding over a couple glasses of dessert wine.

While I was getting lost in the food and wine again, Warrick looked over with pensive look. I wiped my face just in case I had any evidence of his dessert lingering, "What?"

"There's nothing between you and Lou, right?"

I forced out some laughter, "No, I find him annoying."

I hoped that answer was convincing because I wasn't sure I was able to convince myself.

Still looking at me with the same wary expression, "And whatever was between you and Daryl is done?"

"There's nothing between Daryl and I. Why do you ask?"

"He talks about you quite a bit actually and he didn't hold back on telling your history."

I blushed a little looking down. I wasn't quite sure how to respond to that, but everything in his body language was telling me Daryl didn't hold back any of the details.

My phone started to buzz on the counter and we both looked at it. I internally cringed when I saw Daryl's name pop up on the screen. I didn't need to look at Warrick to know he was watching me with a fiery intensity. I excused myself and answered the phone, making my way back to the master bedroom so I could put as much distance between myself and Warrick as possible.

"Daryl, why are you calling me?"

"I wanted to make sure you were okay," he trailed off.

I sighed, "I'm fine. I don't need you to look out for me. Please, don't call me."

There was a pause before Daryl stammered, "I-I'm sorry. Things felt tense back at the office and I got worried. That's all."

"I appreciate the concern, but I'm good. I can take care of myself. Bye, Daryl. Go have some fun."

I didn't give him a chance to respond before I hung up the phone. I sat on the corner of the bed sighing as I took in the view. The sun was starting to set, dancing off the ocean in the distance. I could hear the piano playing softly from the hallway, so I made my way out there to make sure I didn't spend too long away from Warrick.

I found Warrick sitting at the piano gracefully playing a soft melody, watching his own hands move along the keys.

"I thought you said there wasn't anything between you and Daryl."

I watched his face as I responded, "Warrick, there isn't. He made that clear to me and I don't tend to hang on to what could have been."

Warrick didn't stop playing. He took a second to answer as though working through how he wanted this conversation to go. I heard a sigh followed by him saying, "I don't like secrets, love. That's all."

I scoffed at him, "Don't like secrets? You're the one hanging on to magazines and articles from where I came from and you don't want to spill the beans."

I closed the distance between us and leaned against the piano. I was annoyed at him telling me he doesn't like secrets when he carries the most between us.

Warrick winced stopping the music, "You're right. I have no business trying to get everything I can out of you when I am not willing to do the same."

"Well, I'm happy you can at least admit that."

He gestured for me to sit next to him and I instinctively placed my hands on the keys mirroring the song he was playing. Warrick looked over at me with a slow, apologetic smile spreading on his face. He kept inching closer to me until he was reaching over my arms to continue the song. The agitation melting away from me with each note, I stole another glance. This man who I thought had no ounce of human in him was showing sides of himself he kept tucked away. It was hard not to let the butterflies stretch their wings for a few moments in this situation. I looked back down at the piano keys in front of me and reminded myself that despite his hospitality, there was still a lot he was holding back. He had a reason for doing so, too, and one that he isn't quite ready to share yet.

I pulled my arms away, finishing my contribution to the song. Warrick also stopped and looked at me with a concerned expression, "Is something wrong, love?"

"Nothing."

He placed a hand on my arm, "Will you please stay?"

The gesture vaguely reminded me of Lou, making something in my heart ache a little. *Can I not just have some peace, heart?*

My shoulders relaxed and I didn't realize I was holding on to so much tension. I nodded my head, "Sure, but I'm going to run to the bathroom."

I needed a second to regain my composure if I was going to be staying here.

I closed the door behind me and rested my elbows on the counter taking a few deep breaths. I felt my phone buzz in my back pocket feeling the annoyance from earlier seep back in. I pulled my phone out to find a text from Lou asking if I was okay. *Between Daryl and Lou, their ears must be burning.* I sent a quick response back that I was fine and most likely staying over for the night. I put my phone back and ran the water for a second to splash some on my face.

After drying my face off, I made my way back out to where we were. Warrick was still at the piano playing a different tune this time. I sat on the couch watching him a second before asking, "What's the deal between you and Lou?"

Still not missing a beat, Warrick answered with another question, "What makes you ask that, love?"

"More for curiosity. And to understand a little bit of the dynamic."

"From day one, Lou impressed me with how he carried himself. He was driven, a hard worker, someone I could trust that wouldn't ask too many questions. He also helped the company take off. Don't get me wrong, I pushed him a lot of the time, but that was so I could understand how far he was willing to take things. Lou stood his ground."

"Then you changed him. Why?" I interjected.

Warrick glanced at me before returning his gaze back to the piano, "Because I saw him as someone who would be a valuable member to the pack. What I wasn't expecting was how quickly he gained strength. He was quickly starting to match my power and I wasn't ready to have someone overthrow me."

"So, you kicked him out of the pack. Why didn't you just end him?"

That question made him pause. He resumed playing, but this time the song changed to something with a little more anger behind it, "I physically couldn't. I had conditioned him to fear me, so that kept him from realizing what he was capable of. I didn't forget that, though, which is why I had to keep reminding him why he was scared of me."

"Is that why you killed his lover?"

Warrick chuckled at my word choice, "Part of the reason, yes. You know the other part. Lou learned a lot during his time working with me and I know he tries to use that knowledge against me at times, but again, he doesn't fully realize what he can do. I'd like to keep it that way."

I was surprised at how open Warrick was being on a topic that clearly bothered him. I knew this was going to be good information to take back to Lou, but I wasn't sure if that was the best plan. While I buried my internal battle deep within me, I said, "Well, thank you for sharing something difficult with me. Helps with the secrets you're hiding away from me."

That got a wink out of him despite the shadow remaining on his face. Warrick went back to playing a slow song again, allowing that to be the only sound filling the room.

I got up and went back to the kitchen to fill up my glass again then made my way over to the windows to take in the view of the stars and moon as they filled the sky. The moon at this point was almost full reminding me werewolves would be wandering soon.

"What's on your mind, love?"

I took a small sip of wine and turned with a soft smile on my face, "Nothing. Just enjoying the evening with you."

Warrick nodded his head as a way to show agreeance, but it wasn't convincing enough for me to believe him. I made my way back over to him, held his chin in between my index finger and thumb to turn his attention to me, "You seem to be the one with something on your mind."

"I've told you everything that's occupying my mind tonight, love. You don't need to worry about me."

I leaned in and gave him a slow, searching kiss as a way to ease any suspicions that may be lingering. It didn't take long for him to respond and we made our way back to the couch to continue what we had started earlier. The heat was increasing between the two of us, and instead of getting caught up in the moment like I could so easily do, I put a hand on Warrick's chest.

He looked at me, confused, "Is something wrong?"

"Not at all. I'm feeling tired, that's all. I think I'm going to head to bed."

The confused look stayed on his face, but he sat back, "Okay, not a bad idea."

I made my way to one of the bathrooms to start getting ready to sleep and was happy he didn't try to push me more. At least he knew how to respect boundaries.

I headed into one of the guest rooms and started to get under the covers. Warrick made an appearance in the doorway leaning against the frame. He had also made quick work of getting ready for bed.

"Why don't you come with me, love?"

"You sure are calling me love a lot tonight."

He gave a low chuckle, "Take it as a sign of how much I enjoy your company." Warrick nodded his head towards his room before continuing, "Seriously, come with me."

I wasn't entirely sure if I wanted to join him. I gave Warrick a quick glance to see if he caught my reluctance and saw a quick shadow cross his face. Knowing that he was already filled with suspicions around my loyalty, I got up. I couldn't give him the chance to lash out because he doesn't think I'm into him. There was too much risk with that.

He led the way to his room, turning out the lights as I made my way to the bed. We both laid down and as soon as my head hit the pillow, I could feel sleep trying to take over.

Warrick was facing me and traced my jawline with his thumb, "Goodnight, love."

My eyelids drooped right as I mumbled, "Goodnight."

Chapter 17

I woke up to an empty space next to me. I rolled onto my back staring at the ceiling for a while reflecting on last night. Warrick's hard exterior fell showing me the more human side of him again which was hard to ignore. *I can't fall for this.*

I headed out to the kitchen to see Warrick manning the stove with fruit laid out on the counter. I dived right in mumbling good morning and my thanks. He turned around and braced himself with both hands on the island, "Anytime, love. I have to get going soon, but there's something I've been wanting to ask you."

Before giving him the chance to continue, "You're going to leave me here?"

"No," he dropped his head with a chuckle. "I was giving you a head's up. Are you sure there's nothing between you and Daryl?"

I was surprised by his question omitting Lou. I responded, "Getting straight to the point. As I told you before, there's nothing."

He turned back to the stove to finish whatever he was cooking and served it up, "I'll take your word for it."

"Why do you ask?"

"Do you know you talk in your sleep?" he asked as he came over to join me so we could eat.

I looked down in my lap blushing. *Damn my subconscious.* I looked back at him to find his icy blue gaze piercing through me,

"Warrick, whatever I said in my sleep is not the case. At most, it was me reliving a memory I want to forget."

"I'll take your word for it," he said without breaking eye contact. This felt as though it was a challenge and I wasn't going to back down. I also couldn't tell if he was lying in his response or if he was actually going to trust me.

We left with him dropping me at a closed pizza place and him zooming to his parking garage. All of the good feelings from last night were being clouded over by a storm starting to brew and I couldn't help but feel worried.

I tried the front door to find it unlocked. That pushed away all of my other concerns to replace them with a whole new one – why did Lou leave the door unlocked if the place was closed?

"Lou? Hello?"

The restaurant was dark, chairs still on the tables, nothing out of place. I made my way back to the kitchen to find it cold and untouched. There were still a few hours before we opened, but the front door being unlocked made my stomach stir. I checked the door that led up the stairs to his apartment. Also unlocked. The hairs on the back of my neck stood up even further, raising more alarms. He wasn't one to just leave things open. I quickened my pace up the stairs, and just as I was about to test the door to Lou's apartment to see if that was unlocked too, Lou yanked the door open.

There were still signs of sleep in his half-opened eyes, but aside from that, he was fine.

"Everything okay, Val?"

I let out a sigh of relief, "Everything is now. Why were all the doors unlocked?"

Lou skirted past me heading down to the restaurant, "I left them open for you. I wanted to make sure you had a way to get back in if you needed to escape. Did you lock them behind you?"

"No, I was more making sure you were okay and that Warrick didn't send any goons after you."

He disappeared in the main dining area to lock the front door and came back to stand at the foot of the stairs looking at me incredulously, "You think his 'goons' could take me on?"

I threw my hands up, "I don't know! You tell me to be cautious around him all the time and that he's not afraid to hold anything back."

Lou took slow steps towards me with a concerned look replacing his previous one, "Val, is everything okay? You seem kind of jumpy. What happened?"

I crossed my arms nervously rubbing them, "Nothing serious. When he dropped me off, I felt unsettled, that's all."

"Clearly unsettled enough to feel worried about me."

I looked away from Lou, "You're not the only one I'm worried about."

Lou placed his hand on the small of my back to guide me back to his apartment. Once in his place, I took my usual seat while he made his way to his room to go back to sleep leaving me alone with my thoughts.

After a few minutes, I could hear some light snores from his room indicating he was back to sleep. I got up and made myself a cup of tea as quietly as I could trying to let a sleeping dog lie, as the saying goes.

I sipped on my tea letting my thoughts roam wild. Between Daryl, Lou, Warrick, and my dad, there was plenty to try and sort out. I wasn't sure what my gut was trying to tell me, but

I knew it wasn't anything good. I didn't like how Warrick continued asking about the other men in my life, especially Daryl. Daryl may have pushed me away, but I still felt the need to look out for him. The magazines and articles Warrick had about me on his desk didn't sit well with me either. He was hiding something and didn't want to dive into the truth with me.

Lou came back out looking a little more awake this time and started a pot of coffee. With his back turned to me, he asked, "So, a night with Warrick and you survived."

"You sound surprised."

"He doesn't seem like the type to just cuddle up and enjoy a cozy night in," Lou said as a sipped on his coffee and took his place next to me on the couch.

"He actually opened up a bit and revealed a softer side again."

Lou's eyebrows raised, "Again?"

I nodded and drank some more of my tea, "Anyways, what's the plan?"

"I'll open for a little bit and we can work the lunch shift. I've talked with some of my wolves to see if they can run things for the rest of the night and next couple of days so we can keep working in the lab. Time is of the essence now."

I gave him a half-hearted thumbs up and headed towards to the kitchen to clean everything up so we could get moving on the day. There was an hour before the restaurant opened, so we needed to start on the prep work. I was also busying myself to keep Lou from asking more questions.

We got into our easy rhythm of getting everything ready for the lunch shift and prepping pizzas for the dinner rush. I was watching the hands move in their usual dance around the clock knowing Warrick would be picking up his lunch order soon. As if on cue, the door opened and I made my way out with his usual order of a large to-go pizza. Warrick was standing there leaning against the bar with a large gift bag. He met my gaze and a smile etched its way across his face. I returned the smile noticing his wasn't fully sincere which added to the dread inching its way into my gut.

"Gift exchange?" I asked holding up his lunch looking down at the gift bag.

"I would love to be around when you open this, but I unfortunately need to grab the food and run. Lunch meeting, love."

I exchanged the pizza for the gift bag noticing it was on the heavier side. He kissed my cheek before making his way out the door. I stood there for a moment before placing the bag on the bar and Lou came out to join me. Lou looked at the bag and back at me, "You going to open it?"

"Sure."

I dug into the tissue paper pushing it aside to find the gift. My fingers brushed against something that felt like hair making me jump a little. *What the - ?* I put the gift on the nearest chair to give me a better vantage point and stuck both hands in the bag. When I felt the hair again, I inched my fingers down further to feel ears.

"No ... no, no, no, no."

Lou went on full alert, "What's wrong?"

When I didn't answer, didn't look at him, he got even more concerned, "Val, what is going on? What's in the bag?"

I reached back in despite everything in me telling me not to and pulled out the object of the bag. Looking at it without tissue paper obscuring the full view, I saw it was Daryl's head. His lifeless eyes were staring right back at me. Everything drained from my body. One of my best friends was now dead and I was holding his head.

Lou didn't miss a beat and grabbed the head to shove it back in the bag. I was frozen in my spot when Lou came back to me. He grabbed my head with both of his hands trying to get my eyes to meet his, "Look at me, Val. This is Warrick's game. He's trying to attack you so you'll have nowhere else to turn but him. I'm here for you. I'll do anything you need, but I need you to say something, anything."

My eyes slowly made their way to meet his, "I have a plan, but I need your help with getting a few things first."

He nodded pulling me into a long hug. Every piece of me was starting to break. So, these were Warrick's true colors. Nothing seems to have changed at all from when he would play these games with Lou when he didn't get his way. Unlike Lou, though, I was going to find a way to strike back and the first step to do that was to make myself numb.

A few hours later, I got myself all dolled up in a suit with a fresh face of makeup with a gift of my own for Warrick. I had to push away the feelings of sadness. I would have time to grieve Daryl's loss later tonight.

I took a deep breath as I watched the elevator doors close. I heard the familiar ding and made my way out of the elevator towards Warrick's office. I resisted the urge to look over at Daryl's now empty office and instead focused my attention on

Warrick's admin sitting outside his closed doors. She started to tell me I couldn't go in, but I stopped her with a wink as I pushed open the doors.

"Closed doors means I'm –"

Warrick started to get ready to yell at whoever was walking through the doors until he laid eyes on me. I made my way to his desk and sat in the chair across from him. This time, a sinister smile took hold of Warrick's face, "To what do I owe the pleasure of this visit, love?"

I looked at my nails to make it seem like I wasn't that interested in him, "Just thought I would thank you for the gift in person."

"Ah," Warrick said as he leaned back in his chair. "What did you think?"

I cut a look towards him, "I'm not the biggest fan of people who don't trust my word."

That response caught him off-guard. He took a few moments trying to gather his thoughts before responding, "I just thought I would take care of any impediments to our relationship."

I stood up and made my way to his side of the desk sitting down next to where his chair was, "Funny. It seems like you're more jealous than anything."

"I'm not the biggest fan of sharing. I was getting tired of hearing water cooler conversations about his feelings for you."

I leaned closer to him, "Is that the truth?"

"I like this cold side to you, love. I could get used to this."

I let out a bark of laughter, "Of course you could. You still didn't answer my question."

Warrick leaned in so there were only inches between us, "Would I tell you any different?"

There was a dangerous electricity starting to fill the air between us. I chose to ignore that for the moment, "Then tell me why you have a bunch of things at your place with my face on it."

He leaned back putting more space between us allowing for more room for the electricity. Warrick looked around gathering his words before starting, "I'm going to dive right into this because I have a meeting in the next ten minutes and don't have time to keep beating around the bush with you."

That caused the hairs on the back of my neck to ripple.

Warrick continued, "I've been in contact with your dad and know all about the bombs that brought you here. Considering he's the creator of them, I saw the opportunity to get with you as a way to have an upper hand over him to continue growing my pack in other worlds. After all, you are daddy's little girl and I could get whatever I want by leveraging you. I didn't account for the fact I would actually develop feelings for you."

"Why is it not enough for you to be in charge of this world?"

"You really have to ask this question? Have you not learned anything about me?"

I didn't budge holding my gaze.

"Alright. Ultimate power. I see something and I go after it. Now I'm hoping I'll be able to get the missing pieces for a device so I can finally hop between worlds."

It didn't take long for the slime to return. That wasn't news to me, but it sure felt good to finally hear the truth come from his lips. I needed to keep going while he was still in the mood to spout the truth. "Warrick, if you have feelings for me, then why kill someone and give me their head?"

"Because, I needed to know if you were serious. You showing up here tells me you are."

I stood up and walked over to the windows trying to compose myself, "You have a twisted way of going about things, you know that?"

"I made sure to take away something that would impact us."

"You couldn't take my word?"

"Love, you didn't see the way you two were looking at each other yesterday in his office. I didn't want you to have an excuse to run back to him."

"You do realize that by killing him, you've now pushed me away."

That got a growl out of him. Warrick moved so fast out of his chair I didn't have any time to react before he had me pressed against the window. "Wrong. This is how it's going to go. You're going to continue dating me. You'll quit your job at the pizza place otherwise Lou is next. I'm going to get what I need from your dad and I'm going to continue growing my power."

"I thought you couldn't take Lou?"

My question only provoked Warrick more earning me his forearm pressed against my throat. Good to know I can get under his skin.

"Watch me."

"Why?" I croaked.

His icy blue eyes turned icier taking on the color of his wolf's eyes, "Why what?"

I tried to wiggle looser from his grip to make it easier to talk, "Why go through all of this effort? Why not just back down and we could live a life of bliss?"

He only pressed harder, the growl still in his voice, "You make me crazy. You also just said I've pushed you away. I need you not only for my plan, but to stop the hole in my chest from getting bigger."

Warrick pushed off me and went back to his seat. I took a moment to catch my breath and straighten my blazer before walking back over to Warrick in his chair, "So you admit you have feelings?"

"I didn't realize that wasn't clear. I can't let Lou win again and I already took out my other competition."

"Again, why do you let Lou have such a hold over you?"

A deep growl emanated from his chest in response.

"Warrick, you handle things like a little brat, except one who knows how to kill. If you think I'm going to stand here and let you keep threatening me and others, you're dead wrong. Until you figure out how to keep this side of you in check, I'm done."

I made a move to stand up, hoping he would react in the way I expected him to.

Warrick reached out and grabbed my wrist, "No. You don't just get to walk away. Not like this."

Just as I thought. "You don't control me, Warrick."

His grip tightened and started to hurt, "Maybe I don't, but if I can't have you, no one can. I'll make sure of it."

That line set me off. I reached behind me with my free hand and in one swift movement, I plunged a knife into Warrick's thigh. He let out a scream and let go of me causing me to stumble back. I made sure to get his desk in between us again and to put myself closer to the door to hopefully allow for a quick escape. Warrick was still distracted by the knife trying to find a way to grab a hilt. Every time he grabbed on to it, he let out a yelp. Finally, he looked at me with eyes full of rage and wolf.

"What the hell is this?!"

"You're not the only one who plays dirty."

Warrick made a move to stand up and sat back down immediately before trying again. He whipped his head back up at me letting out another growl. He tried grabbing the knife's hilt again to pull it out, but let go as soon as he had wrapped his fingers around it. Through clenched teeth, he asked the question again, "What the hell is this, Val?"

"It really works."

"What does?"

I curled my lip, "Silver."

I turned to leave the office while Warrick kept struggling. I didn't want to waste any more time with putting as much distance between myself and a very angry alpha. I knew my time would be limited to get back to Lou, so I ripped off my heels and started running towards the stairs. *Can't waste time waiting for the elevator.* It also wouldn't take long for his pack to realize he was in pain making me not want to be here when they rushed to their alpha's side.

I got across the street and burst through the door of Lou's restaurant. There were a couple of customers trying to enjoy lunch when Lou poked his head out from the kitchen. I mouthed sorry to the customers and ran back to the kitchen.

Lou's eyes were clouded with worry and searching me to see if any harm had come my way. His hands made his way to my shoulders while he checked me over. His gaze lingered on my neck where I'm sure it was starting to bruise from Warrick pinning me, but other than that, I had escaped free of serious damage. I shook my head to tell him I was fine before saying, "You need to get your pack here to run the rest of the day. We need to go to the lab, now!"

"I take it you were able to deal some damage?"

I nodded my head putting my hands on his that were still on my shoulders, "Thank you for helping me get everything together so quickly. Do you still have the bag from him?"

I couldn't bring myself to admit Daryl's head was still in there despite having seen it earlier in the day. Lou reached down and lifted it up. He paused for a second lifting his head up to smell the air. He brought his gaze back to me, "Head upstairs and take this with you. Don't move until I come up there. Lock the door. Call this number when you're up there." Lou handed me a piece of paper and turned towards the dining area taking a deep breath.

I knew I didn't have the biggest lead on Warrick, so this was only a matter of time before someone came to hunt me down. I turned to make my way up the stairs and as soon as my foot touched the first step, I heard the front door slam open.

"Where is she, Lou?!"

The voice made me move in double time. I got to the apartment door closing it as gently as I could behind me to not draw any attention to myself. I unfolded the note from Lou. The number he told me to call was on there, but so was a quick instruction to log in to his computer to access the security system in the pizza place to see what was going down. I dialed the number while waiting for the computer to load. There was a voice on the other side of the line sounding a little confused by an unknown number calling them.

"This is Val. Lou is tied up right now, but is asking that you come now to finish out the day in the restaurant."

There was no response outside of the line going quiet indicating the call had ended. Lou must've given some sort of warning because that was the quickest phone call I'd ever had.

I put my phone down in time to see the cameras and mics had finally loaded. Warrick and Lou were the only ones left in the dining area meaning Warrick's entrance scared away the rest of the patrons. I was a little surprised Warrick was the one who showed his face here rather than sending someone from his pack to take care of business. When I left him, he wasn't moving too well, but it looks like the knife was removed despite the wound still bleeding. *Guess he hasn't figured out a way to minimize his weakness to silver.* Given the amount of blood still coming out of the hole, I must've hit a good spot.

They stood there for a moment – Lou calm and collected where Warrick's eyes were wild, his body language showed every one of his muscles ready for attack. Lou broke the silence, "I have no idea who you're talking about."

"*Bullshit!*" Warrick yelled letting it fill the space they were in. I flinched, but Lou's body language remained unchanged. "Where is the little bitch?"

"This is very reminiscent of another conversation we've had before."

Warrick took a step closer to Lou who still held his ground, "Stop playing games."

"I'm not the one playing."

"I don't have time for this."

Lou shrugged, "Alright, Warrick, who are you looking for?"

This just made Warrick shake from anger, "You know damn well who I'm looking for."

I got up and double checked the locks on the front door to make sure they were secure. I grabbed the laptop heading back towards Lou's room to hide myself in his closet, closing the door to add one additional barrier. I buried myself under his clothes and turned down the volume just in case werewolf hearing was better than I originally thought. Overreaction? Maybe, but I didn't want to take too many chances. I turned my attention back to the scene unfolding in front of me just in time to catch Lou's response.

"Warrick, I'm going to need a name. You tend to get confused when you're like this."

Warrick erupted with frustration letting animal noises escape. He limped his way over to Lou and grabbed him by his shirt lifting him off the ground. Warrick let out another snarl before slamming Lou down on the bar. Lou looked unphased as Warrick got in his face, "Val, dammit. Where. Is. Val?!"

"You chased her away. Your choice to hold back the truth, to play her made her leave. I have no idea where she's at."

Warrick let go of Lou backing away careful not to turn his back on him. Lou got up and brushed himself off while looking at the bar where he was just at, "You cracked my bar ... I'm adding that to your tab."

"Why can't you take anything seriously? I need you to tell me where she's at. I know you know because she came back over here."

Lou casually drew his gaze back to Warrick, "Oh, I'm taking this seriously. You just can't see past your rage. Are you going to kill her like you've done before? As a way to get back at me and prove a point? That's just going to hurt you in the long run."

I drew in a breath. I don't know why, but I was hoping Lou at least felt something for me with those cozy nights we spent together. With the kiss we shared. His cold response told me the exact opposite. *Pull it together, Val.*

Warrick shook his head, "No. I'm going to make her feel the same pain she's been making me feel since she walked up to me. It's going to be long and *slow.*"

He said that last part between clenched teeth, sending shivers down my spine. I had no idea what he had in store for me, but I wasn't going to let Warrick have a chance to do anything.

Warrick continued, "I need her to carry out my plan. She's my leverage."

"You're sounding unhinged right now," Lou said holding up his hands as a way to show Warrick he meant no harm.

That had the opposite effect on Warrick. He took a deep breath, slicking his hair back as he exhaled. Going through these motions brought about some composure. No longer was there a wild-eyed Warrick, but instead the collected business man I was used to seeing standing in his place.

"You're right. My apologies Lou," Warrick turned to make his way back out of the restaurant. "I'll take your word for now, but if I find her and find out you've been lying, you'll both have hell to pay."

With that, Warrick was gone. Lou stood there for a few moments looking like he was trying to figure out what just happened and what his next steps should be. The pack member I called along with a couple others walked in. They paused seeing Lou standing in the middle of the dining room.

"What's up, boss? Everything okay?"

Lou looked at the woman I spoke to on the phone and nodded. He paused a few more moments still collecting himself until he responded, "Yeah. For tonight, just be careful with the bar. We'll keep her closed up for the next couple of days since the change will be happening." He pointed at the cracked portion of the bar, only getting nods from his pack before he turned around to head upstairs to find me.

I stared at the screen a little longer in a trance. I'm almost certain Warrick was going to kill me if he got his hands on me. I started to shake as the adrenaline left my system allowing all the emotions from today to flood me. Tears started to fall as I curled myself in ball within the nest of Lou's clothes. It was safe to come out, but I wasn't ready to yet.

The front door opened then closed followed by footsteps.

"Val?"

Even though I knew it was Lou, I couldn't bring myself to emerge. His footsteps got closer, pausing only to check the bathroom before making his way to his room. The door opened while Lou's voice softly called out, "Val? You in here?"

I remained where I was still unable to move while the tears continued. The door to the closet opened bringing some light into my dark space. Lou started sifting through the pile of clothes I hid myself under until he freed my head. He gently lifted my chin up so we could look at each other. He crouched down putting his arms around me so he could scoop me up.

"Shh, I got you now. I promised I would keep you safe and I'm not about to go back on that now."

He sat on his bed with me still in his arms stroking my hair trying to bring me some comfort. Feeling the safety that came with his arms, I lowered the flood gates to let the tears flow freely.

When the tears stopped long enough for me to gather a breath, I moved my head to look up at Lou, "I think we should go to my place now."

"Let's go."

He loosened his grip on me so I could uncurl myself and get on my two feet. Lou grabbed an already packed overnight bag and led the way out of his apartment. He was purposefully blocking any view of me from his wolves as we made it in to the kitchen so they couldn't admit to knowing my whereabouts if Warrick came back in a rage.

Once in his car, we quickly made our way to my house sitting in silence. I looked over at Lou to see if I could see any signs of the altercation from earlier. He looked fine aside from the spots of blood here and there. I reached out to touch one of those spots, "Did you get hurt?"

He looked down to where my fingers rested, "No. That's from Warrick thanks to the damage you did to him."

I kept looking at the blood, "You got me the knife."

We passed my house to make sure there wasn't anyone hiding out and turned back around after confirming the coast was clear. Lou pulled into the tight space in the garage and cut the engine as the door closed behind us. He looked back at me, "You knew where to do the most damage. You lodged it pretty deep in his thigh. It'll take a while for anyone, including someone as powerful as Warrick, to heal from that one."

I just nodded my head and let myself out of the car to go into the house. I checked to make sure all the curtains were still drawn then curled up on the couch. Lou ended up on the couch with me putting his arm around me, "I'll have some guys locate Daryl's body so we can give him a proper burial. For now, his head is in my apartment freezer so it doesn't decay too much."

I nodded my head again afraid that if I uttered just one word, I would lose it all over again. Lou picked up on my signal that I didn't want to talk too much letting silence blanket us.

We sat like that for hours. Me, unable to bring myself to talk about all the things running through my mind and what happened, Lou being patient and understanding about me needing to process. The sun was setting by the time I sat up.

"You hungry?" Lou asked rubbing my arm.

"Sure."

I made my way into the kitchen pulling food out of the freezer and fridge, going through the motions. Lou started to help, but I put my hand on his chest to stop him. I pointed over to the chairs on the opposite side of the island where he headed over to get comfortable. I busied myself with prepping dinner, purposefully avoiding looking at Lou.

"I know it's hard right now, but it will help to talk about this," he said picking up on my reluctance.

"I guess." I said mostly to test out my ability to talk and not succumb to tears again.

"Let's start with what happened in his office."

Thankful to not be starting with the "gift" Warrick decided to give me I started, "Okay. I walked in there and started questioning why he didn't trust me. He figured he was doing me a favor by taking Daryl out as he only viewed him as a blocker for our relationship. When I was at his apartment, I found a whole bunch of the articles and pictures we found when we got into my dad's computer and Warrick couldn't answer why he had those then, so I took a shot to ask him about those again since he wanted to bring up the topic of trust. He wasn't a big fan of me calling him out. Warrick also admitted he was using me to get what he wants from my father – more power. It's just as we thought, Lou. He wants access to all the different worlds to grow his power."

I paused catching my breath and letting some of that sink in. Lou nodded at me to continue.

"He also admitted he was starting to grow feelings for me, so I did my best to shut things down. As soon as he told me no one else could have me, I stabbed him. I must've done a better job of letting my anger take over because I got it lodged in there deep. I got out of there after that. I wasn't going to be hanging around to give him a chance at me."

The shivers from earlier came back keeping me from saying anything else. Lou just continued nodding while he was deciphering what I told him, "I haven't seen him that crazed in a very long time. Whatever you said worked. You got under his skin."

"He just flipped. Complete 180 from who he was the night before," I said distantly, recalling how human Warrick had seemed at this apartment.

"That's his specialty."

I finished making dinner rather than responding. We ate in silence with the clanking of our silverware being the only sounds filling the house. As soon as I finished, I headed up to my dad's office to get back on his computer not entirely sure what I was looking for. Lou took care of cleaning things up and checking the security of the house before following me into the office.

I got into my dad's email to see a new conversation started by Warrick. This one started off by asking why my dad sent me and my friends here while also talking about how he was going to torture me unless my dad gave him the information he needed to create the device Lou and I started on. My dad's reply stopped me dead in my tracks. It sure didn't take long for Warrick to try to strike.

"Val, what is it?"

"I – I can't believe what I'm reading," I stammered.

Lou focused all his attention on me, "Something new?"

I nodded my head prompting Lou to come over behind me to read it. It took him less time to read what was on the screen, "Is this saying what I think it is?"

"Yes."

The numbness from earlier was coming back. I told myself it needed to stay this time. Feeling the pain, confusion, anger, and everything else from the day was too much for me to handle.

I looked back down at my dad's reply to Warrick to make sure I understood everything I was reading. My dad admitted to sending me here, but had no way of knowing my friends were going to be with me. He followed that by saying whatever upper hand Warrick has is gone and to do whatever he wants to me. My dad just gave Warrick the green light to kill me.

Chapter 18

I woke up the next morning still feeling numb. I had no idea what I was going to do now that there was nothing holding Warrick back. It's one thing to see my dad admit he knew he was sending me somewhere new, but it's entirely different from him flat out not caring about whether I lived or died.

I slowly lifted myself to a sitting position wiping the sleep out of my eyes trying to figure out what my next steps were going to be. I knew for certain I would be pouring myself into creating the device to start working my way out of here. The more distance between Warrick and myself, the better. I looked around at my room taking in everything that had accumulated here over the years. Was my life a lie?

Before I could continue down that train of thought, my door opened with a soft knock, "Val, you up? I brought some food."

"Yeah," I mumbled in reply.

Lou poked his head in the gap he created and nodded his head. He pushed the door open completely using his back since he was carrying a tray of food. His hearing picked up on the subtle noise emanating from my stomach and raised his eyebrows, "I take it you're hungry."

It wasn't a question which stopped me in my tracks from replying. I gave him a quick glare, but appreciatively took the food. He sat on the same side of the bed I was on and watched as I dived in.

"Did you get anything to eat yet?" I asked with a mouth full of fruit.

Lou nodded his head, "Yeah. I just wanted to make sure you were taken care of before hopping back in the lab."

"Back?"

"Since tonight is a full moon, I wanted to get a head start on making progress. Don't know how much help I'll be while snarling."

"Fair enough," I said as I turned my focus back to my food. Silence stretched out with Lou still watching me.

Feeling prompted by the awkwardness that comes with having someone watch you eat, I asked, "With it being the full moon, are you going to be heading out of here sometime today?"

That question got him to break eye contact, "Yeah, I'll probably head out late in the afternoon. Will you be okay here by yourself tonight?"

I paused for a moment. I wasn't planning on going outside at all tonight now knowing Warrick doesn't have any reason to keep me around. I also didn't know where I was going to lock myself up. It's not like the windows were made with werewolf-proof glass. I looked back up at Lou, "I should be. I'll just go work in the lab or hideout in the bunker and keep all the lights off so it looks like no one's home."

Lou just nodded his head. He scooted closer to me and placed a comforting hand on my knee, "Just let me know what you need today and I'll take care of it for you."

"You're so soft now," I joked with him. "It's like I'm coming to the end of my death sentence."

That last sentence hung in the air. For all we knew, it was true – this could be my last day or last few days considering I stabbed the most dangerous man in this damn world.

Lou gave a low chuckle, "I guess it's only fair since you've helped me through times my demons tried to catch up with me."

"I appreciate you, Lou, despite my joking around," I said as I placed my hand on top of his.

I finished my breakfast willing myself to get out of bed to get dressed so I could help Lou with work in the lab. That was the only thing keeping me going.

We got ourselves back in the lab with plenty of day ahead of us. Lou focused on the electrical pieces of the device while I worked on assembling the parts he handed me. We had a good rhythm going so I decided to break the silence.

"Why do you think my dad sent me here?"

Lou didn't miss a beat as he said, "I haven't been able to really figure out why he would do that. Maybe he wanted to make sure that if you found out anything by staying at his house you wouldn't have a chance to blab?"

I paused for a second to consider this option. It seems like the easy explanation, but not the right one.

"The more probable explanation, though, would be that he sent his house away because all the evidence that would convict him is lying behind these four walls. If you could send away all the evidence of treason, why not? You don't leave behind a single trace and no one would question you. In fact, people would probably take sympathy towards you because you just lost your house and now your daughter is missing. Honestly, it seems like that would be the perfect way to minimize any suspicions of you being involved in something so bad."

I let Lou's words sink in a bit while I pieced together my own thoughts. "But why now? Why not before I was staying here watching things? I mean if he was worried that giving me a heads-up as to what was going to happen was going to risk me exposing him, I would get that. He still could've ordered the strike to happen earlier before I was here. I know you said something about getting sympathy from having a missing daughter, but there has to be more."

"He might've been waiting for the last possible moment before someone did expose him. Someone on your side of the war could've started asking questions and getting suspicious so your dad decided to pull the trigger before it got too far, but this may not have come up until now. And for the record, I'm sorry this is happening, but I am happy it brought you here. You've made things interesting again."

I looked up from my work over at Lou who was still focused on the wires he was soldering together, "Are you flirting with me?"

"It should be no surprise now that I'm into you."

"Is it only because I remind you of the woman you loved?"

Lou sighed and put down his work. He drew his gaze up to me, "Val, while there are some similarities, I'm not Warrick. I'm not trying to relive something that's in my past because you're not the same person. I'm attracted to you not only because you're gorgeous, but because you have a fire in you I haven't seen before. No one has stood up to Warrick, handled all the shit that was thrown at you with such grace to keep moving forward, and still managed to live some semblance of a normal life. You're not a damsel in distress and it helps you're easy on the eyes. You've also seen some of my darker sides and didn't hesitate to step in to help me out. Need I go on?"

I held my hands up in surrender, "Message received. I guess spending all that time around Warrick has made it hard to believe anyone would see me in a different way."

"As you should know by now, Warrick has a lot of issues to work through. He can't necessarily move on from the past because there are parts, albeit small ones, he regrets. I'm sure killing Melody was one of those since he felt like that was his one and only chance of being in love until you came along at least."

Hearing Lou admit his feelings flooded me with relief. It was nice to know that someone was into me for me and not just my looks or the idea they have in their head. It also strangely brought me some comfort in this time when it felt like everything around me was shattering.

"Lou, just know I'm into you, too."

He gave me a soft grin and nodded his head. He got back to work prompting me to do the same. We worked there in silence for a little while again letting my mind drift back to the earlier conversation focused on my father and the possible motives he had for sending his house away. It would make sense if someone was getting close to him and he felt the need to send everything away. That still didn't explain why he was okay with Warrick's threats.

Making sure we didn't lose too much time and continuing with work, I said, "I can't figure out why my dad would be okay with the thought of losing me. I'm his only kid and I thought males were hardwired to want to keep their lineage going."

"I'm not sure how it works in your world, but that's only part of it. As for why he's okay with the idea of you dying, the only thing I can think of is what I said earlier – he may be viewing you as a flight risk with discovering everything you have and reporting him."

"I don't blame him if that's his line of thinking because if, or when, I get back there, my first stop will be to report him. There's also no way my mom is okay with all of this."

"Where has she been this whole time?"

I paused and looked at the opposite wall, "She was supposed to be with him on their 'trip' unless ..."

I trailed off. I didn't want to finish that sentence and I knew Lou would be picking up on what I was trying to say. The thought of losing her too *would* break me. I couldn't deal with that now that we were in crunch time.

"Val, we'll get this all figured out. Just one thing at a time right now."

I nodded my head and went back to piecing parts together. We didn't talk about anything else after that, letting the silence fill the space while we worked. My mind wandered back to Warrick and the look of rage burning in his eyes when I left his office after driving a knife into his thigh. There was no way I'd be able to take him down on my own. Sure, I could do some damage as I saw with the knife, but I had the element of surprise on my side that time. Warrick would be on full alert from now on which also means I have to watch my back.

Lou cleared his throat, "I think I should get going. Time's rapidly escaping us and duty calls."

"Oh," I put down what I was working on not realizing just how much time we had spent in the lab. "Is the coast clear?"

I walked over to the panel with the camera feed of the front of the house to see if Warrick or one of his wolves were staking out the place. Nothing looked out of the ordinary, but before I could say anything, Lou also came over to check. I started to turn around and ran right into Lou's chest.

"You wasted no time in getting over here."

Lou chuckled, "Sorry about that, but looks like I'm good to get out of here still under the radar. Are you going to be okay tonight?"

Trying to settle the butterflies who decided to take flight, I responded, "Yeah, don't worry about me. I'll keep everything locked up tight."

There was a shake to my voice I was hoping Lou didn't catch on to. I gave him a reassuring smile and gestured towards the exit. If he suspected anything, he didn't show it, thankfully. *Phew, it'll be good to get this time to process everything tonight.*

It had been a couple of hours since Lou had left and I was sitting out by the fire pit drinking a warm cup of tea watching the sun set. It would make sense if my dad had been waiting for the last possible second to send his house here if people were starting to poke around, but still doesn't make any of this easier. I just want to know why he got involved with this stuff in the first place – that's the part that doesn't make sense. Either way, I don't know if there's a way I can go back or if the device Lou and I have been working on will even be able to do what we need it to. I'm hoping with a few more days of work, we'll be able to test it out and get out of here.

While I had all the doom and gloom with my dad and Warrick running on a loop through my head, I still couldn't forget about Lou's admission earlier today. I knew he was in to me, but I wasn't sure if it was for the same reasons Warrick was. It also helped push out the weird questioning thoughts running through my head after his latest interaction with Warrick. Hearing Lou's genuine feelings released something in me I didn't realize I had been holding on to since Gabriel exited my life: hope. I had hope for being able to find my friends and getting things sorted out. I had hope for having a promising relationship with someone who wouldn't jerk my feelings around. I had hope for finally starting a new chapter in life.

The moon replaced the sun in the sky reminding me to get inside and shut things down. The night was perfect, though. Not a cloud in the sky, crickets singing their nightly song to lull me into being relaxed, city lights twinkling below. I waited for a few more moments just to soak in the ambiance. The usual evening sounds were disrupted with several wolf howls reminding me I needed to get in the house sooner rather than later.

I stood up and stretched for a second then turned to head into the house. As I was taking my first few steps, I heard the bushes rustling next to me. Every hair on the back of my neck stood on end and I froze in place. I know it's delusional to think it's Lou, but that's all that was going through my mind. *Please be Lou coming to check on me. Please let him be the one to emerge from the bushes to guard me for the night.*

I slowly turned my head towards the direction of the rustling. From the bushes, two ice blue eyes were staring back at me causing everything in me to go cold. I had two options: show I was scared and try to run or stand my ground. Like the smart person I am, I chose the latter option.

I turned my body towards Warrick, held my chin up, and looked him dead in the eyes. Was this me fully accepting the fact I'm challenging a very dangerous, angry alpha wolf? Yes. Was it also me trying to show Warrick I have no remorse for what I did earlier? Also, yes.

"I see you had no trouble chasing me down tonight, but what I can't quite put my finger on is why you're taking the easy way out and confronting me as a wolf rather than a human."

Warrick snarled and started to slowly inch towards me as any predator would do when hunting down their prey. I stood my ground doing my best to suppress any feeling of fear trying to escape.

"What are you going to do, Warrick? Kill another woman you had any feelings for instead of face the music and accept she may have feelings for someone else? You're such a coward."

That got another snarl out of him. I was fully aware of what I was doing and had no intentions of stopping. I was on my own out here and instead of letting him know I was scared as he killed me, I wanted to get him to feel as much pain I could.

There was some good distance between the two of us that was getting smaller by the second. I took a deep breath to center myself and reflect on my life – at least I have had a good one filled with wonderful people and memories. I returned my focus to the snarling wolf in front of me. Warrick looks pissed. *Good*.

I continued with my antagonizing, "At least in this form, you can continue your game of not answering my questions about why you had articles and other shit on me. You're a real piece of work Warrick whose judgment is clouded by wanting to be almighty and powerful."

That got him to snap his jaws at me proving the effect I was having on him. I had nothing else to say, so I continued to hold my ground while he stalked his way towards me. His black fur was rippling with anger and anticipation.

At this point, he was only a few steps away from me, so I closed my eyes and continued to reflect on all the good and bad in my life. At least all the pain I had just gone through would be over. Who knows? Maybe I'd be reunited with Gabriel. *Three.* The snarls were getting louder. *Two.* I could feel his breath on my face. *One.*

I had expected to feel some sort of pain at this point with Warrick being able to latch his strong jaws around my neck, but I felt nothing. Not even his dog breath in my face I had just felt a moment ago. Instead, I heard the sound of another wolf snarling and snapping their jaws. *What is going on?*

I opened my eyes to find Warrick pinned down by another familiar wolf.

"Lou?"

At the mention of his name, he whipped his head towards me. A flood of relief washed over me, but I could tell by the look in his eyes he wasn't happy. I get to look forward to his barrage of questions, but at least I'll get to live to see another day.

That quick distraction for him was all Warrick needed to get out from underneath Lou. Warrick knocked Lou over and lunged toward his throat, but Lou was faster than him. Lou jumped back on his feet positioning himself so he was between Warrick and I. I took this moment to back away slowly to get closer to the door, but wasn't as stealthy as I thought I would be. Warrick snapped his jaws towards me and let out a loud growl which was met by Lou growling back in response. I guess I'll be staying here with a front row seat to the action.

Warrick tried to start circling, but when Lou wouldn't move a muscle, he stopped. Lou continued to hold his ground while Warrick made all the noise and movements all for show. Seeing he wasn't moving towards Lou and that he was just pacing back and forth reminded me of Warrick's admission that Lou was stronger than him. He was trying to put on a show, but deep down, Warrick was scared to be in this situation. I didn't dare say anything, but with everything in me, I was hoping Lou was picking up on this. There has to be a scent or something Warrick's giving off for Lou to understand his true feelings.

While Warrick continued to put on his show, Lou stood where he was tracking Warrick's movements. *Do something, Lou.*

It was as if Lou read my mind because the moment I thought that was the moment he threw himself into Warrick's side knocking him off balance. Warrick focused his attention on regaining his footing giving Lou the opportunity swipe him with enough force to open a good wound opened on Warrick's shoulder. That got Warrick back in the game and he returned the favor by taking a bite out of Lou's leg. Not letting that phase him, Lou went in for another attack, this time also taking a bite out of Warrick's leg.

They went back and forth for a while, both of them becoming bloodier the longer this fight went on. Surprisingly, Lou wasn't showing any signs of pain and kept attacking Warrick with the same intensity as when they started. Warrick, on the other hand, was starting to slow and having a hard time putting any amount of weight on his front right leg. Lou had the upper hand. I was sure this was also motivating him to not show any signs of pain because there was a *lot* of blood coming from his wounds.

Warrick took a step back so him and Lou were in the same faceoff position they were in earlier. He snarled, and in that moment, I saw a flash of silver on one of his canines. *Shit, how is that not affecting him? And what does this mean for Lou?*

Lou must not have seen what I did because he jumped right back into the fight. He hit Warrick a couple more times doing some good damage with those blows. It was taking all Warrick had in him to keep standing, but he lunged towards Lou's throat.

"Lou!" I shouted not able to keep quiet any longer. I was afraid Warrick had just dealt a fatal blow.

Lou let out a whimper and collapsed as Warrick pulled away. Warrick looked satisfied and raised his gaze back to me. I'll never forget this sight – Warrick standing there panting as blood, presumably Lou's, dripped out of his mouth. His head hung low looking like he was ready to attack again, but instead of lunging towards me, he turned the other way and headed back through the bushes he came from.

I waited a few minutes, still rooted to my spot, to make sure he wasn't going to come back. Once I felt confident the coast was clear, I ran over to Lou's limp body and fell to the ground. I put my head near his nose to see if I could hear any breath to be met with nothing. I had no idea where to check for a pulse on a werewolf, so I put my head on his side to try to pick up on a heartbeat, or any signs of life.

I stayed there not willing to give up on him yet as the tears started to fill my eyes. One minute had gone by, nothing. Two minutes, still nothing. Three minutes and I finally heard the faint sounds of a heartbeat, slowly trying to pump the blood through Lou's body.

"Thank goodness," I sighed into his fur. I stayed there, my head still resting on his side and my legs curled up underneath me on the ground. Lou let out a small whine bringing me to full alert. I shuffled so my lap was positioned in a way that could support his head.

"I'm going to lift your head up. It's probably going to hurt, so try not to do anything too rash, okay?"

He looked at me and it felt like he was giving me the thumbs up to proceed. I gingerly lifted his head up making sure I was moving slowly so as to not make his wounds worse or cause more pain than what was necessary and laid his head in my lap. He let out a little growl to signal he hurt.

"I know, I'm sorry. Believe me, the last thing I want to do is cause you more pain on top of what you're dealing with currently."

Lou closed his eyes while letting out a sigh. I ran my hand through his fur marveling at how soft he was. I looked him over to try and assess the amount of damage Warrick had done. There were wounds all over Lou's body – some deep, some shallow. He was covered in blood and I was hoping some of it was Warrick's given how much there was.

"Oh Lou," I said as I gently kept petting his head steering clear of any of his many wounds. "I'm sorry. I got caught up enjoying some of the evening outside, getting some fresh air to help me process and I didn't move fast enough to get back inside. Your pain is all my fault."

That got an exasperated sigh from Lou in response, but he just continued to lie there with his eyes closed.

"You'll recover, right? I don't know how Warrick did it, but he had some silver on his teeth. I'm hoping that means it might take you a little longer to heal, but you'll still make a full recovery."

He opened his eyes and raised his head to give me a nod. That little bit of movement caused him to whimper and quickly lay his head back down on my lap.

I resumed petting him, hoping I was finally doing something beneficial, "Good."

We sat there for a while longer just like that. I would occasionally peek at his wounds to see if they were making any progress. Some were, but the deep ones were definitely still bleeding.

I had no idea how long we had been there or what time it was, but Lou slowly worked his way onto his feet. He couldn't put weight on his front left leg and could hardly put weight on his back left leg, but he turned to face me to give a quick lick on my nose before heading away.

I didn't let him get too far before I asked, "You'll come here tomorrow morning, right? As early as you can? I don't care if you wake me up."

Lou turned to face me, his silver eyes almost glowing, and gave a subtle nod. He turned, moving out the door, leaving me standing there. I don't know where he was going, but all I could hope for was that Warrick wouldn't find him again and finish him off.

I let out a sigh and turned to head back into the house. I locked the door behind me and didn't bother with turning on any of the lights. I made my way up to my room, deposited my dirty clothes in the hamper, showered, and collapsed in my bed.

The least I could do was get a few hours of sleep before Lou found his way back here.

I had no idea how much sleep I had gotten, but my eyes flew open at the sound of something scratching at the front door. I got out of bed throwing on a robe then quietly went downstairs. The scratching continued. *Please let it be Lou this time.* I peeked out the glass that framed the door and recognized the silver eyes staring back at me. With that confirmation, I ripped open the door to see Lou in no better shape than what he had been in before.

"Wait here one second," I said as I rushed off to find something to put on the ground to avoid blood stains.

I laid down a tarp I found and Lou hastily got in the house. Once inside, he collapsed. I sat down next to him, "You're safe here, Lou. Relax."

I watched him lose all the tension in his body after I uttered those words. He nosed his head under my hand and I resumed petting him. It didn't take long for him to fall asleep and for the soft sounds of him sleeping to fill the entryway.

I looked at a nearby clock to see it was just after five in the morning and judging by the way it looks outside, it wouldn't take long for the sun to come up. I didn't know how it worked with him changing back, but I had a feeling I was going to be finding out soon enough. Would the change take everything out of him with some of these wounds?

I took everything in. *This is my life now.* Here we were with me sitting on the floor of the entryway and Lou's head resting on my lap, his breathing labored. Despite everything that had happened, there was a sort of peace filling me. Maybe it was the thought of finally being able to walk away from the lies, all the false feelings I was building up to keep the act going with Warrick. I could finally breathe a little, a feeling I honestly hadn't been familiar with since Gabriel had died. I took a deep breath and let it out slowly to get rid of any tension I had in that moment while looking out the window.

The sun was starting to peek over the horizon, slowly moving out of its hiding spot. With the moon finally saying goodbye, Lou's breathing started to pick back up as he was starting to change. I started to hear some of his bones snapping back to take on their human form. Growls filled the once quiet entryway, and not wanting to risk being in a bad spot, I gently laid Lou's head on the ground and got out of the way. I wasn't risking any werewolf bites today. The growls and bone snapping continued, accompanied with whimpering, as I watched him transform from a large wolf back to human.

When he was done, he was lying there breathing hard with his eyes still closed. I cautiously approached and sat back on the floor to put his head back in my lap. Once there, I took in everything in front of me: a sweaty, bloody Lou whose heart was racing and breathing like he couldn't get enough air in his lungs. My eyes travelled down his body to realize he was lying there naked, but in a way that didn't expose him. Really naked.

Immediately flustered, I said, "U-um, Lou? Do you need me to get you anything? Clothes? A towel?"

Replying in a husky voice, he said, "Val, you act like you haven't seen a naked man before."

Okay, now I can feel the heat on my face. Thankfully his eyes were still closed so he couldn't see my reaction.

"The questions still s-stands."

Lou barely opened his one eye I could see, "Please, sit here for a moment longer. I need a second."

I nodded my head placing my hand on his back in between two wounds. We let the silence blanket us again. I looked over Lou wondering what he needs for his wounds, especially the deeper ones. I also couldn't help but notice all of his muscles again. He was built, but despite his size, I knew he was agile and could move as fast as he wants.

About 30 minutes had passed and he still hadn't moved an inch. "Lou," I said quietly. "I'm going to get you a couple of things and will be right back."

I moved to get up with little protest, so I placed his head back down on the floor and headed up the stairs to grab a few towels along with a big first aid kit to start taking care of some of the damage. I headed back downstairs, pausing at where Lou was to drop those items off before continuing to the kitchen to grab some snacks and water. By the time I got back to him, Lou was starting to try to sit up.

"Here, let me help you," I said as I rushed over.

"You know," he started still sounding husky and in pain, "I've never really had help before. Game changer."

"Don't make it a habit," I teased. I wasted no time with handing over the food and water. Lou started diving into everything while I started to wipe some of the blood off of him careful to avoid the cuts.

"Val?" Lou asked.

I paused what I was doing, "Yeah, what do you need?"

"Can we maybe move this party to the bathroom? I'd like to rinse off."

"Oh, sure. Let me help you up."

I didn't know what I was expecting, but Lou not putting hardly any weight on his legs wasn't it. Makes sense considering he just changed back and took a hell of a beating. We slowly made our way up to the bathroom and I eased him onto the toilet where he could sit. He leaned his head against my side as I reached for the faucet to get the water started. I poured in some soap which was going to sting, but at least would save me from getting flustered again. Once the tub was filled, I helped Lou get into it. The minute some of his open wounds hit the water, he let out an intense scream.

"You okay?"

Through gritted teeth, he said, "No, but I need this."

I offered my arm to help give him more balance as he moved to sit in the tub. As soon as he was in there, we locked eyes and his wolf looked like he was about to jump back out.

"Are you sure you need this?"

Lou just nodded his head.

"Okay," I said as I grabbed a towel to start washing him.

As soon as we were done, I helped Lou to stand and threw him a towel so he could start drying off.

"Val, have you ever given someone stitches before?"

That question stopped me dead in my tracks. Not only had I never done them before, but I was absolutely petrified of needles, "No. I haven't even gotten them myself."

Lou sat at the edge of the tub not quite getting out yet, "I guess it's your lucky day then."

I pinched the bridge of my nose and closed my eyes, "You're really not asking me to give you stitches, are you? Wouldn't this be better done at a hospital where they've done this a hundred times?"

Instead of the chuckle I was expecting, I got a low growl, "We're not going to any hospitals."

"Why?"

"Warrick's got people there. Last thing I need for him to see is that I'm not recovering. Gives him more power."

I sighed and dropped my head, "I don't even have the supplies."

"You sure?"

"Positive," I gestured to the rest of the house. "It's not like we're in a medical facility."

"Go check that first aid kit again."

I let out a groan and turned on my heels to head back downstairs. I don't know why I brought that down there in the first place. I grabbed it and brought it back to the bathroom over to the sink. Thankfully, Lou had wrapped himself in a towel saving me from any more embarrassment today.

I opened the kit looking over at Lou for instruction, "What am I looking for in here?"

"Lift up that top tray and you should see a decent sized suture kit."

I found what he was referencing and held it up. He nodded approvingly then gestured for me to come over to him, "You're going to need to close up several of these." He started pointing at the giant gash in his neck, then one on his arm, and another on his leg.

"Jeez, don't I need to numb you in those areas first and clean them?"

"They're already clean. Don't worry about numbing me, it's not my first rodeo."

I let out another breath of air. *You can do this, Val.* I sat on the toilet lid closing my eyes to try to steady myself for a moment. When I opened them, I met Lou's intense gaze. At least his wolf seemed to calm down. I opened the suture kit, "Lou, you're going to need to walk me through this step by step."

He placed his hand on mine, "That's the plan. Start by threading the needle. You're going to close this one on my neck first since that's the biggest pain in the ass right now."

I nodded doing as I was told. I brought the needle to where he was pointing on his neck and inserted it. I'm not normally a squeamish person, but this sent shivers down my spine making my stomach turn a little bit. Lou continued guiding me through the process, offered kind words of encouragement, and before I knew it, I had closed up one of the three wounds he mentioned.

"Now, tie the knot and get some new thread."

I finished letting out an excited gasp, "I did it!"

Lou softly smiled at me, "You did, now just do it two more times."

And I did. I held the edges of the wounds together, threaded the needle through, and tied it off once I reached the end. There were only a couple of times where Lou tensed up, but besides that, it was relatively smooth.

"You sure you didn't do this in your past life?" Lou asked, cocking one eyebrow up.

"Nope. In fact, I'm deathly afraid of needles, so you're lucky I didn't pass out."

"No kidding. Well, now that we have that out of the way, can you throw some gauze, bandages, the works on the rest of me?"

"Sure," I said getting right back at it. By the time I was done, Lou looked immensely better than he had a couple hours ago.

I helped him back to his feet and we headed into my room. Along the way, his towel dropped, "Um, Lou?"

"Val, really? Can you just ignore the lack of the towel? I'd like to lay down and rest some."

I blushed and focused my attention forward, "Sure."

"Didn't take you as a prude."

I couldn't quite tell if he was joking or taking a jab, but I just kept us moving forward without response. Now that things were calming down a little, tiredness was seeping back into me.

I got us both back to my room and helped him on the bed while somehow not managing to look at him. He got under the covers and wasted no time with falling back asleep. I desperately wanted to be sleeping next to him right at this moment, but I took a second to put some pajamas on, grab an extra blanket, and bring him a glass of water. I gave Lou the rest of the blanket he was under and tucked myself in. As soon as my head hit the pillow, I was out like a light.

It was a few hours later when Lou started stirring causing me to wake up too. He rolled over placing a hand on my shoulder, "Hey, Val, you up?"

I turned my face into the pillow mumbling in response, "I am now I guess."

I rolled over to face him noticing some of the bruising and smaller cuts had vanished. I gave him a quick smile.

"I just wanted to thank you for taking care of me this morning."

"Yeah, it's no biggie. You've literally risked your life for my ass, so it's the least I can do."

Lou gave my shoulder a squeeze before rolling onto his back. I rolled over and propped my head up with my hand, "I am curious about one thing, though."

"Shoot."

"What do you guys do during a full moon? It seems like you're always running off to do something, but I haven't been able to figure it out."

"Well, I can only speak for my pack. Seems like Warrick is spending more time stalking you then anything else."

"You're not wrong there. Can you give me a day in the life?"

"Yeah, I was getting around to that. We typically start the night off by checking the boundaries of our territory. If any of Warrick's goons crossed the line, we typically track them down to remind them not to push their luck. We usually don't have to do that, though, and instead we just reinforce the boundaries. Then, we move on to checking on the people around the city and surrounding towns to make sure they're all safe."

"Why?"

"Warrick's pack has had a history of losing control and killing innocents. Part of his pack being so big and filled with like-minded people who want nothing more than to gain power."

I shivered a little, "That's horrible."

Lou just nodded, "That's why we look out for them. I have a pretty small pack, but we can spread ourselves out enough to keep any serious damage from happening. That's also why I left you last night. I had to make sure they weren't up to anything."

I plopped back down on my back joining Lou staring at the ceiling, "Makes sense. Something else that just popped into my mind – Warrick had silver on his teeth."

His brow furrowed, "You mentioned that last night, too. It's not the first time he's used that trick, hence the scars covering my body. I haven't been able to figure out how he's doing it, but something to do with the many labs he has under his control. That's typically why I don't pick too many fights with him anymore."

"Mmm," I said while processing the last part he said. I felt bad he had to go through that on my behalf, but I was definitely dead if Lou hadn't come in to save the day.

We paused in conversation while Lou took a sip of water. He stopped for a second, looked at the glass, took another sip, then swished it around his mouth. Lou looked confused, but wasn't saying anything leaving me hanging there in suspense, "Everything okay?"

Lou replied, "I can't believe I didn't notice this before, but your water tastes different."

"What do you mean?" I asked a little worried. With something as essential as water, it's unsettling to hear that what you typically drink tastes different.

Instead of answering, Lou gingerly rolled out of bed and threw on a pair of pants. Curiosity mixed with the confusion from moments ago took over causing me to follow him. I found him down in the kitchen grabbing a large pitcher of water. I paused in the entryway asking, "Lou, what's going on? What are you doing?"

He continued his trend of avoiding my questions and walked past me heading out the front door. I followed him as far as the front porch to see him walking to a neighboring house. *At least he remembered to grab pants.* I couldn't see what was going on while he was talking to the home's owner, but when he turned around, he was carrying another cup of water. Lou made his way back into my house continuing towards the lab. I followed him again, confused more than ever about whatever realization was consuming him. Since Lou had a lead on me with getting into the lab, I walked in to find him rummaging through the drawers with the pitcher of water and the neighbor's cup on one of the benches (thankfully away from our device). Once he gathered everything he needed to do whatever it was he was planning, Lou placed his hands on the lab bench leaning on them and finally looking at me, "I'm going to test the water."

I crossed my arms, "Okay, I figured that's what you were going to do, but why?"

"Something you said earlier made me have an idea," Lou said not giving any further details.

"Care to share?" I asked starting to get impatient with his vagueness. Lou was starting to get to work on his experiments putting off yet another answer.

Lou got to a point where he could divide his focus and finally got to work on bringing me up to speed, "There has to be something in the water that's having an effect on us wolves. The only thing that would do that is silver. I'm testing to see if I can detect any traces of silver outside the normal limits to confirm my suspicion. If that's the case, it would explain a lot."

He finished his testing, both of us waiting eagerly in silence. After a while, the results became clear - there was, in fact, more silver in the water that came from the neighbor's house than there was in the water from mine. At least that mystery is solved. Lou pulled out his phone and started typing furiously to let his pack know what was going on.

"Lou, what does this mean?" I asked not able to keep up with Lou's processing speed.

Lou finally looked up from his phone, "My only guess is that Warrick has been adding silver to the water to make us weaker."

So many questions started flooding my mind, but I tried to keep it to a minimum so I didn't interrupt Lou from alerting everyone he needed to, "Isn't that dangerous for humans? Why isn't it effecting Warrick's wolves? Why isn't it in my water?"

"I'm trying to see if anyone in my pack has any idea about the answers for your last two questions. It shouldn't cause too many issues for humans since it's a resource that's naturally occurring and already in the water supply," he said. I was getting ready to ask another question, but was cut off by Lou holding up one of his hands. He continued, "It wouldn't take much additional silver to have an effect on us. Our bodies would pick up anything outside of the normal range and try to fight it since silver is the main thing that can kill us. He must not have it too much out of the normal range, though, because it's not easily detectable."

"How were you able to taste the difference?"

"Honestly, I'm not sure. I think something in the back of my mind was telling me to pay attention after everything that happened last night and in the past."

Before we could continue diving down that rabbit hole, Lou's phone started ringing. He answered the call, quickly becoming engrossed in what the other person was saying. It was my turn to lean on the lab bench eagerly waiting to see if there were any updates to my earlier questions.

Lou hung up turning his attention back to me, "Do you know if you have any filters on your water here?"

"I think there is, but I don't know for sure," I trailed off as Lou turned around to check under the sink for any sign of filtration.

"It looks like you do, so that should answer your last question," he said straightening back up. "As for why Warrick's wolves aren't being affected, it sounds like his pack has access to specific filters that keep the silver within normal limits. This would explain why his pack seems to have a bit of an edge on us."

I have to admit Warrick's strategy is sneaky smart. There's no way Lou would have known about this and who knows what would've happened over a long period of time.

"How are you going to get your pack to stop drinking the water?"

He ran a hand through his hair, "The only thing I can think of right now is to send a couple of them on a shopping trip that's far enough away from here to get filters to bring back. I can't trust that water in water bottles is safe either."

I stood there wishing there was something else I could offer that would be easier for Lou's pack to do, but that was the only thing popping in my mind.

"Val, changing topics," Lou said snapping my attention back to him. "We're almost done with the device. We could probably knock the rest out in a few hours. Have you thought about any plans of action for testing it?"

"The only thing I've thought about is going to a park or open space far away to test it out. That way we aren't dragging one of our houses with us."

"Why wouldn't you want to transport your house?"

"I don't know. I think it made sense to me at the time when I was thinking through everything I had just found out about my dad. I wanted to try to distance myself from the memories as much as I could, but looking at it now, it would probably make sense to bring the house with us so we have a lab, right?"

"Now you're making sense. Let's test it as soon as it's finished and I'm a little more healed up."

"If testing is successful, what are you going to do about the pizza shop? And what are we going to do in the meantime?"

Lou paused for a moment thinking that through, "I'll call some of the pack today and see if they can take care of it for an indefinite amount of time. We should pop back in there for a couple of days before we test the device out, though."

Not following his line of thinking, I asked, "Why? Why not just stay here to finish the device and test it out?"

"I want to see if Warrick will show his face, and I want to make sure to get everything ready so I can walk my pack through what to do. They don't necessarily have the most experience with running a business."

The thought of Warrick coming into the restaurant while I was working made my stomach turn. The last time he came in, he was crazed looking for me. I don't want to see that happen again, especially when there's no way I can stand my ground against him and Lou's in no shape to do that either.

"What happens if Warrick does come around?"

"You stay in the back and keep working on making orders. We'll have you start back there to try and keep your scent in the place to a minimum. I'll handle him."

All I could do was nod my head again. I didn't like the sound of that plan, but I trust Lou.

Chapter 19

Our stomachs were growling reminding us we both haven't eaten anything since we've been up. I made my way back to the kitchen to start making us a hearty breakfast consisting of pancakes, eggs, and bacon. Well, mostly eggs and bacon for Lou. He was looking at me from his spot at the island with a mouth full of food, "Keep this coming, please."

I chuckled, "Are you normally this hungry after a change?"

He had finally swallowed his food when he said, "No, but since I took a beating, that changes things. My body needs more fuel to heal."

"Sure. You just want to eat all of my food," I joked with him.

Lou rolled his eyes and I cooked the remaining eggs and bacon managing to steal some for my plate. I grabbed all of my food to sit down next to him. The silences were getting more and more comfortable each time. I looked back over at Lou who was gazing outside, "Lou?"

He quickly brought his attention back to me, "What's up?"

"Are you still in a lot of pain?"

Lou placed a hand on my knee, "Not nearly as much pain as I was in earlier, thanks to you."

I blushed a little at that, "Just happy to have been here to help. If the device works, are you sure you're okay with leaving your life here?"

He turned so he was fully facing me, "I wouldn't have jumped right in to help if I wasn't willing to leave all this behind. I love my pack and my restaurant, but it'll be nice to get out from under Warrick's control. Don't feel bad about this, I could've walked away at any point."

It felt like he was reading my mind. I just nodded my head for yet another time and went back to my food. This time I was mostly pushing things around on my plate unable to focus on anything else but the thoughts running through my mind. I was scared about the device working. Where would it take us? Would it actually get me to where some of my other friends are? Would they want to join us or would they be enjoying their new lives too much?

Lou cupped my chin and turned my face towards him, "Did I lose you?"

I pulled my chin out of his hand and looked down, "No, just nervous about the potential journey we have lying ahead of us."

"Getting cold feet on me now?"

"Ha, no. I still want to go through with it. There's just a lot of unknowns and it gets nerve wracking with any sort of new change."

"You don't have to worry about anything. I'll be with you the entire time, and even if things don't go according to plan, we'll at least get an adventure out of it. Hell, we could end up back here and just move to the beach or something."

"Sure," I said offering him a small smile.

"Now, come with me. I'd like to enjoy some of the sunshine out there."

We headed out to the backyard and cozied up on the couch that overlooks the pool. There was a slight breeze again, but it was refreshing since the day was already warm. I nestled myself closer to Lou's side and looked up at him to make sure I wasn't causing any pain. He was looking back down at me with a soft grin on his face and before I could ask him what he was looking at, he leaned in for a kiss.

It was soft, but passionate. Gentle, but needing. Everything I could've imagined what actually kissing Lou felt like. Not like the time where he had kissed me before where it felt so right, but so wrong at the same time. The passion, fireworks, and heat from before were back again, but there was something else lingering I couldn't quite put my finger on. Something that left me wanting to get lost in all that is Lou.

I put my hand on his chest and slowly pulled away. The familiar look of hurt came across his face causing my heart to lurch.

"I'm only stopping us because I want to move slowly. I don't want to dive headfirst like I have all the other times before when things didn't work out and I was just trying to fill an empty part of me."

He looked away, "I can do slow. I'm just glad it's not you putting a complete stop to this again."

He brought his gaze back to me and gave a goofy grin to help reassure me. I squeezed his hand and went back to looking out over the city. Casual conversation about random things went back and forth between us until we finally landed on a topic we wanted to dissect more: the device.

Lou asked, "What else is there to do for the device?"

"I just think we have to finish putting it together and then test it. Of course, if the tests don't go as we planned, we'll have to jump right back into it."

"I'm planning on that. Do you remember if there's any other wiring that needs to be done?"

I stood up offering my hand to help him, "Rather than trying to remember, let's just go take a look." I started heading back in the house with Lou by my side. "If all the wiring is done, I can finish assembling it so you can rest some more before we embark on a new journey."

He cocked an eyebrow at me, "Embark on a new journey, huh? What is this? Your odyssey?"

"Who knows? It could be."

We made our way into the lab and over to the bench where our device was laying. By the looks of it, Lou had gotten all of the electrical parts taken care of so that just left the assembly to me. There were a lot of little pieces, but thank goodness for the blueprints and drawings I had next to me to guide me through.

I looked over at Lou who was now standing across from me, "I didn't even realize you got all of your parts done before you left. Why'd you leave the engineering field anyways? You clearly have a talent."

"I'm just that good," he said while inspecting everything that was done on the device. "But, seems like you don't need me at the moment, so I'm going to crash for a little bit and hope I can get some more healing going. As for your question, I just wanted to distance myself from that world with Warrick trying to run my life and all. The pizza shop is a much better pace and a lot less stressful, too."

I gave him a thumb's up letting his words soak in. I can't say that I blame him for wanting to make the career change with everything Warrick must have put him through. Lou made his way over to me to plant a soft kiss on my forehead then exited the lab.

I turned back to the lab bench taking in all the parts laying out in front of me. I had about half of it assembled, so in theory, there wasn't too much left to do. *Takes me back to when I would help dad with his cars and when I would work on my bike.* In this moment, I was thankful for my dad teaching me how to be handy.

I picked up my tools and got to work putting one piece in place at a time. I only paused to grab myself something to drink (leaving it far away from where I was working, of course) and to turn on some music. It didn't take long for me to get into a rhythm.

I heard the door to the lab open, but I kept working away. Lou's steps paused causing me to look up, "Feel any better?"

"Loads. Still have a decent amount of pain, but nothing I haven't dealt with before," he pointed to the screen showing the camera feed of the street in front of the house. "Looks like we have company."

I put down what I was working on, silently cursing Lou for disrupting my progress while I walked over to join him in what he was looking at. Sure enough, Warrick was sitting there in his car keeping an eye on the place.

"Damn it," I muttered under my breath.

"If we stay in here and make it look like no one's home, he'll probably go away."

I shook my head, "No, I'm not being held hostage in my own house."

I stormed out of the lab without saying anything.

"What are you going to do?" Lou called after me.

"Don't worry about it."

He started after me, but I put a stop to that,"Lou, stay put. Enjoy the show on the big screen."

I closed the distance between myself and the front door ripping it open to storm my way across the street to his car. Upon seeing me, Warrick moved to get out of his car and it gave me some satisfaction to see him moving slowly, still in pain. He had some good cuts and bruises covering his body along with some stitches. *Good, Lou was able to do some damage.*

I stopped in the middle of the street, "Can I help you?"

"Just wanting to check in, love," Warrick said as he leaned against his car to get the extra support.

"No, you don't get to call me love. Not after you showed up here last night clearly wanting to kill me. Now you're here parked in front of my house on some sort of stakeout. So, can I help you?"

Any sort of good nature he had in him left being replaced with darkness and anger, "People don't get to stab me and get away with it. I don't like your new bodyguard, either."

I crossed my arms still keeping distance between us, "You don't get to have a say in who I choose to spend my time with. I'm not a piece of property, you don't own me. How is your little stab wound doing by the way?"

Warrick snarled at me but still didn't make any moves towards me, "You mean this?"

He lifted up the bottom of his shorts to reveal the spot I had stabbed him in. The wound looked freshly stitched, but was showing the first signs of infection. It makes sense why he's not putting a ton of weight on that leg. Surprising since Warrick struck me as the kind of guy who takes great care of his body.

I pointed at the wound, "You might want to get that looked at, it doesn't look too hot."

Warrick let out another snarl and next thing I knew, he was right in front of me, hand around my neck and lifting me off the ground. I was starting to struggle to breathe.

With a curled lip, he said, "I don't know who you think you are, but your days are numbered."

"By the looks of it, yours might be too if that gets any worse," I gasped out.

He was sweating from the effort. Being up close to him, I looked back down to see if I could get a glimpse of the wound again and just saw the bottom of it poking out from under his shorts. It looked much worse up close. The redness I was seeing was actually branching out and covering a lot of his leg. There was pus trying to ooze its way out in between the stitches. Warrick's hand felt warmer than usual to the touch.

He must not have liked that last line because his hand tightened so much around my throat that he took away any chance of me talking back, "You listen to me. Your death will come to you when you least expect it. It will be painful, and best of all, slow. There is nothing that will save you from that now."

Warrick held me like that long enough that I started seeing spots around my vision. I tried kicking out with each kick losing power the longer he held me. After a good amount of time passed, he finally dropped me then turned to return to his car. I was too busy gasping for air trying to get something back into my lungs to come back with a retort. My hand went up to my throat to try and give me some reassurance that I was free from his grasp. By the time Warrick got in his car, I was standing back on my feet watching him leave. He gave me a little finger wave then sped off. *Sick bastard.*

I got back into the house to find Lou standing right on the other side of the door completely out of any line of sight anyone may have had on the outside of the house. He wasn't looking happy with me, "Did that go according to plan?"

"It got him to leave, didn't it?" I rasped out.

Lou put his arm around my shoulder and guided me to the couch, "Don't worry about talking. Just rest."

"But the device. I need to finish it."

"Stop. I'll take care of the rest of it. You need to sit. It may not have felt like it, but he was holding you there for long enough to do a decent amount of damage."

Lou made his way into the kitchen to grab a bag of ice. I opened my mouth to speak, but he shot me a look that made me think otherwise, "Val, I'm serious. Don't talk. Just put this ice on your neck and hang out here. Did you see any spots when he was holding you there?"

I nodded my head and held up my fingers to indicate just a little bit.

"Okay, I'll check back on you after I finish the device to make sure there isn't more damage."

He patted me on my shoulder and left the room. I wanted to be able to ask Lou about the knife he had given me. I didn't think that just a silver knife would do that kind of damage, so there must have been something else there. Did he coat it with something? I pulled out my phone and started writing out all the questions I had for him regarding that knife. Was it coated? How did he get ahold of it? How long had he had that knife? Was that always his plan or was it being saved for something else?

A wave of tiredness crashed over me making it hard to think of any other questions. Still holding the ice to my neck, I laid down on my back and closed my eyes. It didn't take long for visions of Warrick to start playing. Him as a wolf hiding in my bushes that first full moon here. Him still in wolf form coming out to attack me. The look on his face as he was strangling me. Again, the look on his face right after I had stabbed him.

I don't know how long I had been asleep for, but when I opened my eyes again, I was under a blanket and Lou was in the spot right next to my head.

"Morning. How did you sleep?" he asked.

I started to sit up, "How long was I out?"

My voice was still pretty raspy. I was caught off-guard by the pain caused by talking.

Lou took the melted ice bag away from me and scooted over so he was right by my side giving me something to lean on, "You may not want to talk for a little while. Give your vocal cords a chance to recover. I called over one of the guys in my pack to check you out. He's a doctor and is the one person I have working in the main hospital here.

I raised my eyebrows curious why Lou insisted on avoiding the hospitals all this time when he had one of his own working there.

Picking up on my question, Lou said, "Too much corruption. Warrick has so many people in his back pocket that if I were to take you anywhere for medical attention, he would know and it would just fuel the fire. We have to lay low to keep suspicions down and to keep this from happening again. My guy isn't afraid to make house calls in case you were wondering."

I nodded showing I understood what he was saying. I looked around for my phone because I wanted to dive right into the questions I had written down earlier. I found it buried under the blanket and trying to fall victim to the couch cushions when Lou put his hand over mine to stop me.

"Val, I want to show you something."

I made a move to get up and he stopped me again, shaking his head. I gave a little pout but stayed put. Lou reached behind his back and pulled out something that looked like our device, except completed.

I looked at him with raised eyebrows and excitement as I reached out to take the device from him. He nodded and handed it over. I felt like a kid getting the biggest present off my Christmas list from Santa. Here I was, holding the device we had been working on for a surprisingly short amount of time that could hopefully take us to different worlds. The search for my friends could begin, but so could the search for a new place to live away from Warrick, away from what my life had been before I came here.

It was a small, black handheld device with only two buttons on it. It fit perfectly in my hand to where I could close my fist and you wouldn't be able to see I was holding something. No wonder Lou got through the electrical piece so quickly. There wasn't a lot there and my dad already had the specialty wires needed to conduct the kind of energy to transport people from his bombs.

I looked back up at Lou to see he was smiling, "We did it, Val. At least the first part. I was thinking we could start testing it next week to give us some time to be more healed up. You good with that?"

I nodded my head, but there was a part of me that wanted to test it right now. The only thing stopping me from arguing with Lou was the fact that he was still pretty beat up and I was right there with him now.

He took the device back from me, "I'm going to put this back in the lab so it's locked up and safe. I'll be right back and then we can go over whatever you were wanting to show me on your phone."

He stood up as I gave him a thumb's up and I wrapped the blankets around me more. While Lou was gone, I gingerly touched my neck where Warrick had held me wincing at the pain I felt as it throbbed. I guess I shouldn't second-guess the strength behind that grip of his.

Lou returned plopping back down in the spot next to me. I handed over my phone with the list of questions there. He started reading through his brow furrowing more and more after each question.

He handed my phone back, "Good questions, I'll start with the easy one. It was coated with the only type of venom that Warrick had discovered as damaging to a werewolf," Lou held up his hands continuing. "I don't know how he figured that out or how he got his hands on it, what he was going to use it for, so on and so forth. He kept all of his research pretty close, so the fact I even found out about this knife was surprising. As for how I got it, I stole it from Warrick during the days I was working with him, so I've had it for quite some time. It was right after his scientists developed it. We were in a meeting at the time going over the recent numbers when they barged in. I started to make my way out as they started talking about it. I heard Warrick mention where he was going to stash it after hearing what it was."

Lou took this moment to pause and run his hands through his hair. I knew this was going to be a hard story for him to tell judging by his expression reading through my questions.

After a deep breath, Lou continued, "He didn't know I had taken it, but I was going through a hard time, a dark time in my life. It was near the end of my time working for Warrick and I had already gone through so much abuse, especially after being turned when I didn't necessarily want this life. I viewed this knife as my way out. I brought it home and buried it away to be saved for a night when I just couldn't take it any longer. There were a couple of times I sat on my couch holding back the urge to grab that thing to plunge it through my heart."

His voice was shaky at this point. I put my hand on his knee to give him a reassuring squeeze. Lou nodded his head taking another breath to center himself, "Eventually, as you know, I found my way out of Warrick's company and pack. I had distanced myself enough to the point where I was forgetting about it. One day, not too long after you had arrived, I stumbled across it and instantly knew it would have to be used on Warrick. It could only be used once with the venom because the venom immediately transfers over to whoever was stabbed with it. I guess the reason for these questions is that you saw his wound?"

I nodded and wrote in my phone, "It was looking really infected and he couldn't put any weight on his leg."

Lou nodded, "Ah, must mean he hasn't been able to find an antidote. Probably because he used all the venom he had on the knife before his team could develop something. Shows he was cocky in thinking his own weapon would never be used against him."

Before we could continue with the knife discussion, there was a knock on the door. The knock was quiet, but in a distinct pattern. Lou must've recognized it since he quickly got up to answer the door.

"Hey Raf, thanks for coming on such short notice."

"Anytime boss. Where is this world-famous Val hiding out?"

I turned to look over at the two men in the entryway to give a little wave. Where Lou was tall and built, Raf was shorter, slightly muscular but more on the lean side. He had dark brown hair and was clean shaven. He has a kind face which I'm sure comes in handy when working on patients. I mean, I'm instantly feeling a little better just by looking at his chocolate brown eyes and kind smile.

Lou was the first to speak, "I think you can find her."

"Sure can," the doctor responded heading over to where I was sitting. He took a seat on the coffee table across from me and started introductions. "I'm Rafael, you can call me Raf. I've been practicing medicine for quite some time and am pretty familiar with all injuries, illness, you name it that have been caused by Warrick. What do we have –"

Raf had finally finished with fishing out a notebook and gloves when he looked at me. I guess the marks on my neck were worse than he thought because it stopped him dead in his tracks. He looked between Lou and I, then back at Lou, "She's the spitting image of –"

I looked back at Lou. He closed his eyes, "I know. Completely different person."

Raf turned his attention back to me and lifted my chin up a little bit to get a better look at my neck. He looked back at Lou as he said, "I forgot how strong Warrick is. This is –"

"Bad? I know. Hence why I called you over here," Lou said finishing Raf's sentence again.

I let out a grunt and started typing on my phone. I handed it over to Lou who let out a laugh the minute he read it.

"What is it? Do I look funny?" Raf asked.

"It's not that," Lou said regaining his composure.

Before Lou could continue, Raf turned back to me, "Can you speak and let me know what you typed on your phone to Lou? It'll help me understand some of the damage done."

I took a deep breath, "You have a hard time finishing sentences."

My voice was barely there and I grimaced once I was done. The pain was starting to set in now that the adrenaline had worn off.

Raf shook his head letting out a soft chuckle, "Just caught by surprise, that's all. Not sure why Lou found that so funny."

I was a little confused by this. I thought I had met him a while ago when I met Lou's pack, but he must not have been there which would explain why he was caught off-guard upon seeing me. As for my neck, I hadn't looked in the mirror since everything happened earlier today, so I couldn't tell how bad it was.

Lou started running Raf through all the symptoms I had been facing since the incident, all light-heartedness from moments ago now replaced with business. Raf was attentive, nodding and writing down notes as Lou explained everything. By the time Lou finished, Raf looked back at me and got to work examining the damage.

He made a few more notes, Lou waited silently, and I sat there anxiously waiting to hear what Raf had to say about what I could do to start feeling better.

"Well, Warrick isn't one to mess with, but we all knew this didn't we? He did some extensive damage in a pretty short amount of time. Judging by the sound of your voice and the feel of your neck, you're not going to be talking for a little while. You should be able to start talking in a couple of days, but until then, give your voice some rest. You'll still sound hoarse, but you should be good to go if it doesn't hurt to talk. It's best to let your vocal cords heal. It doesn't look like there was any extensive damage to your brain from lack of oxygen, which is a great thing. Your neck is definitely swollen and you're going to have some bad bruising for a while. You have some puffiness in your face that should go down over time, too. Just get some rest and take some pain killers to help with any pain."

Raf started packing everything up. Lou reached down to squeeze my shoulder as he said, "Thanks again for coming over so quickly. I'll make sure she takes it easy."

Raf arched his eyebrow up, "Sure." He directed his attention back to me, "I don't know what you did to piss Warrick off that much, but I'd watch your back if I were you. I can do a lot of healing, but I can't bring you back from the dead."

Raf made his exit and Lou came back over to me, "Judging by his reaction, from what I saw earlier today, I'm surprised there wasn't more damage done."

I shrugged my shoulders. I'm a tough one, but not invincible. Wanting to change the topic, I pointed to my stomach to indicate I was hungry.

Lou laughed, "Already ahead of you. We should have pizza here in about ten minutes."

I gave a thumb's up. I got myself up from the couch and headed to the bathroom to take a look at the damage. Looking in the mirror, I startled myself a little bit. There was definitely bruising across my neck where Warrick had held me, but I also had the start of a couple of black eyes. There was more swelling than I had anticipated. I reached up to touch the bruising on my neck just to wince. I'm happy I survived, but if this is the type of damage Warrick could do without trying to torture me, I didn't want to see what he could do intentionally.

I walked back out where Lou was sitting, scrolling through movie options on the TV. He finally selected one when I sat back down next to him. We didn't say anything else to each other, just started the movie and grabbed the pizza when it was finally here. It was good to finally feel a little normal.

Chapter 20

We made it through the weekend focusing on taking it easy and healing. My voice was still not back to its former glory, but I was able to start talking without being in too much pain which meant I could at least go back to work. The bruises were still very prominent, but I took some time practicing covering them up with makeup.

I had just put the finishing touches on my latest round of makeup when Lou came into my bathroom. He had been moving a lot better with minimal injuries still hanging around. We took some of the stitches out and covered the bigger wounds with bandages to help coax them across the finish line with healing.

"Looks like you got the hang of it," he said looking at me approvingly. "Now I won't have to explain to my customers why my best waitress looks like she got strangled."

I rolled my eyes, "Ha ha, very funny. How are we getting there today?"

Lou turned to leave, "My car's still here. We'll head out once we make sure the coast is clear."

"I thought you took your car," I said as I followed him out of my room and downstairs to start closing everything down and to triple check the lab was all closed and locked up.

"Nope. It stayed here the entire time. When I left before changing, I just headed out on foot. No sense in trying to park my car somewhere only to try and remember where it was."

"Makes sense."

We finished getting everything ready to go then set out for our first day back to work in the pizza place since everything happened. It feels like a lifetime ago since I helped serve up some food to our loyal customers.

We pulled up to the pizza place behind the alley where Lou parked his car in his typical space. Once in the kitchen, it was like riding a bike – Lou busied himself with prepping pizzas and some of the regular orders, including Warrick's, while I got ready to head out into the dining room to set up the chairs and give everything a quick wipe down.

I looked over my shoulder at Lou in the doorframe leading from the kitchen to the main dining room, "You really think Warrick is going to show himself today?"

Keeping his head down to stay focused on his work, he responded, "If not him, at least one of his goons. That reminds me, stay back here for a while."

"Nope," I said over my shoulder as I proceeded to get everything ready.

I was out of there before he could say anything or before he could try to stop me. I went into my usual rhythm, and by the time I had everything ready to go, we still had about 15 minutes before opening. I looked out the window to see a long line of ready customers.

"That's odd."

I didn't hear Lou come up behind me, so when he placed his hand on my lower back, I nearly jumped out of my skin, "What?"

"We have a line of people waiting. That's unheard of for the lunch period, or at least is unheard of since I've been here. This place is usually a ghost town."

I could hear the smile in Lou's face as he said, "Well, let's not leave the hungry customers waiting."

He moved to open up shop and instead of coming back in, he greeted everyone at the door. People filtered in and found their spots which was my cue to get to work with taking down orders and bringing them out.

I was back in the kitchen with Lou helping him get ahead of some of the orders while we had a break when the front door banged open. The dining room got eerily silent and both Lou and I froze.

"Shit," Lou muttered under his breath. "Just when we were getting good business, too."

I didn't say anything. Instead, I made my way out there with the usual pizza box to find Warrick leaning against a bar stool looking angry as ever. *Kill him with kindness.*

I plastered a smile on my face and mustered up everything I could so I could talk normal, "Hi Warrick, leg still bothering you?"

He curled his lip, "I'm just here for my lunch."

Warrick took a look over my shoulder. Judging by the sinister grin taking form, I knew Lou was watching from the kitchen. I was going against everything we had planned with me avoiding Warrick, but I don't go down without a fight.

"Here you go," I said making sure I placed the pizza on the counter with just enough distance that would make it hard for Warrick to grab me.

Instead of saying anything in return, Warrick grabbed my arm and yanked me over. Silly me thinking I could stay out of arm's reach.

"I know what you're doing. Yesterday was a warning, don't push beyond that," he snarled in my ear.

Not being able to resist, I came back with, "Sounds like this is your final warning."

His grip tightened to where I could feel my bone threatening to break, "I know what you and Lou are up to. Don't think for a second that I don't have the ability to jump between worlds. You're not the only one with that power."

That stopped me dead in my tracks – Warrick must have completed a device. I needed to get to Lou now.

Warrick released me, grabbed his pizza, and limped as fast as he could out of the restaurant. As soon as the door closed, it was like everyone could breathe again. People did their best not to stare at me, but I could feel the occasional wandering eye linger on me while I was rooted to my spot.

I took a deep breath, brushed off my shirt and headed back to the kitchen where Lou was standing with his arms crossed. When I got in there, I held up my finger, "Don't. I'm handling things."

He held his hands up in defense, "If you say so. What was that all about anyways?"

"We need to test our device now. Tonight," I was looking at the floor trying to figure out the best plan of action.

"What do you mean?"

"We don't have any more time, Lou."

Lou gently turned my face toward him so we were making eye contact, "Why so soon? What did Warrick say to you?"

I put a hand over his, "Warrick figured out how to jump. We got lazy and stopped keeping tabs on what Warrick was doing."

"He told you this?"

"Surprisingly, yes."

Lou took a step back, "I'm going to take care of some of the customers. You sit for a second."

I did as I was told. There's no way Warrick could have figured out a device that quickly when he didn't have access to all the information we did, but he does have access to a lot of scientists and equipment. We know that he was working on figuring out a way to travel between worlds which we had a general idea of where he was at in that process by monitoring his email inboxes. The downside is that we had been so caught up in our own progress that we forgot to keep an eye on how he was doing.

Lou came back into the kitchen and rushed right past me up the stairs to his apartment. Confused, I asked, "Where are you going?"

"Make a couple cheese pizzas. I'll be right back."

I started whipping out a couple of pizzas and was just getting them in the oven when Lou came back down with his laptop in hand.

"What are you doing with that?" I asked.

"I'm going to check Warrick's emails to see if there's anything that gives him away. What he said could be a ruse to get one of us to go snooping in his office so he can torment us."

"Are you sure?"

Lou looked up at me, "Positive. I've known him long enough to understand how he plays the game. He's powerful, but he's not tricky enough to change his signature moves when he doesn't have to pull them out often."

He buried his head back in his laptop. I sat back down to think through this possibility. I know he's been trying to get to me so he could kill me. This would be an easy way to pull me into his office, his territory, to take me down. It still doesn't make sense why he would say he knows what Lou and I are up to. There's been no one around the property. We only talk about the device in my house where Warrick has had no time to bug the place. I looked back over at Lou. There's no way they could be working together, could there? I mean, I barely know Lou in comparison to how long those two have known each other, but I still can't see him playing me like that.

Before I could ponder that any longer, Lou motioned for me to go over to him, "I'll have you look through for a moment while I head back out to take care of people, but I'm not seeing any sort of progress. The only thing I'm seeing is Warrick getting pushy with his team on a timeline for when they'll have a device ready."

I nodded and got to reading. After about ten emails, I was only seeing what Lou was seeing. Warrick was putting pressure on his team for a timeline for when they would see progress, but not because Lou and I were creating something. This was more because he was feeling the need to grow his empire.

When Lou got back to the kitchen, I asked, "You don't think he knows what we've been building, do you?"

He looked at me confused, "No, we've kept it under wraps. Why?"

"Warrick mentioned he knew what you and I have been up to. I don't think I gave anything away, but it still doesn't sit right with me."

"He never mentioned that in his emails. I know he would call that piece of information out because the last thing he would want to do is lose to us."

Still not completely convinced, "Are you sure he couldn't detect us copying his files or hacking into his emails?"

"No. Val, are you not trusting me right now?"

"I am trusting you. I just want to make sure I ask my questions so I'm not stewing on them all day. Warrick saying that didn't sit well with me."

"That's him trying to see what he can figure out by how you react. I saw you, I don't think you gave anything away, so we should be in the clear."

I nodded while heading back out there, "Let's hope so."

I wanted to get out of the kitchen before Lou could grill me about potentially not trusting him. It's not like he hasn't been looking out for me or taking care of me since day one. He has done nothing to make me question his actions. It's only Warrick who's getting in my head to make me second-guess everything that has been going well for me here.

We made it through the rest of our day and were heading back to my house. I didn't realize how tired I was until I sat down in the comfortable leather seats of Lou's car. I started to nod off with the only sounds coming from the radio lulling me into sleep when Lou asked, "Do you really not trust me?"

Damn, he's not letting go of that. The hurt in his voice made my heart lurch enough that I had to take a second to gather my thoughts before responding.

"Don't take my hesitation as confirmation of that. I can see where you're coming from with that question, but I do trust you. You've taken care of me, been there for me, and are somehow into me. I can also see how much pain Warrick causes you mentally to know there's no way you would be going around behind my back," I reached over to put my hand on his thigh. "I shouldn't have asked those questions earlier. I was spooked and that's no excuse. I'm sorry."

All Lou did was nod his head once, but the fact that his body relaxed was enough for me to know he believed me.

To try to lighten the mood, I asked, "Would you be up for a swim?"

He looked at me out of the corner of his eyes, "After we test the device."

"Okay."

We went back to letting the radio do the job of filling the car with sound. Lou was still tense, but not as much as he was earlier. Here's to hoping the device works and we can enjoy some time in the water to unwind.

Lou was the first one in the house heading straight for the lab, "Can you check the emails one more time before we try testing this thing?"

"Sure," I said as I detoured to the computer. I wasted no time with getting logged in. Back in Warrick's emails, I went scrolling through each message to see if there was any true indication of him having a device like the one we built. There was nothing. The only thing I could see that was relatively close was an email between him and my dad where he asked if he could get any sort of schematics to which my dad responded that he no longer had access to those. For once, I was thankful for the rigid and quiet nature of my dad. There was no way he was going to spill his guts and tell Warrick everything. At least there were still some secrets he held close.

Confirming there was nothing else we needed to worry about, I headed into the lab. Lou cleared a space for us to test and was waiting for me. When he looked up, I gave him two thumb's up, "We're in the clear. Warrick has nothing."

"You sure?" Lou asked in a tone of disbelief.

"Yes, not a doubt in my mind. There was even a recent email sent today after he grabbed his lunch where he was asking my dad for schematics or anything else that would help point him in the right direction."

"Did your dad give him anything?"

"Nothing, zip, zilch," I said confidently. "Ready to test this thing out?"

Lou straightened up and grabbed the device. He jerked his head telling me to move next to him. Once there, he went over how the device works despite me studying everything we had on it to know all the ins and outs, "We kept it relatively simple in looks, but there are certain sequences to press to activate it. Using the number codes for the different worlds your dad seemed to know about, we start with the top button."

He went on to explain that we hit each button the specified number of times based on the numerical code in my dad's log books. Once we're done with the code, we hit both the top and bottom button at the same time to activate it. To deactivate the portal we were likely to create, we hit the top button twice immediately followed by the bottom button twice.

"Anywhere in particular you'd like to go?" he asked in an excited tone that made any of his negative emotions from earlier vanish.

"Let's go to this first one here," I pointed at the list we had printed out.

Lou started entering in the code followed by the activation sequence. We waited for a minute thinking it was slow, but nothing happened. We waited for a couple more minutes and still nothing. I looked over at Lou who was looking just as confused as I felt, "Did we miss something when we built it?"

"I didn't think so."

He turned the device over in his hands to see if there was any sign it wasn't working.

I let out a quick laugh, "I think maybe we got ahead of ourselves."

"What do you mean?"

"Well, isn't it rare for something to work perfectly on the first go when you're developing something?"

"I have heard that."

"Let's take it apart and see if there's anything we did incorrectly."

Lou nodded as he started moving back towards the bench with all our tools. He jumped right in with taking it apart, examining every piece he took out and disconnected. I was getting a little more worried when he started getting to the last few remaining components. He stopped and looked at me, "I think I found it."

I moved next to him to get a better view, "What is it?"

"I think I forgot to make a few connections with the wires. There wasn't any definitive pathway for the currents to travel, so there was nothing translating the code we put in."

"That would make sense," I said nodding my head in comprehension.

Lou jumped right in with making the fix then putting everything back together in record time. It wasn't long before we were standing back in our original spots ready to put the code in again.

Lou punched in the sequence and told the device to activate. This time, we watched as a portal opened to us showing a world that looked much older than the one we were standing in. Just like here, it was night, but there was no one around. Lou and I looked at each other both shaking our heads, so he shut it down.

Once the portal closed, Lou set the device down to pick me up and spin me around, "It worked!"

"I can't believe we did it!"

We were smiling, laughing to give our excitement an outlet. When Lou put me back down, he grabbed my face to kiss me. There was no holding back and as I was starting to let my hands search, Lou was the one to pull away, "Let's go for that swim."

He took my hand to lead me out of the lab to the backyard, closing everything up behind us of course. Before I could do anything, I was flying through the air heading towards the water. Lou was close behind me once I splashed into the water and I felt his arms circle around me.

We spent the rest of the night swimming, kissing each other, and sharing our excitement of what we had just accomplished. Now all we had to do was figure out when we wanted to leave.

Lou still holding me in his arms while we both looked out at the city said, "I'll just have to go pack some things and talk to the pack about who's going to keep things running while I'm away."

"Is that going to be an issue?"

"No. If anything, they'll tell me a vacation is good for me and chase me out the door. That's one thing I hear from them a lot."

"That you work too much?"

"Exactly," he confirmed as he rested his chin on the top of my head. "To be honest, when Melody died, I poured myself in my work without taking any time for myself. No breaks outside of the change until now."

"I'm glad I'm giving you a reason to step away. Although, I don't think this is going to give you the rest and relaxation you may be looking for."

"I'm counting on that. I'm sure there are big bads similar to the one we face here wherever we go."

I let that sink in. Not that I had been telling myself there wouldn't be people like Warrick, but I didn't want to face that thought. Warrick had been a lot to handle here. To deal with more similar-minded people? *Ugh.*

Lou took my mind off that as he continued, "I'll plan to grab stuff tomorrow when we're at the restaurant. Then, we can plan on leaving tomorrow night, if you're good with that?"

"Sure."

Big changes once again. I think this is just going to be my life for a while until we end our journey.

We were back into our rhythm the next day, serving our lunch crowd that was smaller than yesterday, but still larger than normal. We had a couple of Lou's wolves helping us to get ready for the transition for when we'd be gone. There was no appearance by Warrick today. He sent over his admin instead to pick up a larger order since it sounds like there's a large meeting taking place. I can't begin to describe the amount of relief I felt when she walked out the door, knowing I wouldn't be seeing Warrick again.

Lou had everything he wanted to take with him in the back of his car. If you looked at it, you would think he was moving in with me which is exactly what his pack thought was going on. They were excited we were going on a trip for an indefinite amount of time and that their alpha was happy enough to take on living with me. It was something like that, but we weren't going to let them on to the whole truth.

We were hanging around the pizza place after closing with the whole pack at the sendoff they decided to put together. We were all laughing and joking mostly about Lou into the small hours of the night. People started filtering out telling us to stay in contact, send them pictures. All that jazz that comes with going on a long trip. Raf was the last one when he came up to both of us handing over a large box, "I don't know where your adventures will take you, but make sure you take care of each other. I don't want to hear about either one of you dying."

Lou pulled him into a big hug, "Thanks, Raf. Means a lot. Make sure to take care of everyone here, especially if Warrick thinks he can run this town."

"You got it, boss."

I said my goodbyes to Raf as well, thanking him for the care he provided not that long ago. I knew everyone was in good hands with Raf taking charge of the pack while Lou was away.

We closed everything down taking one last look at the pizza place. We didn't have to say it to know that both of us were thinking that we hoped this was still standing by the time we made it back, if we make it back.

By the time we pulled into the driveway, it was almost three in the morning. I looked over at Lou, "I think we should make this journey tomorrow. Get some good sleep so we're rested and ready to go."

He yawned for a while before saying, "Yeah, I'm good with that."

We unloaded Lou's things dragging all of the boxes up to my room, double checked the house was locked and closed up, then crawled into bed. It didn't take long for us to fall asleep despite the excitement and nerves plaguing us ahead of leaving.

It was a rainy day when we woke up. I rolled over to find the other half of the bed empty.

"Lou?"

There was no response. I got myself up despite my body telling me to stay in the comforts of the bed. I poked my head out the door to see if I could hear anything. There were a couple of clanks followed by some muttering.

I took a few steps down the stairs, "Lou?"

"Down here."

"Everything okay?" I asked as I headed into the kitchen.

"Yeah, why?"

"Just heard some muttering."

He turned around to face me with a plate full of food, "I was just trying to figure out where things were, that's all. Eat up."

"Okay," I said starting to cut into the hearty breakfast he made.

He joined me at the island with his own plate. In between bites, Lou asked, "How are we going to make sure this entire house comes with us?"

"Hmm," I started tapping my fork against my chin. "I'm going to check my dad's notes after we finish eating, but I think if we do this outside and aim the device at the house, it should do the trick."

"How did you come up with that idea?"

"I was thinking about the bomb and how that worked to transport houses it didn't destroy. It wasn't like it crashed through the roof and landed in this house, so the portal it created was generated outside."

"I can see that. Not a bad idea to read through your dad's work to see if there's anything noted."

"Exactly."

We quickly finished eating and while Lou got busy with cleaning things up, I went back into the office to start researching. It wasn't long before Lou joined me and I tasked him with reading the handwritten notes.

Lou had gotten about halfway through my dad's notes when I stumbled across a section in his digital journal, "Lou, I think I found it."

He sprang up from the chair he was in so he could read over my shoulder, "You were right. We have to go outside and aim the device at the house, just not directly at it."

"Right," I agreed. "We have to aim it slightly above so that it pulls the house with it."

"Does that mean we have to open the portal, then run back into the house? Will we have time to do that?"

I looked back at Lou, "I was wondering the same things, but hear me out. One of us will stand outside to open the portal while the other is in the house. As soon as whoever is controlling the device sees the portal start to open, get at least to the porch if not completely inside."

Lou was still reading through everything that was written down, "That could work even though I'm not the biggest fan."

"Why?"

He shifted his gaze to me, "That gives a chance for one of us to be left behind. I don't like that risk."

"Don't you have super speed or something that allows you to move quicker since you're a wolf?"

"Yes. I'm not sure I'm liking where you're going with this."

"When we opened the portal last night, it took a second for it to be fully formed. Do you think you can make it back before it's fully opened?"

"As long as I don't have to stand on the complete opposite side of the street."

"We should be fine then."

Lou nodded, "I guess the only thing left that we need to do is make sure the coast is clear. We have the weather on our side today. There's not going to be a lot of people out and about, but we don't know what your stalker is up to."

I made a face at the thought of Warrick, "We'll just check the camera. Considering it's the middle of the week, I would be surprised if he was hanging out there."

"Me too, but better safe than sorry," Lou said as he made his way to the lab.

I followed wanting to see with my own eyes. If the coast was clear, I didn't see why we couldn't make the jump.

Looking at the screen, there was not another soul in sight. Not a car, person, or animal. I looked over at Lou who was examining every inch of that screen, "I think we're cleared for takeoff."

"I would agree," he said as he turned towards me. "Well, this is it. Ready?"

"Let's go," I said with no hesitation. I didn't want to give myself a chance to second guess everything and miss our window of opportunity.

Lou headed outside and I remained in the entryway with the doorway open and ready for Lou to run in. He went so he was just on the street. Lou lifted up his arm with the device and took another look around along with a big sniff to check for anyone. When he returned his focus back to the device, I knew were still in the clear. I watched as his fingers entered the code. Lou took one more moment before hitting the activation sequence. As soon as he finished and saw the start of the portal, he sprinted back into the house, slammed the front door shut, and locked it.

I took a steadying breath and counted down, "Three. Two. One."

Lou and I were holding hands, both with our eyes closed. It got eerily quiet and for a second, all the air escaped from our lungs making it hard to breathe. In an instant the feeling was gone and we were back to feeling normal. We both opened our eyes first looking at each other, then headed towards the back door.

As it slid open, we took in the landscape. Gone were the mountains I was so used to seeing behind the house. Instead, it was replaced with an open field with rolling hills and plenty of flowers. The rain we were just experiencing cleared out and the sun was brighter than ever. There was no city for the pool to overlook, just more of the field. I went to go out the front door to find the street was no longer paved. There was gravel over a layer of dirt. I stepped out to look at the front of the house to see that it was the same. We were sitting on top of one of the hills and I could see a city at the bottom. There were some taller buildings poking out, but nothing like the skyscrapers we had left behind.

We were in a completely new place with no worries of Warrick. Our device actually worked.

I went back into the house, closing and locking the door before turning to Lou, "We did it."

Lou smiled, "Now, just to figure out where and when we were transported to."

I nodded my head spouting out the first thing that came to mind, "Three seconds was all it took. I guess the journey has just begun."

Acknowledgements

I have to take a minute to breathe ... I've had my head down, typing away for a while now, so seeing this dream manifest is absolutely mind-blowing! First and foremost, I owe a huge THANK YOU to my wonderful husband! You've been so patient as I've been knee-deep in writing. Not only that, but you've dealt with my wine-enhanced ramblings at one in the morning when ideas click into place. You've listened to me as these characters took shape, you gave me encouragement when I needed it most, and you didn't let me give up when the doubt started creeping in. Thank you, and I'm so happy to be sharing this journey with you.

Thank you, mom, for being willing to take on the editing when you already have so much on your plate. I very much appreciate your eagle eye and for helping to strengthen the story. It was a lot of fun getting to see your initial reaction! And, hopefully, the commas have found their places.

Finally, to everyone who supported me from the beginning – this dream of mine really wouldn't have been able to come true without you. You all stood by me during the million teasers and annoying "something exciting will be happening soon" promises. The promise has been fulfilled and I can't wait for you all to keep going down the path with me on this journey. Your support has helped motivate me, gotten me excited for what's to come, and put a smile on my face. Thank you for reading and here's to many more!

About the Author

Torie is a passionate adventurer who finds inspiration in the beauty of the outdoor world, especially in her backyard of Colorado. When not hiking through the mountains or torturing herself with running, she enjoys the company of her loving husband and their two cats, who serve as her trusty sidekicks as she types away . A lover of engaging storytelling, she often loses herself in a good book, movie/tv show, or video game. Eager to create her own worlds, Torie is excited to share her adventures through writing, inviting readers to embark on journeys of their own.

Read more at toriegwriting.com.